SAY YES
ON
SATURDAY

Based On a True Story

LAWRENCE SCHNEIDER

BALTIMORE, MARYLAND

"I smiled every time I reached for this book--laughed and cried while enjoying this enchanting story you have shared with all."

—Lorraine Bazzell

"I was surprised at how this novel prompted me to become so invested in reading about Clarence's life. The story telling invites one to join in learning about the life and experiences of a young school boy who advances in years to the point of becoming an octogenarian not quite ready for retirement. The prevailing wondrous truth in this story is that persistence is a sure predictor for success and that gentle genuine humor securely paves the way."

—Pat Lackey

Copyright © 2017 by Lawrence Schneider.

Lawrence Schneider
www.LawrenceSchneider.com

Say Yes On Saturday: Based on a True Story
By Lawrence Schneider — 1st edition.
ISBN 978-0692753743

Cover design by Jesse Gordon.

The author's favorite inspirational quotes following each chapter are by several wise humans, and one smart android.

Internal book sketches and images are by the author.

Dedicated To
My Descendants

I pursued genealogy research for years but realized that it didn't reveal what my ancestors thought or how they felt. I'm telling my story here so that my yet-to-be-born descendants do not encounter that disappointment when they wonder about my life.

I chose fiction to describe my experiences so my descendants will be entertained enough to absorb the life lessons I offer, and to find the courage to follow their dreams. I also hope that other readers might enjoy my story.

Acknowledgements

This book would not exist without my wife, Irene Schneider, the primary inspiration and an important contributor to its production.

Others who advised, edited, and supported me on the storytelling journey include:

Kevin Anderson
Jane Bede
Terence Bragg
Victoria Bragg
Lorraine Bazzell
Drew Dorbert
Karen Dorbert
Flora Logie
Jim Logie
Renate Meise
Alison Schneider

Anne Schneider
Janet Schneider
Joe Schneider
Lindsay Schneider
Paul Schneider
Janice Starr
Sue Tomko
Margaret Wright
Cliff York
Janice York

Contents

"Go confidently in the direction of your dreams. Live the life you have imagined."

— HENRY DAVID THOREAU —

CHAPTER ONE

A Boy's World

The Secret

I had carried an unbearable burden through my life — the name Clarence. Then one day in the third grade, I had to rebel.

The day had been terrible. I came home from school in tears and told Mom how other kids teased me about my odd name. "Why'd you give me that awful name?"

That's when she told me her secret.

"When you first came into the world I showed you to my father — your Grandpa Joseph. He held you, his first grandson, and his face seemed to shine with joy. He predicted that you would do special things when you grow up and you would need a fitting name. So we named you Clarence, a name to grow into, a name that was fit for a saint or a hero."

I listened hugging my knees. What did it all mean? I wanted to believe grandpa's prediction because the tests proved that I was dumber than other kids. Now, I was worried that I'd disappoint everyone if I didn't become what grandpa foretold. But, what did I need to do? My quest to discover this required a lifetime and led to many adventures — and finally, to an answer.

I'll start as far back as I can remember; it was the day I got my first real haircut.

Haircut

Cleveland, Ohio — 1940, Age 5

Our family was busy moving into a new house on West 47th Street. I sat balanced on the front porch rail and watched as the grownups worked, carrying box-after-box past me and through the door. Three of my uncles, Dad's brothers, used the oldest one's 1934 Ford Fordor car to move the few pieces of furniture we had. Owning a home pleased my Mom the most; she had never liked renting someone else's house. My parents married during the Great Depression of the 1930's and they now worried less because Dad had found full-time work. Dad strutted around like a new man because he finally had a steady job at a large commercial bakery. My

parents still scrimped because of the low pay, but Dad bragged to his brothers about his promising situation, which was better than the short-term menial jobs that he had during the last few years.

We could never have afforded this house if it was not for Mom's father. Grandpa Joseph had loaned us money for the down payment. He had even recommended that Dad contact the bank about buying this foreclosed house. The small two-story house that we were moving to was of white clapboard and included a front porch and a one-car garage.

On the day we moved in, Mom could not stop smiling. I was excited too, thinking about sleeping in my own new bedroom for the first time. I looked up and down the street, which was crowded with similar houses. While most of the houses were occupied by families, some were empty and rundown. Most of our neighbors were young families, where the adult men were factory workers. I was hoping to meet a new friend that very day.

Everyone we met seemed extremely friendly. I stopped to listen because Dad started talking with the guy next door about the Indians baseball game. I came up behind them while they talked and slid my head under Dad's arm. He held me tightly and absentmindedly messed with my long hair. I lost interest when the neighbor said that they did not have children — *I would find no playmate here.*

Racing back to the kitchen, I complained to Mom, "I like our new house, but I can't find any friends."

"Keep looking; you usually do not give up that easily."

"Okay."

I continued moving. Later, when I referred to our house as new, Mom corrected me. "Our house isn't new; another family lived here before us."

"Why'd they leave?"

"Well...bad times forced them out." She paused and then added "It was empty a long time before we bought it. Then Dad and I worked hard to fix it so that we could all move in today."

"Where are the kids who were here? Where'd they go?"

She glanced up to the heavens, which she often did when she was tired of answering my numerous questions "I don't know."

Her answer didn't satisfy me. "Did they go to live in the park?" I had heard Mom and Dad talking about people living in Brookside Park during the depression.

"I do not know, Clarence. They left a few years ago. We never met them. We only talked to the man from the bank about buying the empty house." My energy had faded, so she no longer needed to hang on to my sleeve to keep me still. She asked, "Do you feel bad about the family that had to move out?"

I nodded. "It's not fair."

"Things like that happen in life, sometimes to people who don't deserve it."

"Will it happen to us?"

"We'll try our best to not let anything like that happen to us by paying off the house loan and saving for the rainy days, which always seem to come. If things do go wrong, we'll stick together and do whatever is needed. We will be prepared, and we'll do just fine." She stood up. "Let's go up to your room. You can help me put sheets on your bed."

I had the smaller bedroom, which was next to the bathroom. I looked out of my window at leaves of a large cherry tree. It was so thick that it blocked my view. *It will be fun to climb that tree.* I tried to think of a plan to overcome Mom's objections. *I'll just get up in the branches when Mom isn't looking. Then, when she sees that I can do it, she might not order me to get down.* I smiled. *I can't believe I'm so lucky to have a house, where my sister and I each have our separate bedrooms.*

After a few days, I finally met a new friend. Tim lived three houses up the street and was five years old, just like me. I liked playing with him because we took turns being the leader. I brought him home to see my room. I grabbed his sleeve and pulled him towards the stairs. "Look, Tim, I have a room, just for me, with a slanting ceiling on one side." Tim followed and I continued, "See, my head touches the ceiling on this low side." I talked animatedly, pointing out things, just like the guy who had sold us the house. I felt a little guilty because Mom had said that it's wrong to brag. "My bed's almost as long as the room, and this is my chair and pine chest."

Tim looked away. "You're lucky. I share a room with my brothers." Since Tim didn't care about my room, we went outside to climb the cherry tree. *I should not try to show off like that.* Dad was the king in our house, but since he didn't have the time to play with me, I needed a friend like Tim.

* * *

Later in the evening, Mom called me in to wash for supper. "Dad will be here soon."

Bang. The back screen door slammed sending a tremor through the wood frame house. *Dad is home from work.* He made more noise, moving through the house, calling out to me.

"Buddy! Tomorrow we'll get you a haircut." He didn't expect an answer, but the news resulted in a twist in my stomach. *At times, Dad drinks too much when he has money. Today was payday. Will tomorrow be a good or a bad day for me?*

Dad did like to drink with his friends, but he rarely drank too much. He was slim with dark combed-back hair and a thin mustache — people said that he was handsome enough to be a movie star, despite being a little short. He never acquired much schooling because his father had made him quit after the eighth grade. Without the high school diploma that most of his friends at work had, Dad was unsure of himself around them. He made up for this by working harder than other guys. This meant he got home too tired to play. Dad's need for relaxation and his unwillingness to do new things frustrated Mom, who liked new experiences.

The next day, as I prepared to leave with Dad for the barbershop, I heard Mom's voice. "Joe, tomorrow after church, let's spend the day with my family." Mom's parents lived on the East Side of Cleveland, which required a long streetcar trip with two transfers. We were always welcome to the Sunday dinner with their big family. I liked to go there because the Kreiners usually prepared roast chicken and mashed potatoes on Sundays, which were two of my favorite dishes.

Dad shook his head. "No, that's a long streetcar ride. This was my first week at the new job, and I'm tired and plan to rest. And your father never talks about anything I'm interested in, just politics and life back in Austria."

I noticed the look of disappointment, on Mom's face.

Dad ended the conversation, "Buddy and I are leaving to find the barbershop." He found me waiting for him at the back door, shifting from one foot to the other. "Let's get your summer haircut. We'll explore our new neighborhood while looking for a barbershop."

"Good, I like to explore."

Several years before, to save money, Dad had bought a used hand hair clipper. I hated those haircuts because that old clipper pulled my hair. He would let my hair grow long in winters and give me a crew cut each spring. This time would be my first experience of visiting a real barbershop. I loved when Dad took me out for adventures that he called outings.

Dad pulled me in our rundown wood wagon, briskly walking towards Denison Avenue, the nearest commercial street. The wagon was old, but still solid enough for Mom to use for grocery shopping each Friday. I had grown big enough to perfectly fit in it, sitting against the back rail with legs stretched out and feet pressed against the front. I tightly held the sides as he bumped over curbs and steered around turns. He teased me by unexpectedly moving the handle sideways and pretending to dump me out. I laughed every time, which made him laugh too. I sat up and looked around. I felt like a king riding in a royal coach, proud, and happy to be with my Dad.

I bent my head back to gaze into the trees whizzing overhead. Then we approached a beer joint with a bright electric sign, which was turned on even during the day. A worry welled up inside me. *Today's Saturday and sometimes Dad gets drunk on Saturday. The problem is when he drinks a lot, he's mean, and I'll need to stay out of his way. I think if I have to, I can get back home by myself from here, but I'm not supposed to go this far alone. I hope I'll be okay.*

We passed a yard, which was surrounded by a chain-link fence. A big growling dog baring his long teeth raced toward us. He was like a large wild wolf. I jumped in my seat and hunched my shoulders to make myself smaller. I grabbed the sides of the wagon. With front paws on the fence, that dog looked as tall as Dad; in fact, he was big enough to jump over. Luckily, the fence stopped him with a clatter of steel. I wanted to cover my face, but I had to hang on to the wagon because Dad moved along faster.

By the time we got to Denison Avenue, I wished I was home and climbing my tree; I no longer cared about the haircut. If I closed my eyes, I could only see those sharp white teeth. So, to divert my attention, I recalled Dad's promise of a surprise. *I saw him put money in his pocket before we left home. Maybe he'll use some to buy the surprise.*

We finally found a barbershop. A bell tinkled when we opened the door, and I saw that the customers inside glanced at us. Two men sat on chairs against the wall waiting and another sat on the barber's chair getting his hair cut. There were no boys like me in the room and I smelled cigarettes and soap. The barber smiled at us. He had a big smile, a pencil-thin mustache wider than his mouth, and no hair on his head. It didn't seem right that a barber wouldn't have hair.

I glanced up at Dad and whispered. "Don't barbers have hair?" Dad opened his mouth, but before he could answer, there was an outburst of laughter. Everyone in the room, including the barber, had heard my remark and grinned at me. My face was hot. I hated being the focus of attention. Moreover, I wasn't sure why they laughed.

Dad stopped smiling and led me towards a chair. He leaned forward and said, "No, not all barbers have hair."

We took seats lined up against the wall facing the barber's chair. After a few minutes, Dad let out a deep exhale and brought his head down close to me and said, "Looks like we're in for a wait."

He also wishes we could leave.

Our chairs faced a long mirror on the wall behind the barber, who worked on his customer. The tops of our heads reflected in the mirror. On the wall above Dad's head, I saw the reflected picture of a naked lady. *I bet Mom wouldn't like this place.* Dad didn't seem to pay any attention to the naked lady.

The next man in line stood and went to sit in the barber's chair. We all shifted one seat, like musical chairs, one person closer to the beginning of the line. In time, I found myself in the last chair, and then finally, it was my turn. The barber reached under his sink, grabbed a wide board with one hand, and with a smooth, practiced swing, placed it on the armrests of his chair; it was a homemade booster seat for me. He motioned for me to get on the seat and with some effort, I climbed up. He fastened a gigantic baby blue bib around my neck using the biggest safety pin I had ever seen. It was too tight and it pinched, but I didn't complain. The bib hung almost to the floor. He rotated the chair so I could see myself in his mirror. I looked strange and small with only my head visible.

Then, he did something with his foot and I was startled because I began rising in short jerks. When the barber thought the height was just right, he asked, "What'll it be young man? Shave and a haircut?" I looked down, unable to talk.

Dad answered for me. "Just a regular haircut, short."

After the barber finished snipping my long hair off with his scissors and buzzing around my head with his electric clippers, he looked at me and asked, "Short enough?" I pulled an arm from under the bib and warily touched the top of my head with my palm. I liked how it felt; just like a soft brush. I smiled and slowly nodded twice.

With a dramatic flourish and a grin on his funny barber face, he picked up a ceramic shaving mug with a blue American eagle pictured on its side. He added a little hot water to the mug from his sink and rattled a shaving brush around inside. He then brushed soapsuds on the back of my neck and the warm, clean-smelling bubbles felt fantastic. He briskly rubbed a straight razor back and forth on a strip of leather hanging from the chair side — zip, zip, zip. My eyes got wide. *What's he doing with that sharp razor? Dad had clearly told him, "Just a haircut?"* I glanced at Dad in the mirror. He watched with a smile, so I figured it would be okay. I felt scraping pressure as he shaved the hairline at the back of my head with a few strokes. It did not hurt at all.

Next, he put a warm, damp towel on my neck. I savored the wonderful sensation for a few minutes before he snatched the towel away and wiped my neck. He sprinkled liquid from a small bottle into his palm, rubbed his hands together, and dabbed his fingertips on my neck. It stung my skin a little and smelled awful, just like Mom's perfume. I closed my eyes tightly and did not make a sound because I was trying to be brave. He picked up a large, soft brush, like a furniture duster and smothered my head in smelly talc powder. I sneezed. Then he finally whisked the bib away and stepped back to admire his work.

"There!" he said, "You are all finished, little man. And, you did get your shave. No extra charge for the shave. What do you think about that?" His mustache made his grin look even wider. *I think I like this barber. I guess he's done cutting my hair.*

I pointed at the picture on the wall behind Dad. "Why don't you get your wife some clothes?" There was another outburst of laughter from the customers. The barber coughed once, and his face turned pink. Once again I wondered what was so funny, as Dad took my place in the barber's chair. I noticed that Dad was also smiling and his eyes were watering.

After Dad's haircut, I climbed into the wagon, and we headed home. The smell of the perfume and tingling feeling went with me. Dad walked faster. *I hope there won't be any trouble on the way back.* As we bumped along, I remembered Dad's promise and wondered what the treat might be? I didn't ask because he might get mad. However, what I wanted most was to go straight home. I called out to him, "Dad?"

"Yeah?"

"I told my friend, Tim that I'd play with him as soon as I got home. Can we go right home?"

"We need to make one stop." He slowed as we approached the beer joint, and my shoulders slumped.

"We'll get your treat here." He parked the wagon by the door and grabbed my hand to help me up two steps. It was dark inside and it smelled bad, real bad; like an awful mixture of sour beer, cigarette smoke, and a dirty bathroom. Several men were perched on stools at a long high table — a gray haze over their heads. Dad picked a small table near the door. The tabletop was sticky.

Dad said, "Wait here" and he pointed towards the long high table. "I'll go to the bar for the treat." He returned with a small glass of beer for himself and an ice-cold bottle of Bireley's orange drink with a frosted glass for me. I had never seen a frosted glass or tasted Bireley's orange. *This will be a real fine treat.* Dad poured my drink. I slid to the edge of the chair to sample it, while he went back to the bar. It was sweet and icy. I had never had anything so cold since the last winter when I ate a handful of snow.

Dad told the bartender: "Let's make it a boilermaker." The guy filled a tiny glass with whiskey, which Dad drank in a gulp. He then got another small beer. A few minutes later, Dad came back smiling, and his cheeks glowed. "How do you like that treat?"

I looked up, "Umm... it tastes good, not so fizzy like the other soda pops."

While I sipped my drink, Dad went back for another beer. He started talking with a guy he seemed to know. I watched, waited, and finished my drink. A long time passed and I got tired of sitting on the hard chair. I was ready for supper. So, I walked over to him and tugged his sleeve but he didn't even look down.

"I'll be there in a few minutes Clarence. We'll go soon. Want another orange drink?" Dad usually called me Buddy. Whenever he said 'Clarence', I knew he was serious.

I shook my head and then shuffled back towards our table, feeling sorry for myself. I kicked an empty cigarette pack aside. *I wish I could kick that guy, who Dad's talking to so that we could leave now. Mom wouldn't like this one bit. She doesn't like when Dad drinks whiskey. I don't even think I'm allowed to be in a beer joint.* I glared at him. He was still talking and didn't notice. *He isn't paying any attention to me. This outing isn't fun anymore, and I'm getting hungry, and I need to pee. There must be a bathroom here someplace, I can smell it but I'm not going to look for it. What can I do? Dad will not talk to me and Mom's back at home. I shouldn't leave him, but I've got to do something. I could walk home myself; I remember the way to go, but that dog might get me.*

After several minutes of growing discomfort, I slipped out of the door, grabbed the wagon handle with both hands behind my back, and trudged home with my head down. *I know he will follow when he notices.* I walked along slowly so that Dad could catch up. I glanced up and down the street when I passed a hedge. There was no one in sight, so I slipped behind the hedge to pee. *I should hurry, so I don't get caught by some stranger.* I felt like a bad boy, but I was relieved.

Now I tried to figure out what to do. *There is a dangerous wolf-dog ahead. Maybe I should go back and wait for Dad. Then I might not even get in trouble if he doesn't get to know that I left.* I imagined him drinking at the bar and decided to continue walking home.

I scuffed my feet while thinking about the bad dog on the next block. Once Dad had told me, "Always be prepared." So I picked up a thick stick for a club and put it in the wagon, just in case. When I got there, the scruffy wolf-dog was angry to see that I was back. He charged and leaped high against the barrier. Chain links rattled and I was surprised to see the entire fence move back and forth. *It isn't as strong as it looks.* I thought about running, but I had the wagon. He jumped again and again, barking and snarling. He made a terrible racket, but nobody came to see what was going on. *He must be a dumb dog that he can't figure out he can't get me.* I stood with hands on my hips, faced him, and gave the dog a hard look. This made him furious. He started digging with renewed energy, trying to get under the fence. Dirt flew behind him. *Maybe he actually can get me.*

I picked up my club and hit the chain links as hard as I could. It caused a louder clatter. My hands trembled, my eyes were open wide. "Go. Get back." I took a deep breath. "Bad dog!" My voice was squeaky, and I felt weak, but I managed to swing at the fence again. The growling animal moved back, preparing to charge. *No help is coming — run.* I took hold of the wagon handle and got away fast.

I was soon out of breath, so I slowed to a shuffle. Then, breathing heavily, I stopped, bent over with hands on knees, and looked back — no sign of Dad. *Where is he?* I kept moving anyway. I finally turned down West 47th Street — still no Dad. Now, past the danger of the angry dog, I walked faster. *That was actually great fun, a good battle with a fierce animal.* I arrived wide-eyed and breathless and found Mom in the kitchen.

"Let me see your haircut. Where is your father?" More questions followed at a dizzying pace. I blurted out answers and soon she knew nearly everything. However, I didn't tell her about peeing behind the bush. She gave my shirt collar a vigorous shake. "You should have stayed with your father. You are old enough to know better. Go to your room and stay there."

I sat on the bed thinking about the outing. *I'm glad Dad isn't back because he'd spank me. I wonder what will happen when he comes home. I hope he's okay.* Much later when he did get back, I heard my parents arguing. I opened my bedroom door a crack. Dad's voice slurred and I heard dishes rattle. *He must have bumped into the kitchen table, which was set for supper.*

He shouted at her, "Don't tell me what to do. I'm head of this house. I'll do whatever I want. And don't you try to boss me around."

I crept to the top of the stairs where I could see them below. Mom hollered loudly; I'm sure the neighbors knew they were fighting. Her hands were on her hips and her face was near his. "You need to take better care of your children. You should stop drinking, and not waste our money." That made Dad angrier. He pushed her away from the table, picked up one of the plates, and smashed it to the floor with a crash. Pieces flew in all directions. Mom raised her hands, screamed, and ran towards the stairs. I ducked back into my room just in time. She rushed past my room to their bedroom and slammed the door. I could hear the sounds of sobbing.

After a few minutes, I heard Dad stagger upstairs and go into the bathroom. I snuck out of my room to listen at their closed bedroom door to Mom crying. When I passed my sister's room I heard Diane's worried sobs. I found myself trapped when Dad came out sooner than I expected. I was unable to get back to my room without passing him in the narrow hall. He noticed me scurry past. With an off-balanced attempt to grab me, his hand caught the back of my head. I screeched as I skidded through the open doorway of my room. My foot smacked the bedroom door with a *clunk*.

I touched my leg but found no serious harm. Mom heard the commotion and opened her door. One look turned her into a lioness intent on protecting her cub. She rushed out with fire in her eyes and a snarl in her throat. *Bang*. The sound of the kitchen screen door was the final exclamation as Dad disappeared into the yard. Before I had time to cry, Mom was holding me in a breath-robbing grip. She cradled me close for a long time, whimpering softly. After a while the house became quiet. She made me a slice of peanut butter bread and sent me to my room. Then she began to clean the kitchen.

I lay there thinking, unable to sleep. I heard him come in later that evening and I left my room to peek down the stairs. He looked pale and unsteady; then he threw up, which created another mess for Mom. He crept up the stairs with eyes downcast. I didn't get spanked.

In the morning, he didn't go to the Sunday Mass with us. The atmosphere at home remained tense for days. I knew their fight was my fault — I'd left Dad and walked home alone. I wanted to cry, but no tears remained, just a throbbing head. On Monday morning, I didn't feel like going out to play so I stayed in bed with my face buried in the pillow. Mom noticed. She sat on the bed and put her hand on my back. "Why are you crying?"

I didn't want to make things worse, but I knew she would not leave, so I admitted, "I'm sorry I made you and Dad fight. Will you get a divorce now?"

Mom sat straighter and her eyebrows shot up. "What makes you think that you caused us to argue? And where did you hear about divorce?" She moved in front of me and held my shoulders. She brought her face closer to mine and I saw that her eyes were bloodshot. Her tone became measured and her words deliberate. "You did not cause our fight — and we are not getting a divorce." She added with conviction, "The Catholic Church doesn't allow it and we do not want one. We are a family and families stick together."

She took a deep breath, gripping my shoulders tightly. "Now, tell me where you learned about divorce."

I was compelled to tell her before she shook it out of me. *I hope this doesn't get my new friend in trouble.* "Tim told me." I looked away hoping I had said enough. She put her fingers on my cheeks to turn my face back, looked me in the eyes, and waited with lips pursed. After a moment I went on, "He said his dad got drunk too much, so his parents got a divorce."

"Well..." She swallowed hard and blinked a few times. Her hands trembled. "Your father and me...well, we just had an argument." She paused and then took a deep breath. "And we are not getting a divorce. And this was *NOT YOUR* fault. So, stop thinking like that." She reluctantly released me.

After a while, I went outside to sit on the high limb of the cherry tree, where no one could see me. I thought about all that had happened since I got my haircut. It was too confusing and I couldn't figure it out.

The next weekend Mom and Dad surprised me with a new swing for the yard. It looked like a real airplane with stars painted on the wings. I had never seen anything so wonderful before. Dad spent Saturday afternoon hanging it from the thickest limb of the cherry tree. When it was ready, he gave me a ride and I couldn't stop laughing. I noticed Mom smile at him. I felt so good that I even allowed Diane to take a ride on my airplane.

I guess my parents made up because everything returned to normalcy. Dad didn't stop drinking, but he cut way back and only seldom got drunk. Whenever he did drink too much, he got sick, so after a few years, he entirely stopped.

My wish was to have another fun outing with Dad. Fishing was one of his favorite things to do and my number one dream was to go fishing with him some day. But when I asked, he said, "You're too little, and it is dangerous."

"But I'm getting bigger. Next year I'll be in the first grade."

"Do not argue with me!"

I looked down, stuck out my lower lip in a pout, and left the house. I sat in my tree, trying to imagine what a day at school would be like. I decided to climb higher and was rewarded with a view of Cleveland's Terminal Tower, along with a whiff of some far-away factory's smoke stack.

Student

I'll always remember starting school because it was the first time I had realized that Mom lied to me.

I was enjoying another warm summer day playing marbles in the dirt behind Tim's house when I noticed that Mom had arrived to talk to Tim's mother. After a few minutes, I heard her mention my name.

Mom was saying, "I want Clarence to get high-quality schooling. He'll go to the Catholic school, St. Boniface, so that he can learn about his religion." Mom was quite spiritual but Dad didn't see the need for church. However, he went along with her on such matters, and they agreed that my schooling would include religious instruction. Going back many generations, their families in Austria and Germany were Catholic. Now, my parents had decided to sacrifice, so that their children could go to St. Boniface Catholic Grade School.

"I'm sending Tim there too. You know that they charge tuition?" replied Tim's mother.

Both Tim and I stopped playing to listen. We were curious about school. With no kindergarten in our neighborhood, children waited to start first grade at the age of six.

Mom said, "I know it will cost a little more, but I have been saving for it."

"It's also a longer walk than to the public school."

"I also had to walk a long distance to my school. It will be good for him."

* * *

Later at home, I went to the kitchen, while she cooked supper. "Mom, is school hard?"

She boosted me up to sit on her high kitchen stool. "School is fun! I had a fantastic time at my school. You are going to love it, you'll see. It will start in just a few weeks."

My mother loved escaping into books and movies. We didn't go to movies often, but she read a library book to Diane and me most of the evenings before bed. She said, "You will learn to read better in school, so you too would be able to enjoy stories whenever you want."

Just as she promised, a few weeks later Mom woke me early one morning and said that it was time to dress for school. The big day had finally arrived. I held back tears. She said, "It is time, and there is no way out. We have to go." After breakfast, she ordered, "Here, put your jacket on; it's cool this morning." She wore her usual outfit, a buttoned sweater over a homemade cotton dress, which smelled of Ivory laundry soap.

Before we left home, Mom told me more about what to expect — teachers, classmates, desks, lessons, and homework. That was when I suspected that school wouldn't be fun. I had to leave my backyard and toys to go to a place for "big boys." It sounded like work and rules, not fun. Now my head started to ache. I was worried about school since the day I overheard Mom talking with Tim's mother. My sister was curious and listened intently to all that was said. It was decided that Diane would stay home with a sitter, while Mom took me for my first day of school. *At least, my friend Tim will be there with me.*

Mom led me by the hand and we walked the half-mile to school. We walked fast and Mom's tight grip was hurting. I whimpered just to let her know that I didn't want to go. As we walked, she recited a new encouragement every few seconds. "It's time for you to be a big boy", "You're not a baby anymore", "You'll make new friends and learn new things." I wondered if her moist eyes contradicted her words, so I resumed whimpering. She looked down and realized that her comments didn't convince me. "Oh, stop whining!" She gave my arm a tug. I bit my lip to stop the urge to cry and we continued in silence.

Before reaching the school, I had realized that Mom had shaded the truth. I was disappointed in her. Until now, I had believed everything she said, but after this incident, I started questioning most of what she told me.

Our family walked this same route to church every Sunday, but I had never paid any attention to the school building next to the church. But today, I carefully observed the people entering it. Mom led me up half a dozen steps, opened the large green door, and we stepped into a crowded hallway that smelled like floor wax. Many voices chattered at the same time and I couldn't understand the confusion of words. Mothers and children looked serious, and few of them smiled.

Mom continued to grip my hand, while pointing in specific directions, "Those doors on each side are classrooms, and one of them should be yours."

I looked at everything and finally asked, "Is Tim here?"

"Yes, but in a different classroom."

She frowned. "We just have to find the right classroom for you." She peered at small, hand-printed signs that were Scotch-taped to each classroom doorjamb — *Third Grade, Second Grade.* "Ah, here it is...First Grade."

I peeked around Mom's dress and saw the child-sized desks arranged in perfect rows. A few mothers and children stood in a line that was leading to a larger desk at the front, where a lady dressed in black sat. A black hood covered her hair and framed her face. Under her chin, she wore a large, stiff white bib. She looked strange and scary. Mom whispered, "That's your teacher; you must call her Sister." I glanced up at the sister's face and her expression was very solemn.

Then it was our turn. I was tall enough to see the few items on her desk — a glossy black fountain pen aligned neatly with a pad of white paper.

Mom introduced me, "This is Clarence Arnold. He has just registered at the school."

With a flick of her pen, Sister checked my name and then looked at Mom. She said, "You may go now." Mom patted me on the shoulder, turned, and left the room. With my mouth open, I watched her go, horrified. *She never said she would leave me!* Sister stood and looked down at me. "Come with me." When I did not move, she gently took my hand and led me to an empty desk. "Clarence, this will be your desk from now on. Will you remember where your desk is?" I nodded. "Keep seated in your place when the bell rings. I will tell you about the bell and other things you need to know after everyone gets here." After that, Sister went back to her desk to greet the next child in line.

I studied my desk. It looked old, mostly made of wood with fancy iron legs. The desk and seat were one unit. A new, sharpened, yellow pencil rested in a ditch in the sloping top. The shelf underneath was empty. Someone had recently scratched 'Ted' on the desktop, which was otherwise covered with old marks and scratches. *I bet he got in trouble for doing this.*

Desks in the room gradually filled with children. Then Sister stood and told us about the rules. I tried hard to remember everything.

One of the things I learned that day was to listen to the toy cricket that Sister used as a signal to us. Each day when the big round clock on the wall showed 8:30, Sister picked up her polished brass bell by its wooden handle and rang it with enough energy to send the sound far and wide. Children became alert and moved with urgency to their assigned places. I think she liked that bell more than anything because she continued to ring it longer than necessary. Before she finished, everyone was in his or her seat, both hands on their desk, waiting, and paying attention. Sister began each day by taking the attendance. Then, like magic, a little tin cricket appeared in her hand.

She used her cricket to tell us when to move. *Click* once meant "sit" and *Click-Click*, twice meant "stand." A hand signal to the first child in line started us marching towards the next destination. On this first morning, it was the church. We attended the Mass to begin each school day. After Mass, *Click-Click* would start the procession back to the classroom. The brief exposure to fresh air was distracting because I got a hint of what I'd be missing once back at my desk.

Then I noticed Mom standing off to the side talking with other mothers. They all stared at us marching past with our hands folded like little angels. I was relieved to know that she was still waiting for me.

Mom and I were soon walking home for lunch on this short-ened first day. She asked, "What do you think about school?" I de-cided not to answer. I was angry at her. She lied to me; she had said I would like school. I hated it. She had walked out and left me with a mean stranger. *I'm not going to talk with her ever again.*

When I didn't answer, Mom sensed why. She stopped walking, faced me, knelt, and pressed my head against her own. "I'm sorry you had a bad day, Buddy. I should have warned you that I would leave you in school; I thought you knew how it worked. But I did wait for you. Always remember that I love you. I would never do anything on purpose to hurt you. Will you forgive me?"

I waited a few seconds longer to ensure that she knew how I felt. Then I said, "I forgive you." She gave me a kiss on the forehead and we continued walking.

"Now, do you want to tell me about school?"

"Ugh." I stuck out my tongue. "I hate it."

"Is that all you have to say?"

"Yes." Then I added, "It feels like a jail."

She smiled. "Well, did you like anything there?"

I had to think for a while, "Her toy cricket." That was the only fun thing I could remember. "Sister used it to tell us what to do."

"Yes, I saw her do that in the church; fascinating."

Mom continued to walk with me to school during the rest of that week. She said, "Next week you will be on your own, so pay at-tention to the route." I was confident I could find my way; *I'll be walking with Tim.*

Getting to school on my own made me feel more grown up. Tim and I were best friends now and allies in battles with robbers, pirates, and all sorts of bad guys. We loved to wrestle on the grass, climb the cherry tree, and trap birds. Now, we floundered together in first grade.

A few children in the class had gone to kindergarten. They seemed to know how to do everything right. I had a hard time figuring out most of the new things.

* * *

My introduction to art happened one afternoon during the first week. After lunch, Sister smiled at us, spread her arms, and said, "Time for some fun, time for art." I didn't know about art and wanted to learn. Fun activities in our house involved things like Saturday afternoon neighborhood movies, watching softball games at Brookside Park, and spending a day at Euclid Beach Amusement Park once each summer. *I am ready for some fun.* For this first art lesson, Sister gave each child one piece of paper and three crayons. Mom had bought me a coloring book, so I knew about crayons and coloring inside lines, but I had never associated crayons with a blank paper.

She said, "Draw a picture!" and then paused for questions. There were none, so she sat down to work with some papers. Sister stayed at her desk without explaining how to draw a picture. *I guess she thinks we all know.* I waited. No one else asked and I was afraid to raise my hand.

Everyone was busy working on their picture, which caused me to stare at the paper, lick my lips, and wonder what to do. *They all know how to do this. I could peek at what the guy next to me is doing. But Mom had told me that copying was cheating, and cheating would get me into big trouble. I better figure this out myself.*

Then I remembered the neat paper airplane my cousin Jason had taught me to make. He was a few years older than me and knew how to do everything. I did not see him often because we only got to play together at family gatherings. He had a motorbike, and I looked up to him. He could identify every airplane design, old and new. I loved listening to him talk about aviation. I was fascinated by airplanes, even before Jason told me about them. A few years before, I was startled in my yard when a small, sleek airplane flashed by overhead — low, loud, and fast. Dad said it was practicing for the Thompson Trophy air race, at nearby Cleveland Airport on the weekend.

I said, "Will you take me?"

He waved his hand, "No, it costs too much. We might see some of the planes from here."

One glimpse of that racing plane was a thrilling and long-remembered event. I never forgot how excited I was; I sat in the shade and daydreamed about flying like an eagle.

When Jason showed me how to make a paper airplane, I thought that it was amazing how he transformed a piece of paper into a toy that could fly.

As I considered what to do in the art class, the paper airplane seemed like the perfect answer. So, I made one with the blank paper. When Sister returned to pick up our artwork, I handed her the paper airplane. By that time she had collected a small stack of colorful drawings. I didn't need to use crayons, because my airplane was white. She reached for my folded airplane with thumb  and forefinger, but then glanced at me with a questioning look. *Did I do something wrong?*

I guess Sister figured I wasn't trying to be a smart-aleck because, after the hint of a smile she continued collecting papers. To fit my paper neatly into her stack, she unfolded it. I couldn't believe what I saw. *Why did she destroy it?* I was confused and disappointed because I thought making that airplane was a great idea. Now, I was positive, I didn't like school, Sister, or art.

Later, when I told Mom about what happened, she said, "Oh, it's okay. Sister doesn't have your imagination. Try to forget about it." I never did.

By the end of the school year, I was terrified of Sister and well trained to do as she asked. I had the feeling, that in spite of being obedient and doing my very best work, I had not made a good impression. Fortunately, my end-of-year report card promoted me to second grade. A handwritten note told my parents that I encountered the most trouble with numbers.

One thing I hated about school was the feeling that I was being critically judged, and that too harshly — with one exception — that note on the report card also said, "Clarence is creative." *Maybe Sister did like my paper airplane.*

Finally, it was the time for summer vacation, so Tim and I could play every day if we wanted. I was happy to just sit on a high limb in my cherry tree and imagine Sister being punished for scaring the kids.

Fishermen

One Saturday morning I went into our basement and peeked at Dad emptying his favorite tackle box on the workbench. He held it up to the light and looked through a hole that had rusted clean through the bottom. "Holy Shit!" A loud crash followed this exclamation when he threw the ruined box on the concrete floor. Then he kicked the box to confirm it was dead. I backed away because I didn't want him to know I heard him say a bad word.

When it seemed safe, I stepped forward to watch. I tried to imagine what it would be like to fish on Lake Erie. Except for being at nearby Euclid Beach Amusement Park, I had never seen the lake up close.

Eventually, he managed to put together enough gear for his first day of fishing. That was when my dream to go fishing became a serious goal. "Dad, can I come too?"

"No." He shook his head emphatically. "It's too dangerous for a kid on those big rocks. The water is deep."

I sucked my lip holding back my real feelings. He noticed and softened, "Someday when you are older; maybe next year." Once again I'd be left out. I sat on our back steps and put my chin on my fist, *Someday. He always says someday.* I watched as Dad went fishing and I waited for his return.

He came home lugging a bucket with just enough slimy lake water to keep a half dozen greenish fish alive. He called them Lake Perch. Mom celebrated the catch with him and began preparing fish for dinner.

I knelt on a kitchen chair to watch her turn them into thin breaded strips, waiting for the frying pan to heat. She handed me an old tin pie pan with stinking fish heads and guts. "Here Clarence, throw this in the garden. Be sure to dig it into the dirt good; we don't want to get a rat." After dealing with the smelly remains, I didn't think I could eat those fish. Later, I got hungry and found out that they tasted great with fresh tomatoes and green beans from our Victory garden.

In the spring of '42, World War II was underway. Dad showed me how to collect aluminum foil liners from discarded cigarette and gum packs as a way to help with the war. After about a year, I was proud to turn in a baseball-size ball of aluminum, which I imagined becoming the part of a P-47 fighter airplane. Mom helped me use some of my saved allowance to buy 10-cent saving bond stamps at the Post Office. Our meals seemed like a continuation of depression days. Rationed sugar meant Mom hardly ever baked sweet things. Dad liked meat and potatoes for supper, but we now ate cheap cuts like liver or kidney because the best went to our fighting men in service. Fresh fish was always a welcome treat.

Grownups in our neighborhood were busy trying to help win the war. Mom worried about three of her brothers fighting in the Pacific with the Navy. Dad was excused from fighting because he was old and had two children. He thought he might help by learning to weld, a needed skill, but after just a few classes, he got discouraged when he could not seem to master it. Dad continued working at Spang Bakery, now in a night job, loading delivery trucks. That meant he slept until early afternoon on most of the days. This frustrated him because fishing was best done early in the morning, so he found less time for his favorite activity.

* * *

A year later, it was again time for Dad's springtime ritual. I heard him rummaging in the basement and hurried downstairs. "Whatcha doing?" He didn't answer. After following and pestering him with unanswered questions, I gave up and went to the kitchen.

"Mom, what's Dad up to?"

"He is going fishing. He needs a break, and we could use some fresh fish for supper — if he's lucky."

When I went back downstairs, Dad looked at me with a grin, "You still want to go fishing?"

I jumped up and down. "Yes, yes." Of course, I did.

SAY YES ON SATURDAY · 39

But Mom did not like the idea. "Joe, you know I'm afraid of deep water," Mom said. "You don't swim and it's all deep water around the breakwall, where you go."

"I wanted to take him last year. He's big enough now. We cannot treat him like a baby forever, just because you are afraid of water." She considered that with a frown. *Wow, Dad is sticking up for me. Guys need to stick together.*

She said, "Well, I guess...I've been telling him to act like a big boy, but don't you bother coming home without him." I couldn't have been more excited, even if it was Christmas Eve!

That evening Dad took me to the vegetable garden and he started digging with a spade. I held the flashlight so that he could look for exposed worms. He taught me all about using night crawlers as fish bait. Dad said, "We call them night crawlers because these worms come near the surface at night. That's good for us because they're easier to catch." When we had enough worms in a tin can, he said, "Now it's time for bed, because I'll wake you up very early."

The next morning when Dad called I was out of bed and dressed in a flash. After a light breakfast, Dad gathered our gear. He carried the empty bucket, a new fishing box, two thin steel rods with reels, and his dented work lunch box. The fishing rod he picked for me was old, but I was glad to have it. Dad said, "We have a lot to carry. You take this canteen of water and the worms. Be sure to keep the can upright. We don't want to lose any."

We began walking down the street. It was a breezy day. Dad wore his grimy white floppy hat, which was reserved for fishing trips. It fit tight so the wind could not blow it away. I had on my faded Cleveland Indians baseball cap. The canteen strap pressed into my shoulder. I had covered the worms with grass blades, and I smiled when I imagined them hiding. *They will soon get a wet surprise.* Then I thought of something and my expression clouded. *If I drop them, Dad will never take me fishing again.* I tightened my grip as we came to the streetcar stop.

Dad said, "We'll take the streetcar downtown. It goes almost all the way to the lakefront."

As we waited, I stepped to the street's curb every few minutes, so I could look back along the steel tracks that ran through the center of Detroit Avenue. We waited for about 20 minutes on this early, quiet Saturday morning. The streetcar arrived, and its big train-like wheel stopped right in front of me. The car was orange with brown doors that appeared to open magically as soon as it stopped. There were large windows on the side of the car, and I could not wait to look through them. I had been on the streetcar before, but this time I hoped to learn more about how it worked.

I said, "Dad, where's the engine to pull it?"

He pointed at the top of the car, "Look up there, it gets power from the pole attached to that electric line. There's an electric motor that turns the wheels."

Once on board, I hurried to kneel on a seat by the window and flattened my nose against the glass. The streetcar moved smoothly, swaying from side-to-side, making a *click-click-click* sound. Between the stops, it moved so fast that the buildings and people outside streaked by, and I couldn't absorb it all. I sat back and focused on a uniformed man sitting up front. After carefully watching, I realized that he was opening and closing the doors at each stop. *What a neat job he has.* By the time we got downtown, I could hardly sit still, so Dad put a hand on my arm and said, "Stay on your seat, Buddy."

I flopped back on my seat. My fanny tried to remain in place but every other part of me kept moving. "Dad, how much longer?"

"About ten minutes, and then we walk for another ten minutes."

After getting off at our stop, we set off walking along a gravel path headed to the lakefront. I smelled oil that had been applied to keep the dust down. The sky was overcast with a stiff breeze from the lake. The oily odor gave way to a fresher smell as we got closer, a scent that I've associated with Lake Erie since then. At the top of a slight rise, I was excited to see blue-gray water in the distance. I looked closer, but it wasn't what I expected, it looked like fish were churning the surface.

I touched Dad's arm and pointed. "What are the white things on the water?"

"Whitecaps, the wind is making the water rough. We might not catch much in this weather." Dad sounded excited. He motioned towards the water. "Can you see the breakwall? That's where we're going." I saw something that looked like a black, L-shaped line far out in the lake; something like a bent finger.

"What's a breakwall?"

"It's like a large rock wall built right in the lake. On stormy days, it protects small boats and the shore from rough water. Today we can sit on it to fish."

We walked past a temporary-looking plank shed. Nailed to it was a handmade sign that read: FRESH BAIT, under it another, MINNOWS 35¢, WORMS 25¢. Dad pointed at it. "See; we saved a quarter by getting our worms from the garden last night. Hang on to the can." I pressed the can to my chest. He reached down and grabbed my free hand as we approached the step-up to the breakwall. The dark gray rocks were much bigger than they looked a few minutes earlier. The top of the breakwall was flat and broad enough for walking, and there was also sufficient space to sit and fish.

Eyes wide, I looked at the water and clutched the can securely before Dad gave me a boost on the nearest rock. The water-filled canteen got heavier with each step because the shoulder strap rubbed on my neck. We continued walking above the choppy waters, stepping with care from rock to rock and over the wide cracks separating the sandstone blocks. Dad looked for a fishing spot with plenty of room for the two of us. We encountered an old guy, who sat with three fishing lines in the lake and a cigarette clamped in his lips. The water made a menacing grumble as it sloshed between the rocks. The wind tugged at my hat, so I pulled it tighter with my free hand.

Dad asked, "Having any luck?"

The old man looked up. "Not much good enough to eat, but I caught a Pike using a minnow; he gave me a good fight too."

I said, "Wow!"

Dad said to me, "Northern Pike is the primary predator fish of the lake. They are harder to hook but more sporting than other fish."

I said, "Can I see his fish Dad?"

The man heard me. He waved me over. "Here, come boy and take a look."

I saw a long gray fish that could hardly fit in his bucket. The old man picked up the slim, foot-long fish by its gill, and held it in front of my face so that I could get a better look. I gawked at it and took a step back. It flipped its tail a few times and looked right at me. Cold water splashed on my face and shirt.

I yelped, "It's still alive!" I took another step back, startled because that Pike looked dangerous. I saw a pointed nose and many sharp teeth. As we turned to go, the wind loosened my hat and I grabbed for it, causing the can to slip out of my grip and fall into a deep crack.

"Oh shit!" Dad said.

"Ha!" The old man gave one loud, involuntary laugh and then he looked away embarrassed.

I looked at Dad and tried not to cry. "Will we go home now?"

The old fisherman said, "Wait. I might be able to reach the can."

Following a few minutes of whispered grunts, he handed my can to me. I looked in and saw that only one worm was left.

Dad said, "All right Clarence, let's walk back and buy more bait."

As we were leaving, the old fisherman grinned and said, "Looks like a worm in the can is worth several in the lake." I know Dad didn't like the homemade joke because he made a muttering sound.

When we returned after buying worms, Dad picked another fishing spot away from the old fisherman. By then the sun was brighter and warmer. The steady breeze kept us cool, a constant reminder that we were on the lake.

The rest of the day was fun for me, and frustrating for Dad. He tried to show me how to tie two hooks on the line, bait the hooks, and select the right size sinker according to the water conditions. On this day the water was rough, the sinkers needed to be heavy.

One of the hooks caught in my pants and pinched my leg. I yelped and Dad came to help. He spent most of the time doing everything for me, as well as casting both our lines into the water. My line always seemed to get snagged on the rocks. When that happened, Dad was forced to climb down close to the water's edge to untangle it. The breaking waves got him wet, and he had to be careful not to fall in. I came to understand why I was still not old enough to manage most of the fishing tasks but was not ready to admit it.

Soon it was time to go home and Dad started gathering our gear. We hadn't caught any fish. He reached for his fishing rod, wedged upright between the rocks. The rod jumped away from his grasp as if alive and the line started to run out furiously, pulled by a powerful force. He yelled, "A bite!" With jaw clamped, he grabbed at his rod, which he missed again because the creature on the other end dislodged the handle from its anchor in the crack. His new rod with an expensive reel bounced erratically, just out of reach towards the water. He scrambled after it in a desperate race.

I jumped up and screamed fearing that he would fall into the deep waters. I saw Dad rushing towards the water's edge — the same edge he had warned me several times to avoid. *I didn't know he could move so fast.* He managed to grab the rod and get himself into a seated position with one foot in Lake Erie. With urgency, he shifted the rod to his left hand and grabbed the reel's crank with his right. My scream caused several nearby fishermen to come to our aid. They soon realized that no one was in danger, but could see that this might turn into a fight with a big fish, so they gathered closer, excitedly shouting advice.

"Let the line play out."

"That's a big one."

"Watch out, so that light line doesn't break."

"Keep it tight so he doesn't spit the hook out."

Dad sat leaning backward. He gripped the rod tightly. Water lapped at his feet, soaking his pants below the knees. I was so scared that I started to sob. The crank would not budge when he tried to reel in the fish. If he let the line play out, it got slack. Whatever was on the other end did not cooperate by running deeper into the lake. The fish liked being close to the breakwall. It seemed to be a stalemate.

Dad looked determined to win, but it was life or death for the fish, so he was even more desperate to escape. The contest continued for over half an hour. Sweat and spray soaked Dad's hair and ran into his eyes. He breathed like a distance runner in the direct sun. Some relief came from cold lake water that hit him every few minutes. The steel rod bent into a bow-like arch and seemed at its breaking point. Dad was almost lying on his back. It looked like he had reached his endurance limit.

I was looking at the entire scene wide-eyed, hopping up and down from one foot to the other, unable to stand still. The old fisherman had joined the spectators, who continued to shout inconsistent advice. Other fishermen made room for the old guy, I guessed because of his greater experience. I was terrified, worried for Dad's safety. I whispered under my breath, "He doesn't know how to swim."

The old fisherman put a hand on my shoulder, pulled me close, and said, "Your Dad is doing a first-rate job. Everything will be fine. Nothing bad will happen. Don't worry." He went on one knee to be at my level. His breath smelled sour. "Well boy, do you believe he'll get his fish?"

His unexpected question forced me to focus on Dad's actions, and not to worry about the bad things that might happen. After a moment, I answered, "Yes. It's his dream."

"Good. A son should have faith in his father."

The old fisherman stood and directed his advice to Dad's battle. He shouted, "Hold the line out over the water as far as you can. The fish is trying to hide under a rock." When Dad followed his advice, the old guy added, "Now gently move the fishing line up and down to tire him out. Don't pull the hook out of his mouth. That's it...keep at it."

Dad continued fighting for what seemed like a really long time. There was no way to know who was winning; it was a tug-of-war between two equals. The fish was in its element and Dad was in his. Observers on the breakwall were transfixed by the scene of the struggle. It was well past lunch, but no one was ready to leave the captivating fight. I sat down; *my dad is doing all the work, then why am I so tired?*

A teenage boy, who wanted to help him, climbed down to sit on the rocks behind him. Dad said something that I couldn't hear. The teenager scrambled back and came towards me. "He wants a drink." I handed him the canteen, and he scurried back, Dad took a gulp and returned to the routine of raising and lowering the line. After another 15 minutes or so, the fish made a move from under the rocks.

I stood again, excitedly jumping up and down, arms flailing like windmill blades. "Holy shit! Holy shit! Kill that bastard!" Dad gave me a side-glance of disapproval, before returning to his fight. My face got red and I stopped cussing. With considerable effort, Dad was able to start reeling in the line. It got too hard to turn the crank on the reel, so he paused to rest and let his enemy swim back and  forth. Then we saw a flash of white near the surface. One spectator pointed and shouted, "There it is! There it is!" Dad continued working the line until the fish came near the rocks. I saw a large fish almost within Dad's reach.

Someone yelled, "It's a Carp, a big one!"

The teenager reached out, grabbed the line, stuck two fingers in its gill, and heaved the big fish on the rocks. It helplessly flapped its tail next to Dad's leg. Dad put a leg over the Carp to keep it in place. Everyone cheered. Dad had won! Exhausted, he laid his head back on the rocks to rest.

I moved closer for a better look. *The fish sure is big, as fat as me.*

The teenager pulled a measuring tape from his pocket, measured the fish, and in a loud voice declared, "Twenty-eight inches long." I cheered again, although I wasn't sure why. I knew it was a good thing but had no idea how great it was. I went closer, sat on my haunches, and stared into the forlorn fish eye. *That Carp is sad because it lost the fight. Is there a little brain behind that eye? Does that hook hurt? Is it smart enough to know it will be killed and eaten today? Or is it sad because it will never see its family again?*

I think that Dad noticed me brush a tear away. He didn't say anything. After a few minutes, he removed the hook from its mouth. Then he patted the Carp's side and pushed it into the lake. There was a buzz of disbelief from the spectators. With a slap of its tail, the fish disappeared. There was another softer murmur of understanding, or was it appreciation. I took a deep breath; I couldn't believe Dad would give up his prize after what he went through to get it.

Dad climbed the rocks with his fishing rod in hand. His hands were trembling, his pants were wet, and there was a hole in the knee. I saw red from the scrape on his leg. He glanced at me and then shook the old man's hand. "Thanks for your help."

The old guy put his hand back on my shoulder and said to me, "The others are glad because a brave fish will live. Every fisherman here will now have the chance to catch that big Carp someday." I was sure that Dad had another reason to let him free, but I knew he would never share it.

Dad came over and hugged me. We had enjoyed enough fishing on that day. After eating our cheese sandwiches in silence, we started for home. I carried as much fishing gear as I could. Dad slouched on the wicker streetcar seat as we rode back. I saw closed eyes and a slight smile. I guessed he was reliving his exciting battle. My grin was even wider than his.

The car rocked us from side to side, accompanied by clicking rhythm of the steel wheel on the track. I was exhausted but felt too excited to nap. Dad was still damp with lake water and sweat — smelling like fish and fear. What I had learned about him this day I would never forget. Earlier, I just considered him to be a payday drinker. But, from now on, he would be my hero.

After a few minutes, I spoke up. "Dad?"

His eyes were half closed. "Yes, what is it, Buddy?"

"Dad, you are the all-time best breakwall fisherman."

He stifled a laugh. "No, just lucky. The old fisherman is the best." He patted my knee. "But, I'm glad you feel that."

"I think that fish just gave up because it knew that it was useless fighting against you. I can't believe how big it was. Wait till I tell Tim. Boy, I wish I could catch a fish like that someday." I sat thinking. "Dad?"

"Yes."

"Did you push him back in the lake because you felt sorry for the fish?"

He didn't answer for a minute. "Not really. For my whole life, I hoped for that chance. It was the fight, not the fish that I dreamed about."

I could see Dad wanted to nap, but I thought of another question before I'd let him rest. "What will you say to Mom, when she asks what happened to the big fish?"

He thought for a while. Then I noticed a twinkle in his eye and a sly grin. "We will tell her it was too big to eat." I realized this was a joke between us fishermen and laughed out loud. Dad seldom said something that made me laugh.

Later, I learned that Mom didn't care about the fish. She was relieved when we were home safe but decided that I needed a good bath because I smelled like worms and fish. It couldn't wait until my usual bath day. All during my cleaning overhaul, she complained about the extra work Dad had caused, but I noticed her smile, whenever I excitedly described another day's highlight. An hour later, I sat on the couch smelling like soap, while I daydreamed about fishing.

After a few more fishing trips with Dad, I did learn how to fish. I enjoyed fishing on the Lakefront breakwall with my friends until I moved away from Cleveland as a young man.

"Money saved is as good as money gained."

— DANISH PROVERB —

CHAPTER TWO

Call to Adventure

Never Give Up

Cleveland, Ohio — 1942, Age 7

Summer vacation was over, and it was time to begin second grade. The dreaded first day of school had arrived. Supporting my head with both hands, I looked at the untouched breakfast with sleepy eyes. I wore a new cotton shirt and itchy woolen pants. My sister finished her oatmeal, anxious to start first grade. She would love school, but I hated it. Tired of my complaining, Mom frowned, as her hands moved like lightning, making peanut butter and jelly sandwiches for our lunch boxes.

Mom looked at me. "Eat your breakfast. You need the energy to work well." I could not eat a single bite; my stomach was filled with knots and my mind with images of forthcoming terrors. I recalled how dumb I felt last year each time Sister asked the class a question. Hands shot up all around before a possible answer even occurred to me. Gradually I learned that my answer would have been wrong anyway if I had responded faster. In addition to feeling inferior to other children, I was worried about the mean nuns. Sister always looked directly at me when she had something critical to say. During the first year, I struggled just to convince myself to leave for school each morning, not that Mom gave me a choice.

She handed me my jacket and gave me a determined look. "Time to go; you can do it and things will gradually get easier." I didn't believe her; the school was unbearable.

With both me and my sister in school, Mom talked to Dad about finding a paying job. With World War II underway, many men were in the military, so women were welcome in the work-force. A few weeks later, she got an office job at the same company, where Tim's mother worked. Dad didn't like it and I heard him argue with her.

"I am the breadwinner of this family. This will look as if I can't support my family."

"No Joe, we are doing fine, but this job will help us get ahead. We will pay off the mortgage sooner and will also be able to buy some better furniture. Moreover, it will also help pay for the kids to go to St. Boniface."

"Well, if you are tired, don't expect me to do any of your house-work chores."

She smiled and took the job. In fact, she worked there until she retired years later. Our family's standard of living really benefited from her employment. She also made new friends, who later be-came her travel companions. She did what she loved – traveled. She enjoyed new experiences using her own earnings and without af-fecting Dad's desire to stay home.

Since Mom was unable to get home from work by the time we returned from school, she hired a lady to watch us for three hours on school days. Her name was Lena, short for Magdalena. Lena had recently emigrated from the same town in Austria, where Grandpa Joseph was born. Chubby and much older than Mom, Lena wore a handmade housedress every day and spoke with an accent. She had no family in America and appreciated having the part-time work. Lena loved children, which was clear from the care and attention she gave to us. We also loved Lena like an adopted grandmother. I especially liked her because she favored boys and gave me more freedom than my parents did.

One Monday, a few months after school started, I came home frustrated and angry because things had not gone well. I dropped my book bag into a corner. Lena was doing laundry in the basement, so Diane and I had the living room to ourselves. I began to jump on the couch, just for fun. Diane yelled, "Lena, Clarence is being bad."

I hit Diane in the stomach, which started her bawling. After a full minute, she was still on the floor screaming. *I must have hurt her bad.* I reached for her shoulder, and she pulled away. "I'm sorry, I didn't mean it." Her screaming got louder in reply, which indicated her crying was an act. So, I tried my favorite diversion. "Oh, you aren't hurt; come here, let's create a playhouse with chairs and cushions."

She stopped crying, and I heaved a sigh of relief. We weren't permitted to play with furniture, but Diane would bend the rule with me because she loved to play with her dolls in my cushion and chair house.

Lena watched from the doorway with a slight smile and folded arms. She often looked the other way if I did no serious harm. Once she made me stand in the corner for ten minutes, but she never spanked me.

After building the cushion house, I let out my frustration by knocking it all down. Diane wailed in protest. Lena grimaced "What's wrong with you today?" I didn't answer.

* * *

There was an advantage of being someone like me, who was quiet and merged with the crowd — bullies mostly left me alone. They targeted smarter children and those who didn't fit in. On the playground, I tried to hide that I was scared of mean boys by sneering at them for effect. I only pretended to be brave when I was playing; imagining I was a hero like in a storybook or a movie.

There were three guys in the school, who were class bullies. They were always together and causing trouble. Today, during recess, the leader decided to call me names. I backed away but he followed with a determined expression and gave me a hard push. I stumbled backward and tried to maintain my footing. I knew what was coming next because I had seen him do it to other boys. I imagined myself pushed to the ground and hearing other children laughing, as he kicked me in the backside, where he knew a bruise wouldn't show.

But that didn't happen; I got so angry at the expected outcome that I lost the ability to think clearly and avoid trouble. *How can this guy, who is my size push me around like this? Dad might hit me when he's drunk, but then, Dad is bigger than me.* Without a second thought, I took a wild swing, cutting my knuckles on his front tooth. He looked startled. I realized that my impulsive act committed me to continue or they would make me pay. So, I put all my fury into a harder punch to the middle of his chest. Before I knew it, he was sitting in the dirt with a bewildered expression. I was even more surprised. I challenged him with bluster that I didn't really feel.

Just like the hero in a movie, my mouth held an exaggerated twist and my eyes squinted at him. "Stand up, so I can hit you again."

Luckily, the bluff worked. He didn't get up and his friends held back. After a final hard stare, I slowly turned and swaggered away, holding my bleeding hand. It hurt like hell. I was glad that Mom gave me a clean handkerchief for school each washday. When the bell rang, I returned to class with the hankie wrapped around my torn knuckles.

I walked past Sister and I tried to look like it didn't hurt. "What's wrong with your hand Clarence?"

"I scratched it during recess. I'm okay." I looked away and hurried to my desk. Nothing more was said.

That afternoon the bullies started teasing in the classroom, where I couldn't hit back without getting into trouble. Their new weapon for bugging me was my strange name — Clarence. There were no other boys, who were named Clarence in my class, perhaps even in the entire school. So, the boys taunted me, whenever they could. "Clarence has a weird name. Clarence is weird." Even I thought it was weird, and I was stuck with it forever.

That evening I asked Mom, "Why did you give me a weird name?"

She looked at me with a start. "What! Clarence is a great name."

Still not satisfied, I crossed my arms and squinted. "And my name is too long. All the guys have short names. I would rather just be Buddy all the time."

She glanced at me out of the corner of her eyes with lips scrunched. "Come here. I'm going to tell you something I have not told anyone and you must promise to keep it a secret."

She held my sleeve as we moved into the living room. I sat next to her on the couch and leaned my head against her arm. It was a comfortable place. I hugged my knees and listened. "I like to hear about secrets."

"We called you Clarence because that is a very special and dignified name. It is not common like names of most of the other boys. It is fit for a person, who does good things, in fact even important things."

"What things?

"I'll tell you as much as I know." She stared at something far away as she remembered. "A few days after you were born my parents rode streetcars all the way from the East Side to see you. You were their first grandchild. Grandpa Joseph held you in his arms and cried."

"Why?"

"Why did Grandpa cry?"

"Yeah."

"Well, I didn't have to ask because I knew. Those were tears of joy because you belonged to him. You are part of his family, and he loves you. That is the cycle of a truly happy life. Some day you will understand when you have a family too. He knew that if he hadn't taken a chance and come to America, he probably wouldn't have had a family. Do you know what that means?"

"What?"

"You would not be here."

"But what about my name?"

There was a twinkle in her eye. "He looked at you and held you for a long time — until you pooped your diaper; then he gave you to grandma."

"Oh Mom, just tell me."

"Relax; I am getting to the good part. That was when Grandpa told me that you were going to be special when you grew up and, so, you would need a special name."

"Why am I going to be special?"

"I know you are special because I feel it in my heart. I don't know exactly why Grandpa was so sure. It will be up to you to find out why you are going to be special. As you grow up, you will make it happen. It will be a quest, like searching for the solution to a mystery or finding a treasure. Remember *Treasure Island*, the story about pirates that we read?"

"Yes, that was good. Will I be like a storybook hero?"

"We don't know your story yet, but I can tell you grandpa's story. When he was a boy in Austria, Grandpa's family was very poor. Their father had died and he and his brother lived with their mother. The Church provided his mother with food and other help to survive. The church pastor helped the boys get an education and guided them as they grew. Because there was not enough work in their village, the pastor helped the boys get to America, when they grew up." She looked at the ceiling again, deep in her memory of what her father told her years before. "The day Grandpa left for America, the pastor blessed him with holy water and said that he would do well in his life. Also, the pastor predicted that grandpa's first grandchild," she touched my shoulder, "that's you, would have special talents and would be very successful."

"Me? But…"

She continued, "It seems you are wondering how did that pastor knew about you, even before you were born?"

I nodded.

"I think that he just assumed that there would be a grandson eventually, it's just a mystery. Grandpa said the pastor was very smart and was able to predict the future." She paused and looked down at me with a hopeful expression. Then she resumed the story. "You were his first grandchild and holding you in his arms reminded Grandpa of that pastor."

I listened trying to understand. What Mom said seemed so strange but now my name made sense in a weird way. Still, that didn't mean I liked it. Mom further explained, "I could not get the idea of you being special out of my mind. When it was time to pick a name for your baptism, Clarence seemed perfect."

"But the other kids are all smarter than me; how could I do something special?"

"Being smartest doesn't always matter. There are many ways to be special."

"Mom, what am I going to be when I grow up?"

"I don't know. I cannot foretell the future. You will discover that in time, during your life journey. But what I know is that you will do well; Grandpa told us that you would."

"What about my weird name?" I asked again.

She sighed. Her expression told me that she was disappointed, "If you prefer Buddy, we will call you Buddy."

"But, in school?"

"I'll ask the Sister to use Buddy in school. Though, I'm not sure she will. She likes Clarence because it was the name of a Catholic saint. But I'll try, is that good enough?"

"Yes!"

"Now, let's read a story together like we used to do when you were little. I picked one up at the library called *Alice in Wonderland*."

"Okay, that will be fun."

Luckily, later when mother talked to the Sister, she did agree. For the rest of the year, I was called Buddy and the teasing lessened. But, I was still left with a mystery to solve. *Will I be special? What must I do? Can I do it?* It seemed like an even bigger weight on my shoulders than surviving second grade.

* * *

When we were children, Mom and Dad took my sister and me to our grandparents' houses to visit aunts, uncles, and cousins from both sides of the family. These were special occasions like a birthday, marriage, or a funeral. For both the families, the highlight of the visit was a big meal. Tables were pushed together so everyone could be part of the conversation. It provided a way for a shy boy to learn about people.

As I listened to the grownup talk, I was struck by how different the two families were. My father's relatives were friendly and generous, but more afflicted with life's tribulations. Adults worried about health issues, job security, and neighborhood problems. They loved German desserts and schnapps. The house where Dad grew up had expanded over the years with do-it-yourself additions and was overtaken by disrepair.

On the other hand, Mom's family seemed more passionate and serious. They discussed work achievements and education. Grandpa Joseph Kreiner, my maternal grandfather, who had emigrated from Austria related the latest news from the "old" country. He was sympathetic to downtrodden workers, unions, and socialistic ideas. He proudly told us that his forbearers fought in peasant revolts. Also, his house in East Cleveland was larger with newer furnishings than the house of my paternal grandfather.

The next time we went to the Kreiners for a Sunday visit, I planned to ask Grandpa Joseph the question that had been burning inside me since Mom told me her secret. Was I going to be special some day?

All the families were busy talking in his living room. Grandpa was dozing in his chair after the big meal. I sat on the floor next to his chair and touched his knee to wake him up.

"What?"

I moved towards him and whispered, hoping that no one else would hear. "Grandpa, did you really tell Mom that I would be special some day?"

"Well, yes, but it's up to you to discover your future."

"What must I do?"

"First work hard on your studies and never give up on your dream. I got my start in the old country, where I learned to always do the right thing. Then seek out adventures and test yourself. I could not get work in Austria, so I came to America. That was my dream." He spoke loudly and the others overheard.

Dad exclaimed, "We know all about that story grandpa." Mom gave Dad a critical look and he clamped his mouth closed.

Mom pulled me away. "Leave Grandpa to rest."

Nothing more was said, and I was no closer to learning what was required of me to become special. *I guess I'll have to discover that on my own.*

I soon learned that Sister did not think I was special. There were no regular studies the following Monday because every second grader in the city took a standard intelligence test. Sister liked the test because it labeled each of us with a single number called the intelligence quotient. My IQ score was well below average, which confirmed what everyone, including my parents, suspected — I was dumb. I was not a moron, but I wasn't in the same league as most of the other children. Sister moved me to a front seat in order to keep an eye on me.

After two years, I had acquired a reputation among the nuns for being slow. Because they prayed, ate, and socialized in their residence house next to the church, my reputation, and now my IQ score stuck with me from grade-to-grade and teacher-to-teacher. It was like a signboard hanging from my neck. Each time I passed to the next grade, the new teacher knew all about my shortcomings. I hoped to start fresh each September, but sadly that never happened.

Once I noticed my teacher talking in the hall with another nun. They studied me as I passed. I heard a few whispered words including, 'retarded' and 'slow.' I was sure they meant me, the hopeless loser. On the last day of the second grade, an older kid warned me, "Sister Mary Ruth in the third grade is mean. Be careful."

* * *

Summer passed quickly, and I now sat in Sister Mary Ruth's third-grade class. I soon decided that the other boy was right about her. Once again I found myself in the front seat. Her constant companion was an 18-inch wooden ruler, which she carried in her hand as she walked between the desks. It served as her pointer. Whenever she wanted to emphasize something or get our attention, she slapped the ruler on the nearest surface. It made a loud, frightening *crack* like a gunshot. I jumped even when I knew it was coming. All day, I remained on the edge, waiting for her to sound her displeasure and my front-row desk got a regular beating.

Each day the arithmetic lesson followed attendance, Mass, and religion studies. Then she asked the hard questions. "Clarence, stand and tell us multiplication tables, starting with eight." Sister Mary Ruth did not agree to call me Buddy, so I was again Clarence in the third-grade.

I'd stand with one hand touching the edge of my desk for extra support. "Eight times one equals eight, eight times two is sixteen...." My wavering voice betrayed my nervousness. Soon after starting, I'd make a mistake or hesitate too long and she would stop me cold with a ruler slap. Someone giggled bringing another slap and her sharp look, which always resulted in silence. Then she calmly stated the right answer and asked me to continue. After a while, I was told to sit so that another student could complete the recitation. A similar routine occurred in the afternoon with spelling, which was another difficult subject for me.

I never saw her hit a student or even utter an angry word, but Sister Mary Ruth's body language and ruler-message betrayed her thoughts about us. I felt terrified every day. Why was I scared? Well, I was sure if I made too many mistakes she would use that stick on me. I also thought that other children would laugh when I'd say something dumb, which they were never permitted to do. I expected to be sent home with a note, which did happen.

Sinner

One morning before class I fidgeted at my desk with trembling hands waiting for the bell, desperate to do well on the day's multiplication drill. I heard rain ticking against the glass as Sister Mary Ruth rushed to close the classroom windows tightly. Children brushed past me, heading to the coatroom, smelling like wet jackets and rubber rain gear. I closed my eyes trying to relax and the idea came to me — a flash of inspiration. With left hand hidden in my lap, I used a pen on my palm, printing answers to the expected questions. Then I sat back confidently.

Soon it was my turn to recite. Sister Mary Ruth saw me glance down before answering her first question. She took a step in my direction. "Show me your hand!" I was caught red-handed and red-faced. I couldn't bear her disappointed and judgmental stare, so I turned away and closed my eyes. The offending palm covered with tiny numbers was exposed and I held my breath, fully expecting a slap on the outstretched hand. It didn't happen. She wouldn't punish me, yet.

As soon as Sister Mary Ruth rang the recess bell, I headed towards the door. But before I could make it outside, she said, "Clarence, come here! I want to talk to you." My head hurt. *Mom hates cheaters. She warned me not to cheat. I've disappointed her.* Sister Mary Ruth's voice was like a snake's hiss, "Sit down Clarence." She spoke resolutely, giving me a stern look, "There will be no play time for you today. This is the last straw. You do not know multiplication, and now you are cheating. Do you know you did a bad thing?" I nodded, too scared and ashamed to speak. "Before you go home, I will give you a note for your parents. Come back to get it. And be sure to tell Father about this sin next time you go to Confession."

The word 'sin' felt like a sharp knife stabbed into my stomach.

Aren't sins things like murder or robbery, not a little cheating on arithmetic?

Sister continued, "Now go back to your seat and wait for the next class to begin."

There were several minutes before the next class started and I kept thinking about the sin. *Will I go to hell now? What would become of me?* I was later surprised when I learned the punishment. The note summoned Mom to meet Sister Mary Ruth after school on Friday. It described specifics of my "sin" as well as my slow learning of arithmetic and spelling.

Mom's meeting with Sister would not include me, so I would only learn about my fate later. That night I overheard Mom and Dad talking after I was supposed to be in bed. They sat, holding hands across the kitchen table, looking glum and talking quietly. I crouched at the top of the stairway so that I could hear. What they said surprised and startled me.

Dad said, "Maybe repeating a grade will be good for him."

"I don't think so, Joe. That should be the last resort because it would humiliate him."

"You mean it would humiliate your family" Dad argued.

She looked down and said, "Yes, all of us."

Mom's family valued education and hard work. Her youngest brother was not only a good student but was about to earn a degree in chemical engineering. At family gatherings, he was referred to with pride and admiration. He was the only relative to have attended college — a high standard to meet. Failing third grade would be a major disappointment for everyone. My parents faced the difficult decision of what to do.

Dad slowly shook his head, "I still don't believe my son can't pass third grade."

Mom said, "I've been thinking about a possible way. I could spend more time helping him. I will talk to the school about it."

Dad looked angry. "I always thought he would get over his problem and grow up to be a regular guy."

Later, I lay in bed staring at the ceiling. Sister Mary Ruth would make the decision to make me repeat the class with the approval of her Mother Superior. My parents could only offer suggestions or state their opinions.

* * *

On Friday, Mom left work early for the meeting. After several days of worry, this was her chance to discuss the plan to become my tutor. She promised Sister that she would do whatever was required. "I've been helping him with homework all along," Mom said. "Now I'll step-up my coaching. What seems to help him is repetition and memorizing. It is hard work though and I'm not sure he will stick to it."

Sister said, "All right, you can try. However, you have to understand that he must improve."

"Yes."

After supper, Mom sat me down at the kitchen table for a talk. I sensed annoyance and determination. "Do you want to repeat the second grade and wait till next year to start third grade all over again?"

"No!" I imagined the little kids in second grade watching me being led into their class. Still, getting through the third grade seemed too hard. I stared straight ahead, undecided.

"Well, what can we do about it?" Mom asked.

"I don't know."

"Would you like me to help you in passing?"

I looked up with hope. "Yes."

Her eyes brightened. In a crisis, Mom was at her best. "Then here is what we can do," she said. "It will not be a certainty, and you will have to work much harder." She paused for a long time, and her expression became thoughtful. "Each day, instead of us just working together, when you have questions we will spend one full hour doing homework." She paused to be sure that I was paying attention. "This will be hard for both of us because I work all day and then come home to make supper. Do you understand that we will do this each school day?" Before replying, I thought about not being able to play with Tim as much.

"I don't know."

"If you mean you cannot do it, then I'll tell Sister Mary Ruth that it's best for you to repeat the grade." She pronounced "repeat" as if it was a dirty word.

"No!"

"Well, then it is settled. Do you promise to do homework with me after school, without complaining?"

I took a deep breath and looked down, holding my head tightly with both hands. "Yes."

"Look at me and say, 'Yes Mom, I promise.'"

Slowly I looked up, "Yes Mom, I promise."

"Making a promise is serious, and keeping a promise is important. If the Lone Ranger tells Tonto he'll come back to save him, he will always keep his promise. No excuses. Do you understand when you make a promise, you must keep it, no matter what?"

I looked away and whispered, "Yes." It was the worst punishment I had ever got. I started to leave, but she grabbed my arm. She had more to say.

"Cheating is a lot like lying. In this case, you tried to fool Sister Mary Ruth into thinking you knew the multiplication tables when you did not. In addition to being wrong, pretending you knew could have kept you from getting help. It would have been better to think about how best to learn than to figure out ways to cheat. It was also dumb because liars and cheaters get caught sooner or later. And you are a terrible liar! Everyone can tell when you are lying." I looked up, surprised. I never thought I was so obvious.

I still had another worry. "Mom, what about my sin?"

"Oh, it was a sin all right. It was not dreadful because it did not hurt someone else; it was a venial sin. I think you will need to tell the priest about it when you go to confession. Then you will be as pure as the angel I know you to be." Every word added to the heavy weight on my head. I decided never to lie or cheat again. It was too painful.

The next day, Mom came home from work with several study aids that Sister thought might help — much more advanced books than I was used to, books I might only understand with assistance. Sister told Mom about a school supply store with flashcards, which were useful for memorizing things like multiplication tables, spelling, and vocabulary. For an hour each afternoon, our kitchen was a homeschool, where Mom helped me read and run drills. All this came as an additional burden on the household budget and her time. I spent many hours trying to keep my promise by working rather than playing. At the end of each work session, she gave me a small glass of Ovaltine chocolate milk as a reward. To entice me more, she said she would take me downtown to a special Disney movie when I would pass the third grade. She never said "if" I passed.

Dad didn't help tutor because he lacked much schooling and had little patience. He paid good money in tuition and expected results. His assumption was that if he put his son into a school a man should come out the other end.

Then I presented another crisis for Mom. After several months of tutoring, and followed by another poor report from Sister Mary Ruth, I became discouraged and decided that tutoring didn't help. It was just a lot of added work that kept me from having fun. The time had come when I couldn't continue.

I told Mom, "I don't want to do this. It's too tough. I don't care if I fail."

"Are you always going to quit when things get too hard?" She asked, getting hold of my collar. "If you do, you will never be as good as I know you can be; you will never be special. Remember, you made a promise. Now I want you to make another one."

My brow creased. "What?"

In her firm motherly voice she said, "When you try hard as you can and still think that you cannot win, you must say to yourself, "Never give up." Do you get that? And then you work even harder. Do not quit, unless you have been defeated for good and forever. Like when a bandit has the drop on the Lone Ranger. The Ranger lowers his gun only because there is no choice. But then he returns to win another day." I opened my mouth to object, but no words were there. So, I closed my lips, and we continued the tutoring.

I never got into trouble again for breaking rules at St. Boniface. I had learned my lesson about cheating and didn't need another. By the end of the school year, I was so well behaved that the other children called me "the good boy."

Of the books, Mom bought, one was called *Modern Machines*. It was my favorite. It was full of machinery drawings and I was fascinated by how gears, levers, and fasteners worked. I spent hours trying to figure out how these parts might run in real machines. Tracing the parts from the book and on blank paper helped me understand what was happening.

Summer vacation arrived at last. Mom's tutoring and our studying together succeeded. She had a big smile as she waved the report card in front of me. "You passed, and I am so proud because you stuck with your promise to study. You worked hard and I know it wasn't easy. You did the work and you won the prize — promotion. Most children your age could not do it. I think you have a special gift of persistence." But this was Mom's victory as well.

* * *

The extra reward came on a sunny June Saturday, Mom's day off. She took Diane and me downtown to an early afternoon show at the Palace Theater. The marquee above the entrance proclaimed: *Dumbo — Walt Disney's Full-Length Feature Production*. While she stood in line for tickets, I looked at a large poster on the wall. I noticed that Dumbo was an elephant with big ears and strange friends, a mouse, and a crow. *Oh boy, I can't wait.*

This show would be my first time inside the grandest movie theater in the city. Its big lobby looked like pictures I had seen of a king's palace. The carpeting was thick and there were huge, old-looking paintings on the walls with wide gold frames. We went up a broad curving stairway. There were big sparkling glass lights hanging from the ceiling and the theater was humongous. There must have been a thousand seats; only half were filled with people today, and there were lots of children.

The show started with a short cartoon, *Donald Duck in the Army*. I liked it. This was followed by *Dumbo* on a big, bright, and colorful screen. I was soon part of the story. When the show ended, and we came out into the sunlight, I was still thinking about Dumbo. Mom asked, "Did you like it?"

I was quick to answer. "I loved Dumbo! I cried when the other elephants laughed at his funny ears when he was little. Then I laughed when his best friend helped him learn to fly. It reminded me of my friend Tim."

When we got home, I ran to find Tim. I told him about Dumbo and the Donald Duck cartoon. World War II had ended, but Tim and I were still interested in playing war, combat, and being soldiers. We passed on stories and news, whenever we learned something interesting, even if it was just from a cartoon.

I said, "Donald was doing basic training in the Army. He went through an obstacle course."

Tim said, "There's still time to pretend before supper." We found our homemade rifles and played Army until we were called to eat.

The remaining grade school years passed quickly, including the routine of Mom's daily tutoring. After eight years at St. Boniface, I was glad that I was leaving. I was happy to be free of restricting discipline and intimidation. I wondered if those nuns, who liked to talk about my learning problems still remembered me. Did they even care enough to think of me? Now, Mom wondered if private schools were really always better than the public schools. My parents decided that I would attend the public junior high school from now on. I was relieved.

In junior high, I was less bothered by my learning problem. While the IQ tests were proven to be largely useless for predicting a student's future performance, they were popular and widely used in the 1940s. I later learned that I was dyslexic. This condition never disappeared entirely but it grew manageable with time.

* * *

Wack, Wack! I heard the now familiar sound, as I hurried past the science room. I smiled, imagining a boy being punished. It was a traditional paddling.

Thomas Jefferson Junior High was within walking distance, but a bit farther from home than St. Boniface. I found the contrast between grade school and junior high refreshing. It felt more grown up. Teachers at Thomas Jefferson included both men and women, which was different than being taught by nuns only. These teachers did much less handholding; mostly letting us decide which classes to take. Discipline was still effectively applied.

I was surprised and impressed by the punishment tradition for boys that had evolved there. It was both physical (paddling) and psychological (embarrassment). Boys in woodworking class made the paddles. They were carefully designed, elaborately carved, and colorfully painted, with easy-grip handles, and holes in the paddle itself. Supposedly holes reduced air resistance when the paddle was swung. A student, who made a paddle would present it as a gift to a male teacher who didn't have one. He would proudly display it on his classroom wall. A paddling punishment was done in front of the class with exaggerated ceremony for our entertainment and amusement. It started with the dreaded statement, "Bring me the paddle." Older students seemed to expect a boy being punished to act as if paddling didn't hurt. It sure looked to me like it did. The teacher swinging the paddle was expected to not hold back, but I'm sure he did.

I was paddled only once. All of the boys in the gym class had done something meriting punishment, so everyone was paddled. It was actually fun. In that instance, I knew that the gym teacher did hold back on his swing — or just got tired. That's when I learned this was a long-established school tradition, like a ritual hazing.

Classes at Thomas Jefferson were a mix of trade-related and scholarly because the school served a working-class neighborhood.

Boys were exposed to woodworking and printing, as well as to history and geometry. Girls also took history and geometry, but then added typing and homemaking. The expectation was to learn a practical trade, find a skilled job, and get married. Later I realized scholarly courses could also be practical. And no one informed us that most of these "practical" trades could drastically change during our working lifetimes, to the point of becoming obsolete.

During junior high, my self-confidence took a leap forward because my grades improved substantially. Now, I figured that I was as smart as most of the other kids of my age, but new challenges lay ahead to test that assumption.

I started thinking more about high school during the summer after junior high. I would soon be in Cleveland's West Technical High. As a freshman, I assumed that most other guys were sure to be older and smarter. Also, I'd be required to choose a career path, which I was not ready for. *Will I be able to do it all and also make new friends?* There was no one at home, who could answer my questions because neither of my parents had completed high school. My approach would be to keep a low profile and to avoid doing anything dumb. I just wanted to fit in and graduate. I felt bad, though because it was not the kind of plan someone special would make. I had decided that grandpa's prediction was total nonsense.

Finding a Path

Cleveland, Ohio — 1950, Age 15

As I dressed on the morning of my first day of high school, a rumbling stomach resonated my nervousness. I tried to stay positive, which was Mom's method to approach the future. *Even if nothing else goes well, I will look sharp today.*

Two weeks earlier, I had gone downtown to a popular men's clothing store and bought an expensive blue long-sleeved shirt with my own money. It was the first time I had shopped for clothes without Mom's advice. *I'll soon be in high school, and it's time for me to start making my own clothing decisions.* I did have some doubts, but when I tried on the shirt, the salesman walked over to me, put his hand on my shoulder, and assured me that I looked great.

"You are right in style. We have a popular accessory this year, suspenders. It's a handsome detail the girls will notice."

I selected a pair of bright yellow suspenders. I showed the purchases to Mom when I got home and I could tell she did not like the vivid shades of blue and yellow as much as I did. She swallowed her comment, which left me uninformed, but content.

Teen years are a time for self-discovery, and mine were no exception. I first became aware of my technical interests and aptitude when Mom bought me the book about modern machines. Now, I was headed to a technical high school, leading to a technical career. I expected to enjoy the classes and for the first time looked forward to school.

Learning was still a challenge, but I knew that if I spent extra time reviewing and memorizing, I'd succeed. If a particular goal excited me, I was able to stick to the job of achieving it for long periods, even plodding through tedious or boring tasks. This was how I had passed third grade. I wondered if destiny gave me a gift to balance my learning problem. Persistence seemed to offset dyslexia.

After spending ninth grade in junior high, I'd be going to a three-year high school for grades ten through twelve. West Tech prepared students for semi-skilled work. Most boys took classes like machine shop, auto repair, and drafting; and girls took dressmaking, typing, and shorthand. In Cleveland, such skills were essential for finding well-paying work after graduation.

The school was on West 93rd Street, and I'd use public transportation — the bus. I knew where homeroom was because I had attended a half-day orientation a few weeks before. So, I planned to arrive early, well before the attendance would be taken. I liked to be prompt when I was not sure of myself. And on this first day, I was far from sure about anything.

It was a beautiful cool, sunny September morning when I got off the bus. West Tech looked large and impressive from the other side of the street, four brick stories with ample ornamental stonework. *It must have cost the city plenty.* I joined many serious-looking students marching towards the building. It seemed momentous like some force compelled us onward to our future.

I looked for the gals first, curious to learn about older high school girls. *Are they more grown up? Would I find a girlfriend someday?* When I saw them fluttering all around in their multi-colored skirts and tight sweaters they reminded me of beautiful butterflies. One even glanced at me and smiled. I looked away with alarm, hoping she didn't guess that I had been admiring her bosom.

There was something strange about the cars parked bumper-to-bumper in front of the school. I soon discovered there was a special car exhibit in the curb lane. This also turned out to be a favorite place for students to meet friends and to chat before school or during the breaks. Even those who walked directly into school without stopping to socialize had to pass by this area. Senior boys with the nicest cars claimed the best parking spots.

These weren't the ordinary factory cars. Cars attracting the most attention were hot rods or beautifully customized versions of older models. They had been lovingly restored, modified, and painted with multiple coats of glossy lacquers in unique colors and dramatic designs. Today, in perfect weather, proud owners described their latest modifications and postured for girls. An effective way to amaze the freshmen girls was to rev up the engine, loudly proclaiming their car was the most powerful of all. The specialty mufflers on these cars roared with the slightest application of power and rumbled menacingly like distant thunder when the engine idled. It reminded me of male lions roaring to impress other lions.

The loud sounds harmonized with excited voices, colorful sights, and milling students. Exhaust smoke hung over everything. I had never seen anything like this spectacular show. That moment was when I first considered that it might be possible for a teenager like me to own a car.

After my first week at West Tech, it became evident that a car would provide opportunities for independence and fun. Cars also represented prestige. Having one would certainly help me fit in. These special cars also appealed to me as mechanical wonders and I came to appreciate the well-designed machine as a thing of beauty. I soon become obsessed with owning a car.

My first problem was to get enough money. I didn't know how much a car would cost but was sure that it would be a lot. It didn't seem within reach. If I did manage to buy a car, how would I get a driver's license? Dad never owned a car and did not drive. I could not see any way to do it, but I resolved to find a way.

It was a while before I realized that life was about to get better for the U.S. economy, Cleveland, and our family. Since the Great Depression, recovery had been slow and discouragement spread throughout the city. Some working class households had given up on the American dream. Now, work and jobs were easier to find and wages were rising. In the 1950s, Cleveland's economy and manufacturing companies prospered. The city was a major center of modern factory production. This could not have happened at a better time for a young guy like me in need of a car. But would I be able to see through the dark clouds of past thinking and set my sites high enough? I was not experienced enough to know that what I really needed was an education and a good career. The problem is a goal is only achievable if it is visible.

* * *

That evening I helped Mom dry dishes. This was one of several household chores my sister and I were assigned so we'd learn to be responsible family members and also earn small allowances while doing that.

Mom said, "What was your first week like?" Starting high school had been a whirlwind of new experiences, which I was yet to absorb fully, so I did not have much to say. Then I remembered the impressive cars.

My expression glowed. "You should see these sharp cars. The colors are bright, and they shine better than new. And, they were built by the guys using old car parts."

Mom said, "I don't understand why the boys put so much effort and money into fixing up junk cars."

She wouldn't understand something like that, so I won't even try to explain. After a few minutes thinking about the best way to bring up a related point I said, "Can we get a car someday for the family? Car companies are making new ones again, and used cars are cheaper than during the war."

"We don't need a car." She pushed a wet dish into my hands. "They are too expensive. We would need insurance too. Dad doesn't even drive. No, using the bus works just fine for us."

This was what I expected, but I was disappointed to actually hear it. All I could think as a reply was, "If we get a family car, I can learn to drive."

"No, you have more important things to learn. Just concentrate on the school work." She turned back to the sink.

For now, my concerns about buying a car had to wait. Mom and Dad were still worried about my doing well at school. Getting passing grades was my priority because I could not let them down.

Several months later, Mom quizzed me again about school. "Isn't it about time for you to decide what your career will be?"

"Not now, but soon. We try out different subjects before deciding on a final career. I've been looking at various programs. I have until the end of the year to pick my technical career."

"Technical! Don't they have college preparation?"

"Sure they have, but not many guys take it. I'm not interested in college." Mom opened her mouth, nothing emerged. Her shocked expression said it all.

The truth is I didn't know what I wanted to do in life. I had enjoyed woodworking in junior high but didn't want to adopt it as a profession. Most senior boys, who had cars took auto repair. Since I planned to get a car, I figured I'd take the same thing. However, when I asked for the auto repair class, I was told that they didn't have any seats available. So, I selected drafting instead.

I thought I might like drafting. Our teacher took the class to visit a real drafting office. My image of a draftsman was someone wearing a white button-down shirt, working in a clean office, at a large slanting table with his sleeves rolled up. He would design machine parts for someone else to make. It seemed interesting and fun.

By the end of the tenth grade, I decided that I liked the subject and the teacher, so drafting became my specialty and future career. I didn't consult my parents. When I told Mom, she did not look pleased.

She said, "I see. If that's what you want, I guess it will be all right. But I had hoped you would go to college like my brother." She hesitated and touched my arm. "If you are going to be a draftsman, be the best...and do not rule out college someday."

I felt important working at the large drawing table with its professional drafting machine. The machine kept the drawing arms in precise alignment and I spent many hours practicing on it.

* * *

Like most teens, I was experiencing the effects of being an adolescent. One day Mom took a close look at my face. "Those sores on your skin are getting worse. You have not been to the doctor for a long time; I'll make an appointment."

The doctor confirmed the sores were acne. "It will probably go away without treatment by the time Clarence is twenty. He may end up with a few scars, though." Then he added, "They discovered an x-ray treatment during the war, but it is costly and requires several visits. It helps most acne cases." He told Mom the details.

Acne was no surprise to me. I spent a lot of time looking at my skin in the mirror. The sores looked terrible and I felt ugly. I said to myself, *Twenty! By then I would have finished high school.* Then it occurred to me; *I will never have a girlfriend.* I was too embarrassed to say it out loud, even to Mom.

On the bus ride home, I whispered to her, "Can I get those X-rays to clear up my skin?"

She waved her hand dismissively. "Too expensive. My acne went away on its own, yours will too."

I struggled to adjust to the school's social life. The acne seemed worse each time I looked. On some days, I wished I could stay home so that no one could see me. I needed a fast cure and I understood that x-ray treatments are the best solution. I pleaded with Mom to pay for them. She identified with my adolescent sensitivity and was sympathetic, but maintained that it was too expensive. After several months of badgering, she gave in, and I received the treatments, which seemed to help. Mom never thought they were worth the cost, though.

Seemingly minor events can become turning points in life, and send us into a new direction. Receiving those x-ray treatments was such an event, although the impact would not be apparent for many years.

With time, my acne subsided enough and I felt that I may be able to attend the school dance. I had learned to dance before high school. My sister and her teen friends liked to practice slow dancing when they got together at our house. Tim and I were starting to like girls, dancing provided the perfect excuse to hold a girl in our arms for a few minutes. The two-step and box-step were my favorites because they were simple and slow.

Dressed in my blue shirt and yellow suspenders, I leaned against the gym wall next to Tim. We planned to observe and learn before asking anyone to dance. A student disc jockey sitting at a table with his stack of 45-rpm records and a microphone added rehearsed banter between dances — just like on the local radio station. He turned off most of the overhead lights so that the lighting was dim. Several seniors, who were the best dancers got attention and admiration as they demonstrated the jitterbug.

I was relieved to discover that the girls expected minimal conversation. I watched a boy dancing in front of me looking at his feet. *I can do better...* Most of the freshmen girls looked just as scared as I felt, which gave me the confidence to ask one of them to dance. This first dance partner preferred to lead, so we struggled to move together awkwardly. My next partner preferred to chat, so I became distracted, forgot the steps, and stepped on her toe. She squeaked "ouch," and limped off, leaving me alone and embarrassed. I was glad the lights were low. After just two dances, I went home, feeling emotionally worn out.

Years later, I recalled the blue shirt and yellow suspenders that I wore as a high school freshman. I wondered how Mom could let me wear the awful outfit to school. When I asked her about it, she said, "Oh I do remember. It was so gaudy that it could get you a job in a circus. You want to know why I didn't stop you from wearing them. Well, at that age you always complained when I picked out your clothes. It embarrassed you. I hoped that you would discover on your own how bad that outfit looked, and then learn a lesson about getting help when you needed it."

"Did I learn that lesson?"

"No."

"Energy and persistence conquer all things."

— BENJAMIN FRANKLIN —

CHAPTER THREE

Attracting Mentors

Car Guy

Cleveland, Ohio — 1951, Age 16

I sat at the kitchen table with my nose buried in the newspaper. On most days, I was only interested in the comic strips, but today was different. My dream to own a car seemed to be slipping away. As the end of the tenth grade approached, other boys had taken all the newspaper delivery routes in our part of town and I had not yet found a job. When I turned sixteen, I was old enough to apply for a work permit at the City Hall. Without success, I searched the *Plain Dealer* classified ads for a part-time job. Dad kept me busy with home projects, but I was not saving money. Buying a car in high school without a paying job no longer seemed possible.

I helped Dad on most of the Saturday afternoons. One day we were working side-by-side at his narrow, old workbench, which was squeezed behind the fat coal furnace that dominated our earthy-smelling basement. The work light was a bare 40-watt bulb hanging by a wire over the bench. We would have preferred to work outside, but it was raining. Dad and I enjoyed a friendly competition as I got older. I had already grown an inch taller than him, but he was stronger than me. He also knew a lot more about fixing things. I was in high school, a level he never achieved, so with the logic of a sixteen-year-old, I figured that I was smarter.

Dad said, "You are in high school, you should at least know how to fix a broken window pane."

"Well, then show me how." I examined the window frame that we had scraped and repainted last week. Our task that day was to replace the glass pane that was broken during the delivery of coal into our basement coal bin.

Dad held a large, dirt-covered piece of glass. "We will make another pane from this scrap glass. You clean the glass while I find my glass cutter. Try not to hurt yourself."

After three attempts and a lot of broken glass, we produced a usable pane. I learned how difficult it was to cut glass with a dull cutting tool. I sliced my hand while handling the new piece. After the first aid break, I was relegated to watching him as he secured the glass in the frame with glazing putty. As he washed his hands in the laundry tub, Dad said, "We will install the window next time." He grinned and pointed at my hand. "Well, you weren't much help today, were you?"

"I think I'll know how to do it the next time."

"We'll see. Knowing how to do it isn't enough. You also need hands-on practice. By the way, I might have some good news for you."

"What?"

"Let's get cleaned up. Then I'll tell you."

We sat down at the kitchen table. Mom made coffee for us, which I now preferred to Ovaltine because it seemed more grown up. Dad took his black, but I required ample cream and sugar. Dad was miserly with most things, like today's good news. I was anxious to hear what I hoped he would say.

He looked at me with a smile. "There might be a part-time job for you at Spang Bakery. They hire high school boys to clean-up on weekends. I told the cleaning boss that you were looking for part-time work." Dad grinned as he looked at my bandaged hand. "I told him how helpful you were around the house."

I held the bandaged hand to my forehead, closed my eyes, and waited. "Well, what did he say?"

"He said that you should go and meet him next Saturday at 8:00 in the morning."

* * *

A week later I arrived early and waited at the bakery's back door, well before the cleaning boss arrived. He was a tall, thin guy dressed in a gray janitor uniform. I saw "Spang Bakery" and "Gus" displayed on his shirt pocket. He looked at me and said, "Everyone makes the minimum hourly rate. You want to start next week?"

"Sure."

"I'll give you a quick tour now. The guys are coming in, but they already know what to do." I looked around the large space filled with bakery equipment and just a few workers on this Saturday. The place smelled like yeast, flour, and frosting. It was a cool day outside, but was extremely hot inside, even with the ovens turned off for the weekend.

Gus said, "During baking days, flour, dust, and other stuff drops on the floor and equipment. So, we clean it every Saturday. We do a careful and complete job because the city health inspector might visit for a check anytime. This is a commercial bakery and hundreds of people work here day and night. In addition to bakery products, they also create a lot of mess." I could see that this was more like a factory than a bakery shop.

"My Dad works here," I said.

"Yes, I know — Joe Arnold. He's here nights loading trucks with the finished bakery products. Some trucks deliver to retail stores and others drive through neighborhoods in the morning."

"Dad told me that some people can afford to buy fresh bakery every day."

"Yes, prices aren't bad. This place uses the latest production equipment to make most of the stuff." He pointed. "Look here at this automated bread oven." The oven was bigger than a semi-trailer truck. We walked past one of the boys sweeping with a large push broom. Gus tapped him on the shoulder and pointed at bread fragments under a table. The boy hurried to pick them up.

"There are six guys in my crew. In addition to the Saturday work, we do heavy-duty summer cleaning projects, each of which lasts several days. Those summer jobs can be hard work for some boys." He pointed, "They do things like climbing on this hot conveyor oven to vacuum the flour dust, or other smelly jobs, like scooping rotting dough from the floor's drain traps." He stopped and looked at me. "Are you sure that you are up for all the hard work?"

I stood straighter. "Sure."

I was soon on my way home with a day-old jelly donut in my hand and a smile on my face. I had a part-time job at last, which would get me closer to buying a car. This job might also provide a chance to learn more about production equipment and conveyor lines.

However, it did turn out to be a difficult and dirty job. I came to appreciate the advantage of training to be a draftsman, who worked in a clean office.

That evening, Mom said, "As long as you save most of your pay, we will not ask you to contribute to the family budget. Dad wanted you to pay your share because that's how he was raised, but I talked him out of it. This way you can get a head start to achieve your goals. If you are still living with us after high school, we will want you to pay a share when you are working full-time."

I saved all I could with the hope that I would have enough to buy a used car before graduation. It would have to be one of the least expensive cars available. Out of about 700 West Tech boys, only a few dozen owned a car and most of them were seniors. In the Cleveland metropolitan area, with its streetcars and buses, even heads of many households decided to forego the expense of a car.

* * *

One day, a year later, our family visited Mom's younger sister and her husband, Uncle Martin. They could not have children, so my uncle was always interested in what was going on in my life. His eyes lit up when I described a hot rod at West Tech.

"I always wanted a car, when I was in high school, but the war was on," he said, "Also, I did not have the money. Do you think you have saved enough?"

I'd been saving for two years now.

"I think I do. I've been looking at classified ads, but I don't know how to buy a used car."

His eyes opened wider, "I can help. How much would we have to work with?" I told him how much I had saved and described the cars at West Tech that I liked best.

After a few weeks, Uncle Martin called me on our shiny new black telephone, which for the last few days had prominently occupied a small table in the living room. We did not use it much and this was my first call on it. Dad said the phone was only for "important" calls, like emergencies.

I held the phone to my ear and heard Uncle Martin's voice. "I found the perfect car for you." He paused. I heard paper shuffling and pictured him looking at notes. "It's a black '42 Chevy coupe, one of the last of the 1942 model year before production stopped for the war. The guy who owns it is just a little older than you. He made one change that you would really like — leopard skin upholstery."

"Real leopard skin?" I tried to imagine how leopard skin upholstery would look.

"No, it is imitation." Then he added in a less excited voice, "I would not have leopard skin in my family car, but it will be perfect for you. It might help you get girls." My face flushed. "If you bring cash, we can see it tomorrow after I finish work."

"Super." I was excited beyond imagination. I never expected buying a car could go this smooth. I went to the bank and took out all my money. I could barely wait the entire day to see the car.

When Uncle Martin came to get me, we decided to take the bus to see the car instead of driving his car, just in case I decided to buy it.

It was love at first sight. The Chevy was jet black and highly polished. I chose not to notice the few small nicks and rust spots. *This could be my car. The leopard skin interior is impressive. The upholstery looks new. It's just right as my first car. Maybe not good enough to get me into the lineup in front of the school, but it sure is a good start. Maybe I can fix it up more. I'll add —*

Uncle Martin interrupted my daydream. "Well, Clarence, what do you think?"

"It's perfect."

We paid for it, and he drove the Chevy to our home. "I'll teach you how to drive on Saturday. Get your license before then."

The next day I took the written test required for a learner's license. I had studied beforehand and easily passed the test. When Dad saw the car, he smiled brightly. "Well, you did it." He was sparing with praise, but I knew he was pleased.

I said, "Do you want me to show you how to drive some day?"

He glanced down. "No, I am getting too old to learn new things." He was 46 years old.

Buying the car marked another turning point in our parent-child relationship. Soon I'd be driving my parents around just like a grownup. Until Saturday, though, the car would just sit in the driveway. For four days all I could do was admire the Chevy, polish it, and sit in the driver's seat. I daydreamed about speeding down the road with a pretty gal next to me. I spent every spare minute after school examining the car's visible parts. Being forced to wait to drive my car was torture.

On Saturday morning, I was more than ready. After breakfast, I sat in the car waiting until Uncle Martin arrived. He demonstrated the rudiments of driving, before putting me behind the wheel. I found steering easy, but shifting was another matter. Each time I tried to move the car from a standing start, it would buck and jump like a wild stallion that wanted me off its back. Then it shuddered, stalled, and died. We went through the starting routine several times. I had almost mastered the stick shift by the time Uncle Martin had to go home.

"I'll be back tomorrow," he said. "Practice driving."

As soon as he left, my friend Tim, who had been watching from our front porch step, came over to the car to talk. Tim was excited for me, but he did not have a car or any prospect of getting one soon. "How's it going, Clarence?"

I smiled proudly. "I'm making good progress. Did you see me driving?"

"Yeah, you looked fantastic. Will you take me for a ride?"

I wasn't sure it was a smart idea, but Uncle Martin did say to practice and I wanted to show off my driving skill. I drove cautiously through the neighborhood, stopping at the first stop sign. I let out the clutch to move through the intersection, but the Chevy bucked violently and  stalled. Two neighbor ladies on the sidewalk watched with critical curiosity.

Tim said, "Wow! What happened?"

My face flushed, and I wished we were back in my driveway. "I haven't got the hang of shifting yet." After a moment to recover, I managed to get us underway. When I reached the next intersection, I decided not to risk embarrassing myself further. Instead of making a complete stop, I shifted into second gear and made a rolling stop.

"Can you do that?" Tim said louder than necessary, "The sign said STOP!"

I didn't answer. I looked around hoping a cop hadn't seen me break the law. I was lucky — there was no policeman this time.

During the next weeks, with a little more instruction and a lot of practice, I learned to drive my new car properly. Each night as I fell asleep I imagined turning my Chevy into a custom car. I settled for cosmetic bodywork, which provided a way to learn. I fixed rust

spots and small dents, removed chrome trim, and smoothed sur-
faces with body filler and touch-up paint. A completely smooth,
chrome-free surface was a popular customized look at the time.
Fender skirts were also popular, so I saved the money and bought a
set. I discovered I didn't like scraping the skin off my knuckles on
greasy, rusty parts, which seemed to happen every time I tried a
major modification. I decided serious auto customization wasn't
for me, but I loved to cosmetically care for my Chevy. Over the
next few years, I managed to keep my car running, which was a
challenge because the Chevy was totally worn out, even before I
bought it.

* * *

Around this time, a different sort of love came into my life. Each
day, Tim and I ate together in the school cafeteria, while we
watched for pretty girls, which was our lunchtime habit. On this
day a beautiful girl with a brilliant smile walked past us. She approached her friends and their faces brightened, plainly pleased to
see her. Whatever she said must have been entertaining, because
they all laughed. She had a cheerful and confident attitude. That
was the precise moment I fell in love. When I became aware of
sounds again, I heard Tim's voice, "Clarence, why aren't you answering to me?"

"What? Oh, nothing Tim. Sorry."

After that day, I always tried to be in the best position to witness
her arrival. I looked forward to her entrance. I asked friends about
her, but all I learned was that her first name was Suzanne, and she
planned to be a secretary. They say opposites attract, and I think I
know why. She had the outgoing personality I admired. I was not
popular, so I longed to be like this girl who was. Also, she was cute
as a button. Getting to know her remained my impossible dream. It
was evident that I would never acquire sufficient courage to introduce myself to her.

I shared my thoughts about her with Tim. Then one day, Tim and I were having lunch, when she came in as usual and we intently watched her. She looked in our direction and I quickly switched my focus to Tim. "Don't let her see us staring."

"Why not?"

"I don't want her to know. Tim got the message and we casually looked at different points on the ceiling. Then, I realized that she was walking towards us. I felt exposed — like a nude swimmer, who had just discovered that his clothes are gone. She saw us looking up, so she too looked for the phantom spot on the ceiling. Seeing nothing, she continued toward us with a pleasant smile.

Tim leaned toward me. "I think she's coming to meet you."

"That cannot be; stay quiet."

She stopped at the water fountain next to our table. When she bent to get a drink, her skirt was close enough to touch. I clasped my hands so they wouldn't shake. She turned to return to her friends and our eyes met, she smiled. I couldn't breathe. Then she was gone. A minute later, everything in our part of the cafeteria was back to normal, except I could feel my heart beating.

Tim said, "Why didn't you say hi?"

I couldn't think of an answer to his question that could justify my lack of courage, and this made me angry. I got up and hurried out of the room to avoid another pointed question.

Of course, I was in love, but it was the so-called puppy-love, and it was a one-way attraction because she didn't even know me. During the rest of the senior year, Suzanne and I moved in different domains. I saw her a few times between classes. She looked happy almost all the time. *She sure has a great figure.* I became increasingly infatuated as the year progressed. Once I saw Suzanne talking to my cousin, Jason's steady girlfriend Jane. Later I asked Jane, "Who was that girl in the yellow sweater?"

"She is my friend, Suzanne. We take secretarial classes together."

"She seems very nice."

"Yes, she has a lot of friends. Her father died a few years ago and she lives with her mom in a small apartment. They don't have much and her two older brothers are married. Yes, Suzanne is a nice girl."

I hoped Jane would volunteer more. She didn't. *I guess Jane doesn't think I'm good enough for her friend.* Like many teen boys, I was reluctant to approach a girl who I didn't know, but I still couldn't gather the courage to ask Jane to introduce us.

Decision

Cleveland, Ohio — 1953, Age 18

As a senior, all I could think about was graduating, starting my drafting career, and buying a better car. Tim, my friend since first grade, was in West Tech's college preparatory program, so we didn't hang out a lot anymore. But one day he stopped me in the hall. "Hi, Clarence." He looked away and hesitated.

I could tell something important was on his mind. "What's going on?"

He said, "I need a favor." He looked to the side. "I'm trying to get this scholarship…you know, to afford college? Then maybe I can get a business degree and be an accountant someday."

"Okay. What do you need?"

"A ride downtown one Saturday next month to take the test at Fenn College. I don't want to depend on an unreliable bus, this test is too important."

Fenn was a small college that would become the nucleus of Cleveland State University in a few years. I should have told Tim that the bus would be a lot more reliable than my old car, but didn't want him to think I had a junker. And, I did want to help so I said, "Sure, I'll take you." I didn't want to take time off work, but he was my friend, and it was the right thing to do, so I felt good about saying yes. Also, I was curious. I had never been inside Fenn or any other college.

A week later, Tim learned that there would be two tests, intelligence, and aptitude. It meant my good deed could involve an entire day. Now, I was sorry I had agreed because it would mean sacrificing an entire day at the bakery job and I was intent on earning as much money as I could, but I wouldn't go back on my promise.

So, I said, "Since I'll have to wait for you, I think I'll take the test."

"I thought you didn't want to go to a college."

Tim had highlighted my confused mindset. My personal dream was to get a good drafting job and a better car, but I also wanted to please Mom, and that meant considering college. However, I was leaning towards the car and an easier career path.

"That's right. I'll get a full-time job as a draftsman and will be driving a better car before you finish your first year at Fenn. I don't need a scholarship, but it might be interesting to learn how smart I am." It was ironic that after years of lacking self-confidence, I now had the inflated ego of a teen having an easy time in high school. Easy didn't mean I was getting top grades; my only goal was to get by and not fail a class. To achieve this objective, I took simpler classes whenever possible. To me, earning the high opinion of other students and becoming a skilled draftsman, who others could respect was more important than grades.

Tim gave me a questioning look. "But you may fail!"

I wrinkled my nose. "That isn't possible." According to me, there was no way I'd do poorly on the test. I had bought a car and I felt successful. It didn't occur to me that Fenn might judge me using some different standards. I had more self-confidence than common sense.

* * *

Fenn had a prominent Euclid Avenue address. As we walked towards the school from the parking lot, I looked up at an impressive high-rise building. Tim and I joined over one hundred test takers, who had gathered in an auditorium-sized lecture room. There was ample space between seats to discourage cheating. *They don't trust us.* Then it occurred to me why they were careful; they planned to award a lot of money. I was surprised that I felt apprehensive.

An official administering the test described the rules and passed out blank tests. He performed preliminaries with formality and seriousness. The official announced, "The two tests are each scheduled for an hour with a lunch break in between." I decided that there was something far worse than being evaluated and graded; it was not being prepared for what lay ahead. I sat with damp hands resting on the test form. A few minutes later I heard, "Start now."

I began. Several student proctors hovered as I worked. The intelligence test was difficult and I wasn't able to finish all the questions. So, I left the room sure that I hadn't done well.

Three weeks later, we returned for our test results. I thought I should complete this last part of the process, even though I expected bad news. I was aware of my underarm dampness as a school official called my name. He took me to a cramped interview room. All was quiet when he closed the door. We sat on the opposite sides of a small round table. He didn't say anything, just furrowed his brow as he studied my file. I watched and waited, trying to be patient. *What is he thinking?*

At last, he said, "Your tests indicate you have a strong technical aptitude. I'm sorry you did not do well enough to get a scholarship." He stopped to let the bad news sink in. I was relieved. *Now I can escape this situation.* I made a move to stand. He lifted his hand slightly, indicating that he was not finished yet. He had paused before administering a follow-up knockout blow. He looked up at me. "In fact, you did so poorly that it is doubtful you could even complete our college program."

"What!" I blurted out.

He sat up, cleared his throat, and removed his reading glasses. "I notice that you always get an 'A' in drafting, but other grades were average or below. I suggest that you continue with your plan to become a draftsman."

Before I knew it, he ushered me out and called for the next person. I stood there stunned. I thought I was one of the smartest guys in that testing room. This result was a blow to my grandiose self-image.

Later, Tim met me with a broad smile and the good news that he won the scholarship. We rode home in entirely different moods. He was elated, talking nonstop about his scholarship and career plan. I was jealous, dejected, and did not say much.

For days, I was unable to forget the interview and I became progressively angrier. *How could anyone tell me that I wasn't good enough to do something, even something tough like going to college? I am smart.*

That was the moment, I resolved to graduate from college, despite what the Fenn guy thought. I went back and picked up the standard admittance forms.

Several weeks later, I was granted a follow-up interview with the same guy to discuss my new application. We met in the same interview room. On his table were my neatly lettered application and his pack of Lucky Strikes. He had a neutral expression, but a superior tone. "I see you have come back, Mr. Arnold. Forgot something?"

"Yes, I would like to be admitted —" I cleared my throat, "if possible... I understand it would not include a scholarship."

"But your test indicates that you are not prepared."

He wants me to give up and leave. 'Never give up' that's what Mom would say. "I have never failed at anything I want to do," I said. "I can do this and I know I can. I will work as hard as necessary."

I noticed his surprised expression. "You want to go all the way and get a degree?"

"Yes," I answered quickly, without considering what that would mean.

"What department?"

"Engineering."

"Um." He looked at me. "It is a difficult discipline."

I stared back at him. "Do I deserve a chance to try?"

"Deserve? No, you must study and earn your way. You are not prepared." My head started to hurt. *I am failing to live up to Mom's expectations.* I guess the advisor noticed the distress on my face because his expression softened. "Well, I suppose we might give you a chance. We still have a few freshmen spaces available."

I looked up with hope. "I will pay my way."

"Yes." He lit a cigarette, leaned back, studied me, and paused for what seemed like a long time. "We can allow you to enroll for the coming fall term on a trial basis. I will send you a letter spelling everything out."

Typed on top of the letter were the words 'ON PROBATION.' Conditional acceptance came with the requirement to earn at least a "C" average during the freshman year to remain in school. I was pleased for winning this first part of the struggle to redeem myself. But, in spite of my bragging bluster, I was concerned I was not smart enough. Learning was still harder for me than for most students. *There is only one way to know, earn at least a "C" average.*

Engineering was the only program that interested me. I figured it would be difficult, but did not seriously consider anything easier. I'd either succeed as an engineer or be a draftsman. A few months before drafting had been my dream job, but now settling for drafting would mean I had failed to become an engineer.

The acceptance letter revealed another problem; tuition was more than my savings. The letter directed me to Fenn's Finance Office. The Finance Advisor met me in her office, which was crowded with bookshelves. I occupied the only visitor chair. Seeing my worried expression, she gave me a supportive smile. "I understand you need a way to afford college. What can we do for you, Clarence?"

I blinked, "Well, I have very little savings, and I spend most of my part-time earnings on my car. Mom and Dad aren't able to help with tuition, but they said I could continue living at home. This way I would not have to pay for room-and-board. The problem is I don't know how I will pay for tuition, transportation, or books."

"In such a case, our Co-op program could work for you. It would spread course load and cost over a longer period. This means that essentially you would attend school for half the year while working to earn the tuition money in the other half. If everything goes well, you could complete a four-year bachelor degree in five years."

It was a difficult choice, but I was determined to go to college, so I selected the Co-op Program. As I stood to leave, she said. "Come back to meet me when you are ready to find a job. I help match students with potential Co-op jobs at the participating companies."

The series of decisions leading to college had not been entirely rational; however, it seemed like the right path. It also meant my immediate future would include a lot more schoolwork.

Each day, I took the bus to Fenn in the morning and returned home by dinnertime. I stayed all day, even when I did not have classes because it encouraged me to stick to a study discipline. I'd go to the library, whenever I had free time. There was one quiet spot there, which I preferred for study, research, and writing. After a few weeks in class with better-prepared student competitors, I realized that my lack of preparation could prevent me from getting the required "C" average. Most of the professors graded freshmen on the curve, which meant that an equal number of us would be below average as those above.

I developed a way to compensate for my learning deficiency by studying high school-level textbooks, along with the assigned course textbooks. My study approach had to be rigorous and repetitious to ensure that I'd remember the information. First, I outlined assigned textbooks and more basic books for material I did not understand. Then I took detailed lecture notes, which I later related to the book outlines.

* * *

When it was time to find my first job, I returned to the Co-op Advisor. She said, "You do not have much experience, but it is more than most of the freshmen students. Also, you have drafting skills. I think all your future jobs should be in drafting, if possible."

"I would like that."

"Also, you can earn more by doing skilled work than the average student, without any marketable experience."

I slid forward on my seat. "Do you know of any drafting jobs?"

"If you can begin today, I do have a possible company." She looked annoyed and gestured with both hands. "They hired a student I sent out last week, but he quit on his very first day. The employer is Swift and Company. They need a proper drawing of a new conveyor system, so their contractor can start building it. Swift is a large meat processing company on West 65th Street. You know them?"

"Yes. I live on West 47th and I guess I could start today."

"I just talked to Swift. They're anxious to have a draftsman to begin working as soon as possible, but I cannot refer another quitter."

I didn't hesitate. "I'll take the job."

"Good. Go to their Maintenance Department and ask for the boss." She walked me to her office door, where another student was waiting.

Killing Room

The company's building on West 65th Street looked like a three-story brick warehouse with oversized, multi-pane windows. Behind the building were several crowded livestock pens, which were continuously serviced by the trucks unloading animals. I drove into the parking lot and was overwhelmed by the bad smell. In the past, whenever I was near this place, I noticed a stockyard odor. Now, as I walked towards a door marked *Maintenance,* the stink was much worse.

I knocked on the heavy steel door. No one answered. I knocked a few more times but to no avail. Finally, I pushed my way in, only to be stunned by the offensive smells and sounds. Instinctively, I took a step back, covering my nose. It didn't help. *This must be the main killing room.* The overwhelming stench seemed to originate from a blend of fresh blood, urine, and spilled intestines. It was humid and warm, and almost unbearable. Loud inhuman screams completely overwhelmed me.

The room seemed to be filled with the relentless movement of men and animals. I saw a conveyor production line for cattle on the far side and another for hogs right in front of me. I stood on a raised wooden walkway, about 12 inches above a concrete floor where the slaughter took place. Hogs entered in single file through a low swinging door. The fat, fleshy animals looked around with wide eyes and reacted with a terror-filled scream, as a worker shackled their back hoof with a chain connected to the conveyor. In another instant, they lost their footing and were hoisted aloft. The loudest sounds were the desperate screams of the hogs. From the other side, I heard lower moans of cattle. Overhead conveyors rattled and chains clanked, adding to the din. The frantic hogs moved along in an upside down position. Seconds later, they added their blood to the mix on the floor.

Most workers wore protective black rubberized aprons. Several had removed their shirts because of the heat. Everyone used high rubber boots to protect their feet and legs as they sloshed around in a stinking soup of animal fluids. Blood and gore spattered everyone. This scene became the source of my nightmares during the next few weeks.

I had an overwhelming urge to run. I turned and took two steps toward the exit, then hesitated. *This job is my first assignment. I shouldn't quit before I start. How will I explain my squeamishness to that Co-op lady?* I forced myself to turn back and resolved to carry on.

It took me a few seconds to get my bearings. The sound level made normal talking impossible, so I shouted to a passing worker. "Where is the boss's office?" He pointed at a grimy wooden staircase against the wall. His index finger continued moving upward until it stopped at a rough-looking, plywood room; then two quick jabs made it clear that was the place. Later, I was told that the man in the plywood room was known only as 'The Boss' by everyone. I never did learn his real name.

I half closed my eyes. *If only I can get away from this chaos.* I proceeded along the raised walkway around the frenzied activity, then rapidly up the steps, hoping to escape the anguish below.

On reaching the top, a man's bald head was visible through a small window of the office door. He had been watching, and now motioned for me to enter. The noise subsided significantly when his door closed behind me. I took a deep breath and welcomed the moment of relief.

Boss was a short, muscular man and was about my father's age. He wore a stained cotton butcher's coat and a stern expression, fitting my image of a tough supervisor. He was white skinned, unlike every one of the production workers below, who were black.

His cramped office contained an old oak desk, a matching swivel chair, and a large drafting table; each piled with papers. There were two small windows overlooking the killing floor. Against another wall was a blueprint cabinet. There was no place for both of us to sit, so we stood for the interview. Surprisingly, he asked no questions about my experience or drafting ability.

He gestured with amplified arm motions. "Your project is to design a replacement conveyor for hog slaughtering." He handed me a catalog of standard conveyor parts. "After you finish the initial blueprint, you will work with the contractor as he does modifications to make everything work. I know from experience your first drawings won't be worth crap. The final drawing must look exactly like the finished conveyor. We expect to install it before the end of your three-month assignment. Can you do it?"

I blinked trying to understand everything but didn't hesitate even though I was not sure what I'd be doing. "Yes, I can do it." *I'll figure it out.*

He continued without slowing for questions. "The current conveyor is worn out and limited. It only goes to the second level. The new one will move hogs entering on the first level to the third. By the time they get to the top, they'll be half-carcasses ready to slide on shoots through the remaining meat-cutting steps."

I was dismayed. *He makes killing these creatures sound like a mechanical process.* I hadn't formed a firm opinion, but I did feel an affinity for helpless animals. I recalled a story about how American Indians prayed to the souls of animals they hunted. Boss continued and my mind abruptly returned to the task at hand.

He pointed toward his drafting table. "Use this table right here." He removed a dirty coffee mug from the slanted table top and then showed me where he stored the building's architectural drawings. I was compelled to make the other needed measurements myself.

"When you come in tomorrow, go to the Business Office first." He looked at a clock on the wall. "Tell them you started today at 9:00 AM. They will put you on the payroll. You have two weeks to finish the first version of the drawings."

As he brushed past towards the door, he handed me a clean white coat like his. "Now let's go down to meet someone, who will help you with your job." He quickly moved out of the office door. I followed him down the steep stairway and found myself back in the chaos. *I guess I am hired.*

After a quick introduction, Boss left me with Sam, the supervisor of hog production. Sam was a tall, pleasant man with close-cropped hair, wide smile, and a gold front tooth. He wore a black rubber bib apron similar to other workers, but he secured his apron with a worn belt holding a leather sheath and his pointed 8-inch-long hog-sticking knife.

During the next half an hour, Sam gave me a tour of the entire process, which included demonstrating his technique for killing a hog. "I'm quicker than anyone else." He was plainly proud of his hog-sticking skill. "Don't want to upset the unfortunate animals more than we need to." Later Sam informed me, "In two days, Boss starts a two-week vacation. It would be best if you have your conveyor ideas ready for him to see when he gets back. I'll help wherever I can."

My heart was racing. *This job is not going to be easy.* I returned to Boss's office to examine his drafting setup. It was lunchtime when I returned to find Sam. Thankfully, the noise and turmoil stopped for the break.

I asked, "Where can we have lunch? Do you want to grab a bite together?"

Sam said, "We eat right here," pointing to the surrounding walkway and staircase. Two workers sat grinning at us.

One said, "We get half an hour for lunch."

I exclaimed, "How can you eat here? It smells too bad!"

"You get used to it." The workers' grins widened. *I shouldn't have reacted like a wimp.* I suspected the men guessed exactly what bothered me. They seemed to be teasing the young college boy, who acted so important, and easily saw through my desire to appear tough. It was another form of lying, and I knew I was not talented in this arena. My mind raced to think of a way to avoid eating in that place.

I said, "I didn't know I'd start working today, so I didn't bring lunch."

Sam said, "It's okay; I got extra." I gave in. We shared Sam's lunch on the stairway. He and I got acquainted and were soon friends.

I learned that he lived with his bedridden father, who had dementia and needed constant care. Sam's sister, who lived next to them, took care of their father while Sam worked. Sam had no other family or time for a social life outside of work.

It took about two weeks before I was able to eat with Sam and the others without thinking about the real purpose of the room. I finally got used to it as they predicted. I came to admire Sam's generous nature, leadership skills, and quick intelligence. Even though he wasn't my boss, after a while, I was comfortable confiding in him.

Once while we ate, I mentioned something about my problem of feeling inferior to people in authority. He reacted with a determined tone.

"No one is better than you! Everybody has some strengths and some weaknesses. You're good at schooling and drawing, I'm good at sticking pigs." As he said this, he showed me a wide smile and made a poking jab with his index finger. "It all balances out. It means that no person is better than you. That's what my Mammy always says to me." He smiled again, and his gold tooth glittered. Then his smile faded. "She's in heaven now. When she was dying, she made me promise that I would take care of Daddy. I couldn't say no to her." He paused. "I was her youngest. She died four years ago." He raised both palms slightly. "Now this is my life."

About two months later, as I neared the end of the Co-op assignment, Sam stopped me. "You're a good kid, but you need to know that Boss is a hard man. I see the conveyor isn't working yet. If it isn't finished when Boss says it should be, somebody will get blamed. Right now, it is you because the contractor says your drawing is shit."

"What!" My posture stiffened. "The contractor never said anything to me." *I need this job to pay for my tuition.*

Sam shrugged. "He's covering his ass. It's the contractor's fault. His best mechanic quit because he didn't get a pay raise, so the contractor plans to blame you for the delay."

"Me! But —" I stammered. "That's not the right thing to do."

"It's the smart thing."

I brushed moisture from the corner of my eye. "What can I do to keep my job?"

Sam said, "I don't know…fight back! You're a college boy, think of something."

Boss was away again, so I couldn't talk to him. I thought hard for two days and rejected all but one idea. It was a simple solution. If it  worked, no one would be fired, but I would need to convince the Plant Manager, the top boss, and a man I had not yet met. The thought of talking to the Plant Manager terrified me, but to pull off the plan, I had to overcome my fear. I did not know if I could do it.

I told Sam what I was thinking and he said that it was a good plan. At that moment, the Plant Manager came into the killing room. Sam's eyes lit up, as he grabbed my sleeve and gestured towards the man who was headed in our direction.

I got the message but hesitated. Sam cleared his throat as loud as he could and gave my elbow a poke. I didn't want to let Sam down, so I took a step forward, introduced myself, and asked for a meeting that would include the contractor.

The manager hurried as he rushed around us. "Why?"

"We should ensure that the deadline is met," I replied.

He hesitated. "Call my secretary to set it up." Then he went out of the door. Sam grinned.

I gave the contractor my latest drawings two days early, so I would have time to revise it if he found something. The contractor said nothing to me about a problem. At the meeting, in the presence of the Plant Manager, I asked the contractor if there were any problems with the conveyor design. He looked uncomfortable. If he claimed my drawings were no good, he would have to give me a reason. The contractor said, "Your drawings are okay, but I will need to work my crew overtime to meet the schedule, which will cost me extra."

My plan had worked. The contractor had admitted responsibility for the schedule delay. Thanks to Sam, I had avoided getting fired and learned a lesson about office politics. I finished the hog conveyor design with time to spare, so I was able to add an extra feature to the overview drawing, a small sketch of a hog hanging upside down from the conveyor. As an inexperienced draftsman, I had debated with myself if such an illustration might be amateurish or unprofessional but then decided it best showed the conveyor's purpose. *If Boss doesn't like the hanging hog, I can always kill it with my eraser.*

What Boss liked was that I gave him more than he expected. The Plant Manager was amused and approved the job a few weeks later, which concluded my first Co-op assignment. The job did leave me with one lifelong drawback; I could no longer eat hotdogs after witnessing what went into them.

The next Monday I was at Fenn facing the bigger challenge — getting a "C" average in freshmen engineering. I knew how to do it — work hard.

* * *

Cousin Jason was also attending Fenn as a second-year engineering student. I had been impressed and inspired by him ever since he taught me to fold a paper airplane in the first grade. Because we now attended the same college, I hoped to see more of him. We had lost touch, and I planned to look him up.

I soon found that Jason had changed. He had thinning hair and was a bit overweight. His stout appearance was eclipsed by a perceptive smile and charismatic personality.

A few months later, Jason and I traveled along US-40 in my car, on our way to an air show in Dayton, Ohio. Our conversation was about airplanes, which soon turned to his airplane design. His face glowed and vigorous gestures emphasized his words. Like his inventor father, Jason was a super salesman when it came to convincing others of his ideas. His father encouraged his son's aviation dreams. By the time Jason graduated from West Tech High School, he had earned a private pilot license and had a clear vision of the unique airplane that he would build some day. He called it the XJ-2. It was a short-takeoff-and-landing design destined to have a place in the aviation history.

He said, "I need you to be my devil's advocate. I'll describe a design idea and you poke holes in it. You have the technical background to ask tough questions."

"But I have just started engineering."

"You know enough to help refine my design," he replied.

"Well, I'll do my best. What are your latest ideas?"

"To take off and land in the shortest distance," Jason said, "It must be able to fly slowly, which is done using several features that have been proven on other airplanes, although they have never been used together."

"Are you sure they'll work together?"

"Pretty sure, but we will test them. The first feature is large flaps that roll out of the wing's interior. It's not a new idea, but in the J-2, the flaps increase wing area more than in most of the planes — twenty-five percent. The second feature is boundary layer control, which helps the plane to fly slowly. I saw it demonstrated at the Mississippi State Aeronautics Department."

"I heard about it at school. Where does the suction come from?"

"From an engine-driven blower, which also cools the engines."

"Isn't that heavy and unreliable?"

"I'm sure it will work." He looked thoughtful. "It could be a weak link, so we will do extra tests."

I said, "Once you showed me a government test report about a shrouded propeller. Are you going to use that feature?"

"Yes, the shrouded prop is vital to increase the takeoff thrust."

As usual, I was impressed by his ideas. It was obvious that he had given this design a lot of thought. *I sure would like to help build the XJ-2 someday.*

"Are you still planning to get an aeronautical engineering degree?"

"After Jane and I get married, I'll transfer to Wichita State because light plane design is a primary feature of their program."

"After I make it through the first two years at Fenn," I said, "I think I'd like to follow you to Wichita and try to get in the same program."

"Wonderful. We can build airplanes together someday."

It was an exciting thought, but I'd have to travel a long road to make it real. During the drive back to Cleveland, Jason talked about the plans for his wedding. It reminded me that I did not have a girl-friend. *I hope I would make some progress in overcoming shyness.*

Since high school, I had been intrigued by the value of self-improvement practices. Defeating shyness was my primary goal. At the library, I borrowed Dale Carnegie's *How to Win Friends and Influence People* and read it twice. The advice seemed to work. Once I asked another student about her favorite sport and watched her talk enthusiastically about swimming. Next time I met her, she remembered me and asked me to come to her swim meet. While she didn't become my serious girlfriend, I did start to make more friends. I continued to work on shyness and discovered guidance from experts to overcome various problems and weaknesses. I tried any interesting self-improvement tip I came across.

Then during my first year at Fenn, I found a tip that proved life altering. The advice was aimed at overcoming the tendency to avoid doing something new, by tricking oneself into trying it. The idea was to choose one day of the week and on that day to accept the first appropriate proposal to do something new. It did not matter who made the proposal, just that the activity was legal, beneficial, and new. This technique assured that I'd have at least one new experience each week; and some of them might lead to personal growth, new friendships, and even adventure. I could also expect it to be fun, but I wondered if it could also be a fiasco. Still, I was willing to try it. I picked the following week to *say yes on Saturday.*

Self-Improvement

Cleveland, Ohio — 1954, Age 19

When my alarm rang on Saturday, I was anxious and curious to find out what my new adventure would be. I did not have to wait long. Jason was at Fenn when I arrived for a day of study. I could see by his body language that he was excited about something. "Hey Clarence, I'm starting a flying club. It's a good and cheap way to learn to fly." He talked fast with animated gestures.

My face turned red. *Oh no, this self-improvement adventure will not be something easy. I hope to learn flying in the future but not now. If I take time now, I will risk neglecting studies and not earning the required grades. Also, I doubt this will be cheap; and flying can also be risky. I'm not ready for this. How can I get out of it?*

I looked down and cleared my throat. "No, I can't do it."

Jason ignored my response. "Each member chips in a little up front. The club will buy a used J-3 Piper Cub. I have already picked out a plane. And, there are eight guys interested. We just need two more, and you can be one of them." I started to turn. "Wait, Clarence, let me finish."

I paused for a heartbeat, but it was enough to encourage him.

"Club members share the cost of the airport tie-down fee and maintenance. There shouldn't be much expense. I checked out the plane yesterday. All the routine work is up-to-date. Then we will each buy flying time by the hour. So you will learn to fly as your time and money allow. There are two hourly flying rates, one for instruction and the other solo time. The great thing is you will end up with a private pilot's license! Do you want to join?"

I searched for a face-saving way out. I barely had enough money to pay tuition and had nothing extra for other things. I needed time to study, and flying lessons would require many hours. The childhood memory of a racing plane flashed into my mind. Despite all my misgivings, some outside force prevented my lips from saying "No". Instead, what came out of my mouth was, "Well...I guess so.

Sure, I'll join." My childhood fantasy was to fly, and this flying club would provide a chance to try, even if it meant risking my standing at Fenn, I had to do it.

Jason smiled. "I knew you would say yes."

"How did you know?"

"Well, you plan to be an aeronautical engineer, don't you?"

"Yes."

"You cannot expect to design an airplane if you can't fly one."

* * *

Two months later, on a Monday morning, just five days after my twentieth birthday, I drove about thirty miles from home to Stan's Flying School near Chagrin Falls, Ohio, for my first flying lesson. I entered the gravel driveway annoyed about the dust settling on my polished Chevy. In the distance were a few light planes parked by a small building that could be the hanger. I didn't see anything resembling a runway. *The ground isn't even leveled. Am I at the right place?* Later, I learned this alleged airport was recently laid out on a farm field. The short grass runway looked like a pasture. I had expected a paved runway surface.

My anxiety increased. This experience would not only be my first flying lesson, it would also be my first time in an airplane. I would never admit it to Jason, but I was as scared as a fledgling chick about to leap into the void. Fortunately, the day was calm. Despite my fear, I hoped to begin a thrilling adventure.

Jason had shown me a photo of the plane, so as I drove towards the hanger, I looked for a bright yellow Piper J-3 Cub, and noticed one like the photo. The Cub is a high-wing airplane made primarily of lightweight metal tubing and covered with painted fabric. To a car guy, it's as substantial as a kite. An instructor with dual controls sits in front between a 65 horsepower air-cooled engine and the student sits behind. Flight controls and instruments are basic.

The instructor waiting was the only person at the field. He had been a World War II Army pilot, who flew observation missions on light planes similar to the Piper Cub. He looked the part with a leather flying jacket and aviator sunglasses. He told me to call him Stan. I was tempted to answer, "Yes sir."

He tilted his head and squinted. "You look scared."

I nodded once and blinked. "Never been on a plane before."

"Fear warns us about the danger. But sometimes it is a false warning and just a distraction. I have trained over a thousand people to fly and have never had a fatality. So, it is likely that you are not in danger." He grinned. "Sometimes we have to decide if the gain is greater than risk. If it is, we take the risk like bitter medicine and move forward. What do you say?" He raised open palms and gave me a questioning look.

I produced a phony smile. "I'm ready." *I hope I am.*

Stan described his program. "I only take students, who intend to get their license. You will need a ground school course and then pass a written FAA test. FAA is the Federal Aviation Administration. There will also be a medical exam and flight test before you get your license." He confirmed the flying school's payment arrangement. "You're going to need a pilot's logbook so we can record your progress. We sell them here. We also carry a basic booklet about how to pilot the Cub, which I recommend. First, I will show you the preflight steps."

With a new logbook tucked in my back pocket, we walked to the plane. Stan said, "A primary reason for the preflight is safety. It is important never to skip any steps on the checklist."

"Where is the checklist?"

"I will tell you the steps, show you what to look for, and you will memorize it."

Stan described the layout of the rural airport. Then we pumped aviation fuel into a small gas tank located in front of the Cub's cabin. I stood on one of the plane's tires holding a gas hose in the opening of the tank filler, while Stan turned a hand pump on a 55-gallon drum.

A 'walk-around' was one of the items on the checklist. Stan said, "We circle the plane hunting for anything that doesn't look right."

"I don't know what to look for."

"You will learn with time. Think of it this way, if something is wrong and you miss seeing it, you could be hosed. Use your natural problem-solving skills." *It sounds sort of hit and miss.*

Next, he showed me how to start the engine. One of us cranked the propeller by hand since the Cub didn't have an electric starter. The other person sat in the cockpit to control the plane. Stan said, "For safety purposes, the engine will not start unless the magneto switch is on." He demonstrated while describing it rapidly. "Stand directly in front of the prop... Grab the prop blade with both hands. ...and swing your left leg under the prop. ...Then pull down hard to turn the engine over, while getting out of the prop's path."

My fear increased another notch. We took turns so I could practice until I had the hang of it. One of us stayed in the cockpit holding the brakes, and the other cranked the propeller. My brain was on information overload, and we were still on the ground. The process was also more primitive than I expected. There wasn't a proper runway, no powered gas pump, and even my prewar car had an electric starter.

Stan announced, "Get your ass in gear. Let's fly!"

I hesitated for a tense moment, then followed and took my place in front of the prop, ready for the real starting sequence. He got in and stuck his head out the door so I could hear his shouted instructions. "This time, before you crank I will yell 'contact.' For a numbskull like you that means the switch is on, the magneto is hot, and the engine should start, so stand clear after you pull the prop and then jump in."

"CONTACT."

I pulled hard. The engine belched a puff of smoke and immediately roared to life.

Stan yelled, "Easy start because we cranked the hell out of it practicing."

I scooted around the wing support and used a footrest under the door to struggle into the empty seat. My eyes started to water from the strong smell of exhaust and gasoline. He closed the clamshell cabin door, while I buckled my harness. We bumped over turf, and the cabin air cleared a bit.

Stan spoke with purpose, explaining and demonstrating how we would get into the sky and up to the practice altitude. There was no radio in the Cub, so he shouted. He showed me how to do turns, climbs, and dives before moving on to more advanced maneuvers like stalls and spins. After each maneuver he bellowed, "Take the stick!" and he talked me through, as I made the plane turn and dive through the air. I was beginning to think flying wasn't too difficult, but then I felt a knot in my stomach, the first sign of nausea. An expert at recognizing signs of student distress, Stan took one look and got us back on the ground before I could christen the cockpit with the remains of breakfast. I got over the feeling as soon as my feet were on the ground. Stan turned it into another teaching point.

He said, "A pilot is responsible for passenger's comfort. Try to remember that when you take others up."

I was beaming like a newlywed, when we returned to his small office, proud of what I had accomplished, and ready to get back into the Cub, as soon as possible.

"You did good numbskull," Stan said, "but you have a lot to learn. It is important to maintain progress by taking more lessons soon. Remembering maneuvers isn't just about mind memory; it involves muscle memory too, which requires repetition."

I scheduled the next series of lessons before I left the airport. I figured I could handle the time and cost of two per week. When I drove through the gate, I didn't notice the dust covering my precious car. The excitement of this new venture eclipsed my earlier fixation on the Chevy. One flying experience had transformed me from a car guy to a new pilot.

Over the next weeks, I looked forward to each scheduled lesson. With time, we progressed to the significant seventh lesson. Stan's plan for the day — landing practice — had kept me awake the night before. It would require me to get the plane back on the ground without killing anyone.

He said, "Today will be about acquiring basic takeoff and landing proficiency. It is called touch-and-go." I didn't realize Stan was about to teach me more than how to land. "You will spend the hour doing one takeoff and landing after another without my hands-on assistance." Since I had not soloed yet, he rode with me. "I will not correct your bad decision," he said, "unless it could be fatal. Remember numbskull, if you break it, you fix it." He grinned at his bad joke.

My first landing was terrible. I can't imagine how Stan restrained himself from taking control. I landed too high and too slow. The Cub stopped flying two feet above the grass, then bounced and pitched several times on its fat tires before skidding to a shuddering stop. I closed my eyes, embarrassed and shaken.

In his consistently calm voice, Stan said, "Taxi off the runway and turn off the engine." *He is going to tell me to leave and never come back.* When all was quiet, he said, "What were you thinking during that landing?"

I pondered his question for a few seconds, "Well, it was my first landing. I wondered if I could do it. I thought I might not get us back on the ground. I just wanted to return in one piece. I guess this proves I'm not ready to land on my own yet."

"You are ready! You know how to land. The steps are simple. I asked earlier today, and you told me what they were and then you watched me do it. Then you landed with my hand on the stick." He paused. "You are just scared, which is natural. It is what most novice performers feel before performing. Think of it this way, suppose you had to balance and walk for one block by only stepping on a six-inch wide curb at the side of a street. Could you do it?"

"Sure, I guess so," I remembered pretending a curb was a tightrope as a child.

"Now imagine the curb at the edge of a 40-foot drop rather than six inches high. It would be harder only because the stakes would be higher, not because it requires more skill or knowledge. Physically, it is no more difficult, but in your head it is." He paused before continuing. "One solution might be to walk on the high curb without looking at the ground. In other words, try to block out the risk by concentrating only on the curb in front of you. That might work until you remember that you are dangerously high, and then you would be afraid. The blocking technique might work even better if you were distracted by something else to occupy your mind." He put a hand on my shoulder. "Here is what you do; this time only concentrate on doing each landing step perfectly. Think about performing precisely. Make each maneuver with precision. Don't let any other thoughts get in the way. The trick is to focus on achieving precision!"

He stopped talking and looked at me. "Now go and make a perfect landing."

We started the engine, and I took off. I thought about executing one step at a time. I concentrated on making turns at the right places, precisely banking at the proper angle, and descending to the prescribed altitude for each leg of the traffic pattern. I didn't have time to worry because performing each step with perfection was difficult enough to fully occupy my mind.

When I was on final approach to the runway, Stan said, "By the way, the Cub is so easy to fly and so forgiving that some pilots say it will land without much help, if the pilot just wills it to land with his mind."

I imagined the upcoming touchdown. As the plane reached the runway, I greased into a perfect landing. It couldn't have been smoother. From then on, I remembered this lesson and heard Stan's advice in my mind whenever I was concerned about performing well. I hardly ever made a bad landing after that, even in gusty weather or when practicing crosswind and short-field landings.

Later, Stan pointed out that his method applies to all performances, and not just flying. Then he offered me another tip. "I don't want to give you the impression that you can do anything and everything by ignoring risk. That is just being a daredevil and not a good pilot. The time to consider failure is well before taking the action; not while performing it. If the risk seems too high, you may need more preparation. However, in this case, I knew that you were ready."

The lessons continued and three months later, I headed back to Stan's Flying School on another beautiful warm day. Today's schedule called for more takeoff and landing practice. After an initial flight together, Stan told me to taxi towards the hanger and stop. He jumped out, while the engine idled and shouted. "You are ready to solo. Make another takeoff and landing like the last one." Then he stepped back displaying a confident smile.

My mouth fell open, and I sucked in a deep breath. *I've had less than eight hours of instruction, but if Stan thinks I am ready, I guess I must be. He has always been right. But what would happen if he's wrong and I make a mistake?* My hands were clammy. I knew I shouldn't think too much, and I decided to trust him.

I taxied to the beginning of the runway, looked in all directions, and pushed the throttle to a stop. The engine roared and without the burden of Stan's 170 pounds, the Cub leaped ahead briskly and was airborne in a heartbeat. This reminded me that my security blanket was no longer with me and I was on my own. That alarming thought diverted my attention long enough and I found myself about 100 feet higher than the proper crosswind altitude. *Concentrate.* I eased the stick forward to recover while making the downwind turn. *Good. I am back on course.* The rest of my first solo landing was routine. I continued takeoffs and landings for the remainder of the lesson as Stan monitored his fledgling pilot from the ground.

On the fifth or sixth circuit, I noticed the Cub's shadow projected on the ground below — a small, distorted airplane shape racing along. It hopped up to the treetops, then snapped back to hug the ground, seemingly independent of me in the real plane far above. I knew the shadow was me. *Holy shit, I am flying.* Not just in the sense of controlling the airplane, but flying through the air like the eagle of my childhood fantasy. I was no longer worried about landing, as I savored the sensation, and then suddenly flying became a delight, rather than a concern. I recalled the boy in the yard, looking up at the racing airplane and wishing he could fly. *My spirit is free of the earth, free to soar above everyone and free to punch a hole in clouds.*

* * *

By the end of my freshman year, I had completed two Co-op assignments, plus six months of college work, and just barely earned the required "C" average. Retrospectively, it seems like a meager achievement. At the time, however, I regarded it as a triumph because I was allowed to continue at Fenn. As a bonus, by the end of the first year, I had learned how to study and became accustomed to the demanding schedule. From then on, each school year was easier than the prior year, not because I was smarter, but because I had discovered how college worked. The advisor, who initially expressed doubts about my ability, now shook my hand to congratulate me. *Perhaps he hadn't really doubted me. Maybe he was just using my teenage pride to trick me into going to college.*

More flying lessons followed until I earned the private pilot's license about one year after I first met Stan. When the license arrived in the mail, I took it to the airport to show him. "Well numbskull, that means you will no longer need me to correct your mistakes; you can do dumb things on your own. How many flying hours do you have now?"

"Twenty-six."

"Well don't call yourself a pilot until you have at least 1,000 hours." His comment immediately brought me back to earth. I continued flying the Piper Cub, whenever I had time. I had the pilot certificate to brag about, but little flying experience or skill.

A New Adventure

A surprise awaited me at Jason's wedding reception. It was a re-play of the high school cafeteria scene — a large space filled with people eating and socializing. Across the room, I saw a young lady looking cute as a kitten and wearing a shapely black dress. It was her, my dream girl from the West Tech high school, the one with the self-assured attitude — the one who I was unable to approach in high school. She was at the reception, conversing enthusiastically with two guys, one sitting on each side. I waited hoping to intro-duce myself. I was still reserved and wouldn't interrupt, so all I could do was hope that they would finish talking soon. After an hour of waiting for the two admirers to leave, I gave up and went home disheartened. It was another missed chance. I was frustrated and angry at myself but could think of nothing to do other than continue with self-improvement, as a possible way to defeat shyness. Then, perhaps I would have a chance in the future.

Soon after his marriage, Jason transferred to Wichita State Uni-versity in Kansas for the final two years. Fenn didn't offer aeronau-tical engineering, but Wichita did. I planned to do the same, after earning enough Fenn credits, which would require at least another year.

Wichita was the perfect place to be immersed in aviation. The city billed itself as the *Air Capital of the World*. There were three major light plane companies in the town — Beach, Piper, and Cessna. A large Boeing Company plant and McConnell Air Force Base represented military aviation. Because of the local demand for engineers, WSU's aeronautical engineering program focused on teaching the designing of light planes — just what I wanted.

A year later, in August 1956, I piled my belongings into a Twi-light Blue 1949 Chevy Coupe, which I had acquired to replace the worn out '42 Chevy. After all, I needed a reliable car to travel be-tween Cleveland and Wichita. This one had fresh tire retreads, so I thought that I could make it back and forth without a breakdown.

My first cross-country trip was a grueling, but an uneventful two and a half day drive. Lumbering trucks dominated the two-lane state highways. Passing was a challenge with the puny engine. I liked to drive, but the Chevy's hard, bench seat was like sitting on a board. My right leg cramped after about two hours of holding the accelerator down. Without air conditioning, I ended the day both sweaty and weary. I figured these minor inconveniences were a fitting test to start a new adventure.

Midwest scenery unfolded from Ohio's rolling hills to Kansas's flat farmland. Aromas in the air improved after leaving Cleveland's industrial haze. I was excited at the prospect of living on my own for the first time and wondered where my budding aviation future would lead.

The Wichita skyline finally came into view. I dragged my stuff into the assigned three-person dorm room. My roommates were large and athletic freshmen — one was an aspiring football halfback from South Chicago and the other was a high school basketball star from a Kansas farm. I was the oldest, so they deferred to me like an undersized older brother. They insisted that I take the bed near the window and bathroom. However, we didn't see much of each other during the school year because they spent their time practicing their sports, while I focused on my engineering.

During the Thanksgiving break, our Kansas roommate took us two city boys to his family's farm, which was about forty miles away. His mother treated us to a traditional turkey feast, which reminded me of my own home. This was the first time that I was not with my family for the holidays. But, I felt comfortable experiencing the same Thanksgiving traditions with my roommate's family. Our roommate also showed us how to use a shotgun, and then how to hunt ducks and rabbits.

I enjoyed being out in the crisp morning air and being challenged to hit a moving target. However, I realized that I would need much practice to be an acceptable shot. Hunting as a sport was another matter; I didn't see the point in killing for fun. It seemed that my roommates and many other hunters loved it, but ending the life of a defenseless animal felt wrong to me. Part of my attitude stemmed from an article I had read about gene research. It had established that humans shared over 88 percent of their genes with mice. So, I concluded that all creatures must be related. While I didn't spoil my visit by debating this with my hosts, I decided not to hunt again, unless I was starving.

Soon after moving into the dorm, I knocked on Jason's door to let him know that I had arrived. He and Jane lived in an apartment with their newborn son. "Clarence! Good to see you. Did I tell you there is a glider club here?" He took me into the kitchen to meet Jane and the baby.

Jason was always excited about something new related to aviation; today it was the glider club, where members participate in the sport of flying an airplane that has no engine or propeller. "Later, I want you to meet some of the guys. One is a B-47 bomber pilot from McConnell AFB and several of them work at Cessna. Most members of the club are experienced pilots, who enjoy the challenge of glider flying. This club is a good place to learn about flying a glider."

While driving to the glider airfield, Jason described the club operations. "A tow plane is expensive, so we seldom use one for training flights. You won't believe this! We use an old pickup truck to get the glider up. The club owns the truck and the cost is reasonable. It's like launching a kite by running with the string. I'm on the flight schedule today, so I can show you how we do it. Since I'm certified to take a passenger, I'll give you a ride."

My eyes gleamed. *Gliders would be a different experience with the added risk of flying without an engine.* There was no doubt I would participate. I anticipated future thrills as a club member.

Jason said, "While the cost is low, we don't spend much time in the air, unless we get lucky and find an updraft at the top of the launch, a six- or seven-minute flight is typical. Since we take turns, we only get one or two flights per hour. You don't fill your logbook flying hours quickly, but you have fun. Moreover, you stay busy between flights helping with glider launches. In addition to the pilot, there are three team launch jobs." It all sounded exciting, and I looked forward to trying it.

The glider airport at the edge of town was one long paved runway. The Wind shouldn't be much of a factor because flying 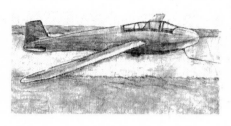 was limited to calm days. There were no big trees nearby and the surrounding land was tabletop flat in all directions, which was important for beginners. Operations were underway as we approached. Jason drove into the parking lot containing a dozen vehicles — cars, pickup trucks, and glider trailers. We walked to the end of the runway, where club activities were happening.

The club plane was a Schweizer TG2 two-seat World War II training glider. I was disappointed because I expected a sleek, streamlined sailplane like those I saw in the flying magazines, more like a falcon than the pigeon I saw sitting on the tarmac. Still, I was glad for any chance to continue flying and learning to keep a glider in the air without an engine.

After meeting club members and watching two flights, it was Jason's turn. This time, I helped with the glider launch. The glider rested at the beginning of the runway, facing a light breeze. A steel cable, one-eighth of an inch thick, was attached to the glider and it stretched forward more than one thousand feet down the runway. The other end was securely attached to a pickup truck's tow hook. I squinted to see someone standing next to the open driver-side door looking back at us.

"You hold the wing level," Jason said. "I'll be in the cockpit. I'll give you a signal when to let the pickup driver know I'm ready."

I took my place at the wingtip and waited.

When the truck driver saw Jason get into the glider, he got into the pickup and inched forward until the cable was taut. There was a bright glint of sunlight reflecting from the glider's canopy, so I shaded my eyes to see Jason inside, securing his harness. He gave me a thumbs-up sign, and I waved to the driver.

The truck took off with a roar, spinning back tires and a cloud of oily smoke billowed from its tailpipe. A fraction of a second later, the plane jerked forward. I ran to maintain a grip while keeping up with the forward motion. After a few steps, the wingtip pulled out of my grasp and the glider was flying. It wanted to go straight up but was restrained, and was being pulled forward by the cable. Just as Jason described, it was similar to a kite being launched by a runner.

After a few minutes the old truck, now almost concealed by the exhaust smoke, abruptly slowed as it reached the far end of the runway. Jason and the glider were 800 to 900 feet high. Inside the cockpit, he pulled the release, and his end of the cable fell back to earth. I watched with my head back and hands shading my eyes.

There were no updrafts to keep him up, so Jason began his landing approach. I smelled burnt tire and truck exhaust, which had drifted the length of the runway. He landed and stopped within inches of his starting point. I watched the entire flight experience intently; I was excited by the prospect of flying the glider myself someday, and before we left the field, I became a member of the Wichita Soaring Association.

During the next few months, I completed the prescribed flight training with a club instructor. I participated as a launch team member, practicing each flying maneuver and launch task. After several practice sessions, it was my turn to solo. I sat in the cockpit waiting and staring down the runway. My right hand tightly gripped the control stick, while left fingers drummed my knee. It was hot in the dome-covered cockpit. I wiped sweat from my eyes. *Calm down.* I recalled my first flight instructor, Stan's advice to concentrate on the process.

I gave the 'ready' signal and tensed while the cable stretched tight. Then the glider jerked forward, gently bouncing up and down several times on its single tire, which was mounted right under my seat. The glider was airborne after rolling just a few feet.

This was nothing like the full-power takeoff that required a long, noisy run to achieve sufficient speed. I pulled against the stick and the TG-2 seemed to go straight up. It was as if a powerful giant had firmly pushed the underside of the wings. The structure resonated a few metallic complaints under the strain, but the primary background sound was a tranquil swoosh of air. Visibility was excellent through the large Plexiglas windshield.

I watched as the runway dropped away and the glider gradually gained motion. The cable slackened, and I concluded that the pickup had reached the end of its run. *The cutoff point is happening too soon. I don't want to stop going up yet!* I had heard of a way to squeeze a little extra energy from the tow and quickly eased the stick forward to capture the last bit of momentum before pulling the cable release. Suddenly, my focus shifted to the invisible atmosphere surrounding me, hoping for any sign of updraft. After a few seconds, I decided that there would be no help from nature this time.

Sounds became quieter as I descended. Turns seemed to be taking place in slow motion, like the gentle swooping of a high-flying albatross. Now that I was free of the cable, wings telegraphed the slightest up or down draft to the stick and then my fingers could suddenly sense the atmosphere's pulse. I was united with this plane much more than the Piper Cub. I was not high enough for maneuvers, so I'd have to return to earth before running out of altitude. Because of the placid nature of the glider's motions, I felt no urgency. I imagined the route through the sky and was soon on course. My goal was to land close to the starting point so the ground team would not have to reposition the plane for the next flight. The main control for achieving the landing precision is to kill lift with small flaps called spoilers on the top of the each wing. On final approach, I moved the spoiler control back and forth to accurately adjust the glide path. Nearing the ground gave the illusion of racing forward faster and faster until the tire hit the pavement a few yards ahead of my aiming point. *I'm on the runway and on target.* I applied the brake with a hand-leaver, which caused a twist and grunting complaint as the glider lurched to a complete stop. I breathed an elated sigh. Surprisingly, I felt no fear during this first landing. The earlier orientation ride with Jason and prior powered flying provided me the much-needed confidence. This experience confirmed my love for aviation and the desire to make it my career.

I continued flying with the club for the next two years. I had no inclination that my current interest in aeronautical engineering would soon concentrate on things much higher than the altitude of a glider's flight.

"The love for all living creatures is the most noble attribute of man."

— CHARLES DARWIN —

CHAPTER FOUR

Testing Fitness

Embracing Change

Wichita, Kansas — 1958, Age 23

Just months before the graduation, I was forced to reconsider my career choice. Wichita was the center of light plane manufacturing, but each batch of aeronautical engineering seniors discovered that the demand for light plane designers was diminishing. A year earlier, Jason had settled to work for a large airplane company, North American Aviation. It was not his preference, but he and Jane were expecting another baby and this was an essential choice considering their impending financial responsibilities.

Now, it was my time to make an important decision. How convenient it would be to have a mentor to ask for advice, but Jason had graduated and we had lost touch, so I didn't have him to call for guidance. I recalled the Logic course that I took at Fenn. It appealed to me for decision-making, because it was structured. *Maybe I should use what I learned; pose a question, examine the facts, and use logic to choose my next life direction.* I decided to give it a try. I took out a notepad and wrote the following:

Question: How can I find a job designing light planes?

Facts: The economy has changed, diminishing the availability of such positions. Good engineering jobs are available in other industries.

Alternatives: Keep searching for a job designing light planes (Low probability of success before graduation).

Redefine dream job to match the new economic reality (Higher probability of success, but it takes me off track).

Decision: Defer or change the dream and look for a different engineering career.

Demand for engineers was high in the Aerospace Industry. After the World War II ended, the Soviet Union and the United States got embroiled in an arms race. A standoff had developed between adversaries with equal destructive capabilities, like two giant dragons spewing flames at each other in a posturing stalemate. Maintaining this equilibrium was essential for coexistence and uneasy peace. This was the Cold War.

Then in October 1957, the Soviet Union launched their Sputnik satellite into orbit. This first successful man-made satellite joined the planets and generated a lot of concern in the U.S. because it led to an upset in the balance of power. A satellite flying overhead may be a nuclear weapon. Sputnik signaled the start of the space race and America was losing the battle.

The U.S. strategy to catch up became a high-priority national effort. America formed NASA, the National Aeronautics and Space Administration and combined the existing space-related agencies into one, and then expanded them as necessity to win the race. The cost was no constraint because the alternative was dire.

Possible consequences of Sputnik, including war, concerned the American public. I was no exception. I assumed that these current events would affect my future, and I was soon about to learn how.

In January 1958, a representative from the Army Ballistic Missile Agency (ABMA) came from Huntsville, Alabama to recruit technical students for expanding their rocket program. They were interested in me as a graduating engineer and I was interested in them as a major player in the space race. I signed up for an interview, suspecting that it might change my career plan. Helping to beat the Soviets was more urgent than a boyhood dream to design airplanes.

Several classrooms were transformed into ABMA interview rooms. When it was my turn, I sat down with a middle-aged man, who was the chief of ABMA's Instrumentation Branch. *Wow! I'm about to meet a rocket scientist.* Rocket scientists had been turned into celebrities by the news media, and I felt respect and awe to be in the same room with him. He did most of the talking in his soft and pleasant voice. I guessed he had lived in the South most of his life. "First, I will tell you about ABMA and our plans to beat the Soviets in space, and then I will describe what we plan for an engineer like you. How does that sound?"

"Good."

He paced in front of me as he repeated what must have been a familiar speech. "ABMA is led by Dr. Werner Von Braun, the famous German rocket scientist. He and about 130 other scientists and engineers worked on the V2 rocket for the Nazis during the World War II. After the war, they immigrated to the United States."

"Was that the entire V2 rocket team of Germany?"

"Other German engineers from the V2 project went to the Soviet Union and are likely to be on the Sputnik team. America persuaded Von Braun to come here by offering him resources to work on his dream of building a rocket that could launch a satellite into space. The United States kept its promise, and Von Braun is in Huntsville with a top team of engineers and scientists. His latest rocket design is called Redstone. It is a proven missile delivery platform, but is yet to be tested as a satellite launch vehicle."

"When will it be tested?"

"That is classified." I must have looked guilty for asking. He stopped pacing and raised his hand, "Don't worry. You were not aware that it was classified. Too many things in our agency are categorized as classified, including whether or not Von Braun is in his office. Last month he called for a car to take him someplace. When the driver showed up and asked if he was at the right door to pick up Von Braun, the guard could not say because that fact was 'classified information.' So, the driver left to find another door, and Von Braun ended up late for his meeting."

I appreciated his attempt to put me at ease. It worked.

"The Navy also has a prototype rocket scheduled for testing before Redstone," he further said. "So, we are in a race with the Navy to see which rocket is the best. It is no secret; I think Redstone is better because Von Braun and ABMA have more experience than the Navy." He took a deep breath. "So… do you have some questions?"

I did not have any because most of what he had just told me, I had already read in the newspaper.

"Now I will share with you all that I can tell you about your job. You will work in my Instrumentation Branch, as a research engineer and would then be promoted to a project manager when you are ready. We invent guidance system instruments that are installed on the rocket to control it during the launch. You will be responsible for proof testing those instruments, before they fly on Redstone, including aerodynamic tests in wind tunnels. That is why we need an aeronautical engineer."

Then I asked a few questions about work and salary.

He replied, "Because our space effort is a national priority, we can offer you one pay-grade higher than the past engineering graduates. We will cover moving expenses to Huntsville and would help you find a place to live. Because this is a vital national initiative, you will also be eligible for an occupational draft deferment."

The deferment was one thing I had not thought much about until now. As a student, I was able to defer the draft, although only a few men were drafted at that time. If I worked in the light plane industry, my current student deferment would end after graduation. I preferred to control my future, which meant avoiding the draft.

In less than an hour, his proposal had impressed, flattered, and convinced me. The job provided a generous salary, kept me out of the military, and began an exciting career. So, I agreed to join ABMA upon graduation. I was pleased with my decision, even though I had put my dream of designing airplanes on a back burner.

While completing the final semester, I looked forward to graduation. Mom and Dad would come to Wichita for the ceremony. That day would be a major highlight for them, particularly for Mom. She had struggled to get me through grade school, while scarcely clinging to hope that I might go to college. Her wish was a big reason for my college decision. My parents were proud and excited enough to endure a long, uncomfortable bus ride across the country to witness this rite of passage.

They planned to return home the same way, but I convinced them to go back with me in my car before I headed on to my new job in Alabama. I felt capable of anything as a college graduate with a fine career in my future, even transporting them in my precarious vehicle.

Mom arrived excited about being in Kansas, which was a new experience for her. Dad arrived troubled about being in Kansas, a strange place. The day after meeting them at the Wichita Greyhound station, I showed them things that had been an important part of my life for the past two years, including the campus, dorm, and glider airport. They were impressed with the formal graduation ceremony, including delightfully inspirational words of a down-to-earth speaker. I saw Mom wipe her eyes, as I walked across the platform to receive the diploma. We celebrated over dinner at a nice restaurant.

After a night's rest, we headed back to Cleveland stuffed into the coupe with our luggage and belongings. The car struggled under the load. Following an overnight motel stop, we began our second day of travel. It was a beautiful day, late in May, but traffic was heavy. My Chevy was on a two-lane highway in southern Illinois laboring up a small hill, when I heard a muffled bang and the car died. Adrenaline kicked in, and I managed to pull to the shoulder off the road. Dad was in the passenger seat and Mom sat in the back. With a wide-eyed expression, he asked, "What happened?"

I employed my most confident and calm engineer's voice and replied, "I think we blew the engine."

Mom asked a more pointed question. "What now?"

I produced a pretend smile. "We will get it fixed at the nearest garage."

After waiting by the side of the road in the sun for what seemed like hours, we got a tow to a populated area with a small auto repair shop. A hefty garage owner in overalls sat in front of his small shop, smoking a cigar. He immediately began removing parts and soon delivered bad news. The engine, now unassembled on the floor in front of the coupe, wasn't easily repairable. The estimated cost of a replacement was more than the car was worth and would require two weeks to order. So, I decided to junk the Chevy right there. The garage owner helped me box and ship most of our belongings, and then he gave us a ride to the nearest cross-country bus stop to finish our trip to Cleveland.

I had started the journey towards home feeling like a winner and ended it like a loser. On this day, I learned that anything can go wrong, particularly when it involves pride.

At home, in the boyhood sanctuary, where I had nursed many past disappointments, I soon got over the travel humiliation. My parents continued to celebrate my graduation by bragging to all who would listen. Mom's advice was to look forward and not back. So, I turned my attention towards my new career.

The race to space remained the most talked about news. Even children referred to it with wide-eyed wonder. Of course, my interest was heightened because I'd soon be an insider, playing my small part in that big production.

My feelings bounced between confidence and uncertainty. *What's it like to be thrown in the deep end? Thrilling? Terrifying?* I was eager to succeed, but also afraid that I might fail. *Is it possible for a new graduate to be at the center of the nation's space race?* Worldwide events were giving me a chance to try, but am I up to the challenge? I knew what I wanted — to help the U.S. win the race. However, this was an ambitious goal for a boy from Cleveland.

I could only guess what my job would entail, since I would be kept uninformed, until being cleared by the government. Forms containing my detailed personal history and requesting a secret clearance were in process, but it would take weeks for approval. With considerable intrigue in her voice, Mom whispered to me that an FBI agent had interviewed several family members and a neighbor. Finally, the process was in action.

Rocket Science

In Huntsville, I rented a cozy, furnished upstairs bedroom in the home of a retired couple, whose children had grown and moved out. It was a comfortable suburban house, much larger than my parent's house in Ohio. They offered the second room to a newly minted electrical engineer, Steve from Minnesota. He was of Swedish ancestors, with a husky build and thinning blond hair. Friendly and talkative, his habitual smile could morph into a smirk, if provoked by what he called "those idiots." Our hostess treated us like substitute sons and provided all the advice we could stand.

Despite different personalities, Steve and I had similar views and soon became pals. Our rented rooms did not include meals, so we frequently ate together at a local diner. In addition to fresh engineering careers at ABMA, we shared the experience of being Yankees in the South and had frustrated desires to find girlfriends.

On the last leg of the drive from Ohio to Alabama, I got a firsthand view of the contrasts between North and South. Roadside foliage became more luxurious and the rural dwellings more impoverished. While driving through the South and even before arriving in Huntsville, I observed signs in public places designating separate toilets and drinking fountains for blacks and whites.

Steve and I were eager to explore the area's social life in our free time. We figured that since the town included the ABMA facility and an Army base, there should be nightclubs and events where we might have fun and meet girls. We were soon disappointed. There were only a few redneck bars and a country music dance hall. They were interesting for a while, but we did not have much in common with the other customers. Also, the girls were older, cruder, and far from beautiful.

Steve asked Ethan, a technician and coworker who grew up in Huntsville, "Why don't we ever see those southern belles we hear so much about?"

"Ha…Where did you hear about them, in movies? Oh, hold on to your dreams, you won't meet them! Established families keep their daughters away from guys who aren't acceptable marriage prospects, and definitely away from Yankees like you in particular." It was disappointing news for two lonely bachelors.

Alabama residents were welcoming, kind, and friendly, but were quick to remind us that we were Yankees. I learned that Civil War enemies aren't easily forgiven, even over generations. So, we were forced to find fun in larger southern cities like New Orleans and Nashville. However, we didn't travel often because of the expense involved. In Huntsville, I had the possibility of a fantastic career, but little opportunity to meet a fantastic girl.

To avoid the looming boredom, Steve and Ethan decided to start a regular Friday evening poker game in Steve's room. They were short of one player, so they recruited me. I always thought playing table games of any kind was a waste of time because there was no useful result at the end. This was an attitude I may have inherited from regimented Austrian ancestors. More importantly, my third-grade cheating disaster had convinced me that I had no talent for bluffing, but Steve talked me into learning poker "just for fun."

Ethan came to the first Friday evening game with a brown paper bag containing a small Mason jar, half full of homebrew. He called it moonshine. We sampled the harsh, transparent liquid, while he showed us how to determine the alcohol content by examining the bubble size, which intrigued me.

He stood and demonstrated, "You give the jar a quick shake, like this, and then check the surface. Large bubbles that pop fast mean higher proof. It takes practice, but it works."

Steve asked, "How can I buy some? This is good. It has a bite to it." I didn't say anything, I just thought it tasted like paint thinner.

Ethan replied, "You'd have a hard time getting it on your own. It's illegal in this state, but that's not strictly enforced, as long as you don't get caught with it in your car. Moonshiners like to sell to neighbors. You don't sound or look like a local, so I'd have to go with you. Moreover, you'd have to buy at least a gallon to make it worth it."

Steve stood, "Let's do it. I want to see how it works. I'll drive."

"I'd like to go too," I said.

"Hold on. I'll need to make a call. Maybe, we can go tomorrow."

Ethan made arrangements, and we agreed to meet at the diner in the morning.

* * *

After breakfast, we set off on our quest. Steve drove and Ethan navigated. I went along for the excitement, thrilled to do something marginally illegal.

It was a foggy fall morning. We went far into the country before turning on a nondescript, unpaved, one-lane road of rutted red clay with narrow weed-covered shoulders. After passing two cornfields, we entered a wooded stretch and continued several more miles. Shoulders disappeared, and trees crowded the road on both the sides. I had not detected any houses or people since we left the paved road. While he drove, Steve showered his friend with questions. "These guys we will be dealing with... How old are they? And how many are there?"

"I don't know. I've never seen them. The one that I talked to sounded young, about our age I guess." Ethan seemed annoyed by Steve's questions.

"Do they carry guns?" Steve sounded concerned, which caused me to look up and wonder if this venture was a good idea.

"No! I haven't seen guns, or anything else other than moonshine. They're very careful, and they won't risk the Feds breaking up their still. They might have a way to see us coming, as we drive in through the woods."

Steve kept it up, "Will we get to see the still?"

"No way! I've never seen it. It's probably at another location." We drove on in silence. A few minutes later Ethan said, "Here we are!" The fog had lifted, but the mist was still evident in the tree-tops.

We had come to a dead end, a vague clearing just wide enough to turn a car around. Tall brush and scrubby trees were on three sides. At the edge of the clearing was a large stump. The top was chain-sawed level and now it served as a rustic table about two feet in diameter and three feet high. A rough-cut wood box rested on it.

Ethan leaned forward and pointed. "See that box on the stump? That's the booze. Pull the car closer."

Steve did as directed. The idling car was the only background sound in the secluded place. I saw no one, although I had a feeling someone was watching. I cranked down my back window and heard only the birds chirping in the bush. It looked and smelled like someone had recently mowed the weeds in the clearing.

Ethan said, "Everything's cool. Give me the cash. I'll get your booze. You stay here." He got out, walked a few steps to the stump and lifted the overturned box. Underneath was a gallon-size glass jug. He grabbed the jug with both hands and shook it vigorously, then squinted at the liquid's surface. Satisfied, he thumbed the cork out, boosted jug to shoulder, and sampled the moonshine without spilling a drop. He looked our way and called out, "It's a good batch. And, Steve? Since you're driving, it's best that you don't sample the booze yet." He replaced the cork, transferred the cash from his pocket, and covered the bills with the wooden box. Ethan stepped back to the car, opened the trunk, put the jug in, and slammed it shut with a loud bang. The twittering birds became quiet. I again looked around but saw no one.

We were soon bumping along towards the highway. My heart was beating much faster than usual, which surprised me. Doing nothing more exciting than watching a moonshine buy had caused my adrenaline to soar.

Steve and Ethan sipped moonshine during the next Friday evening poker game. It was the only time I ever won.

* * *

Later that week after driving through ABMA's front gate on the way to my workplace, I heard the deafening roar of an explosion. I pulled out of the traffic flow to the shoulder and looked in all directions for a cause, but saw nothing unusual. The sound diminished after a few seconds and I was left sitting as other arriving workers drove past me as if nothing had happened. Traffic had slowed and a guy pulled next to my car, leaned over his passenger seat, rolled down his window, and shook his fist at me. "Keep moving dummy! That was a Redstone engine test." My face felt warm. Every few weeks after that, I heard a similar sound. The rumble of a Redstone engine undergoing a static test near our building shook the ground for miles and sent frightened birds flying in all directions.

The Soviet Union had roused ABMA like a provoked tiger facing another predator. After a slight pause to get its bearings, the Agency tried to propel itself into action. I had been one of the first new engineers to arrive and I started learning more with each passing day as I waited for the security clearance.

ABMA was part of an expansive Army base near Huntsville. The workplace of my Branch was in two buildings — a three-story brick office plus an identical-looking building next door, which was referred to as the 'lab' as it included rooms equipped for fabrication and testing. My olive drab steel desk was in a small cubical.

On my first day, my boss said, "You will work on a sensor that is part of the Redstone guidance system, controlling the rocket from launch until it leaves the atmosphere. It is a classified secret because of the advanced design and critical function to control the rocket's path. An initial concept design was done here at ABMA last year. We contracted detail design and fabrication to a specializing company. Final acceptance tests will be done here and you will be involved in that. However, for now, your clearance is still pending."

"Can I start doing anything to help?"

"Not much. My experienced engineers are overloaded, so I will conduct your orientation, which means that you will need to track me down and ask questions if you wish to learn anything useful." He smiled. Since I did not understand his attempt at humor, he did not get the expected response. The shortage of staff seemed like a serious problem to me.

He coughed once and continued, "Your clearance should arrive soon. Until then, here is an unclassified test report to study."

I took the document, which I assumed would be a meaningless time filler.

"Now it is time for your pep talk." He grinned again. "Seriously, this isn't simply a race with the USSR. It is a lot more critical. They intend to wipe us out, and they're getting closer. You might think that you have a small role here, but everything we do is essential. We never know if a single well or poorly performed step might be the difference between a successful launch and a disaster." He stood up to leave. "I'm glad you are part of the team. There is much to do, and we urgently need you."

It was frustrating because everyone else in our building seemed to work with urgency and purpose. I was ready to go, but the starting gun had not been sounded for me. He left, and I looked at the unclassified document. I was bored before lunch.

Three weeks later the clearance arrived, and I was in the race at last. Normal procedure was to apprentice a novice engineer to an experienced project manager for a few years. However, in the current emergency, I was christened to be a project manager with the wave of my boss' imaginary magic wand. Need trumped past practice and common sense.

My first project would be to test the sensor destined to control future versions of Redstone, a gigantic, seventy-foot high rocket that was originally designed to launch a nuclear payload at a target. Now the expanded US goal was to use the rocket to launch a satellite.

With my clearance came more specific direction and an initial look at the sensor. My boss showed it to me, "This untested control  sensor is an advanced version of an older model, which was used for lower and slower ballistic missiles. Your job is to test the new design to ensure that it will work for higher and faster space launches."

I said, "It sounds like the primary difference is that this new sensor will function at supersonic speeds."

"Right, but we're most concerned about transonic speeds. You will have to conduct several tests. First is calibration of the sensor's electronics, next are wind tunnel tests at both supersonic and subsonic speeds, and the last is a transonic flight test."

With considerable help from an experienced technician, who knew more about my job than I did, we designed a test bench in the Huntsville labs. Its primary purpose was to calibrate the instrument. Subsequently, I would test it at a government facility near the Cleveland airport for the subsonic and supersonic wind tunnel testing. The Cleveland wind tunnels, like the ABMA, would soon be a part of the NASA.

Even though it was the sensor that had to be proven and not me, I personally felt responsible for a positive outcome. The classified sensor was carried from Huntsville to Cleveland beforehand by a secret courier. Cleveland engineers installed it in their wind tunnels, connected wiring to recorders, and operated their equipment. I had already provided them with the required test conditions and would now record the results. It was thrilling to witness these large, powerful wind tunnels devoted to my tiny sensor. To my relief, the tests went well. I had not won the lottery, but it felt as if I had.

While I was proud of my role, I was a little disappointed to learn that there was a good chance my sensor might not fly in space because Redstone was a backup to the priority Navy rocket. As it happened, Redstone proved to be more important than any of us realized at the time. It was soon recognized as the most successful large US space rocket when it launched America's first earth satellite, followed by the first two astronauts into orbit. As my boss had said, when I came to Huntsville, that honor had belonged to the Navy. However, their launch pad explosion changed America's plan, so ABMA got the nod to try.

My parents' home was near the airport, the same home I left for Wichita a few years before. That evening, I looked forward to a home cooked meal with Mom, Dad, and my sister. My family had a vague idea why I was in Cleveland.

Dad said, "We hear you're a big shot now?"

I was pleased my family was proud of me, but I felt self-conscious, when they exaggerated my importance. It was all classified, so I could not describe my job. Like much of the general public, my parents eagerly followed news about the rocket launch attempts and other space related events. Mom was prepared to quiz me.

"Clarence, which space rocket are you working on?"

"I can't say, Mom. It's secret."

"So, you are working at those airport buildings with the big wind machines?"

"Sorry, I can't tell you. That's a secret too."

"Do you like your project?" she probed further.

"I can't say."

Now she was grinning. "Do you like the chicken?"

"Yes. It's wonderful." Everyone laughed. "I haven't had anything as good since my last visit."

I soon discovered that Mom and Dad knew more than I did about what was going on in the space race by watching the television news. I considered taking notes about what they told me.

While at home, I stopped to see my old friend, Tim. A strange man wearing long underwear answered his front door.

"Is Tim here?"

"Who?" he asked.

"Tim. He lived here."

I heard a woman's voice call out. "They moved two years ago. Their son got a big job in Chicago."

"Do you know how I might reach them?"

"No" she replied.

"Okay. Thanks." *It sounds like Tim is doing well. That's good.* It was a reminder that all things continuously change.

This brief visit was a welcome break and a reminder of the family support that I enjoyed. It also reminded me of Grandpa Joseph's prediction, and my quest to discover why I deserved the name Clarence. *Is being a rocket engineer something unique or special? No, I do not think so. I work with many rocket engineers, who are no more special than me.* I'd have to keep searching.

My ABMA career goal was to be a successful aeronautical research engineer. Today, it meant that I would have to do my best on this project, given its tight schedule. The most critical step remained, testing the sensor while it is exceeding the speed of sound. Several Huntsville engineers argued that it would not work properly or might even fail due to the vibration. Passing through the sound barrier could be a violent affair. There had been many meetings with the ABMA manager responsible for vibration and flutter analysis. He was one of the repatriated German scientists and was considered to be a genius by his peers. He had indicated that the sensor's cone shape would work in all probability, but one can never be sure until it is tested.

The next test could not be done in a wind tunnel because transonic airflow is unstable. At that time, only a few military planes could achieve such speeds. My boss arranged for this final test on an F-105 fighter jet at Edwards Air Force Base in California. He was sending a beginner to do a professional's job. I worried if I was good enough to be the project manager. Simultaneously, I hoped to meet one of the famous test pilots who worked at Edwards.

Each step was new and challenging, even the routine things I had no experience with, like mastering airline schedules and business meetings. While I got advice from my boss and help from other employees along the way, I was forced to carry on without a lot of day-to-day guidance. I used the trial-and-error method or, in my case, the "try not to embarrass myself" method to efficiently carry out the work assigned. Luckily, I was dealing with  understanding professionals, who may have remembered their youthful mistakes. I imagined them smiling behind my back at my blunders. It helped that we were on the same team in this race with the Soviets and were not competing for standing or promotions.

The trip to Edwards AFB started with two airline flights from Huntsville to Los Angeles — the first leg was on a well-used DC-3, and then cross country on the Constellation, which was the premier airliner of the day with its distinctive triple tail. The sleek and powerful design had set some flight records. I thought it was a beautiful airplane and was eager to ride in it.

I never flew above 2,000 feet in the Piper Cub, so I requested a window seat to see the view from 20,000 feet. After boarding I approached my assigned row and was surprised to see an attractive young lady with short brown hair sitting next to my seat. I estimated that she was a year or two older than me. There was no wedding band. I blushed, as I settled in place and buckled my seatbelt. I smelled her perfume and she gave me a warm smile. She talked about nursing, tennis, and her hometown — Los Angeles. She asked about me, which got me talking more than usual. She was even interested in what I had to say about airplanes and cars. I wondered if she too had read *How to Make Friends and Influence People* because she was a skilled conversationalist.

At one point I admitted to being a shy and reserved person. Of course, my introverted persona was obvious to everyone. I said, "I wish I could make friends as easily as you."

She brightened, "Oh, I will tell you my secret for starting a conversation. It works every time, even with strangers. If you are ever at a loss for what to say, 'thank you' always works. Follow with a reason — whatever seems appropriate for that person. Almost anything will do. It might sound too simple, but it is a winner." She gestured toward me, "For instance, 'thank you for sitting here with me' or 'thanks for being such a good listener'. Or 'thanks for telling me about you'. Get the idea?"

"Yes," I said, "It sounds easy enough. You think it will work if I'm talking to an important person?"

"Oh heavens, yes. Receiving a thank you from anyone is a positive recognition. People who are important, or think they are, like to be recognized, and it may get them talking about themselves. Try it."

"I will."

I asked her name — Sunny. It suited her perfectly. I was attracted to her and we spent most of the long flight in conversation, which was most unusual for me. The Constellation descended into Los Angeles and I spoke up, "I have had fun traveling with you, Sunny. I'm sorry the flight is ending."

Her smile widened. "Me too, maybe we will meet again someday." She giggled. "Oh, it sounds like a line from a movie, doesn't it?" She laughed nervously again and changed the subject. "Do you make this trip often?"

"No, this is my first time. I have no way of knowing when I might return." *It seems she wants to see me again.* I gathered courage from the possibility, but it's still a mystery where my next faltering words originated from. "Could I visit you, while I'm here?"

She hesitated and slowly shook her head. "No… I'm sorry."

Did I hear a hint of regret in her reply?

She quickly added, "I would like to, but can't."

I tried to hide my disappointment, "How often do you come to LA?"

"I visit my family for one week every year. Then I have to get back to my kids."

I was surprised and stunned. I took a deep breath. Then I managed to ask, "How many kids do you have?"

"Forty-eight." She saw my puzzled expression and guessed why I was confused. "I help out at an orphanage in Kenya. Next year, I hope to take my vows."

I couldn't believe what she said or didn't want to. *She is almost a nun!*

The Constellation made a silent descent as props no longer labored to keep the stately airship aloft. We were quiet for the last few minutes of preparing to land. I struggled to absorb what she has just said. *Had I been lusting after a nun?*

As we gathered our things and moved towards the exit, she leaned forward, smiled and touched my arm. "Thank you for being my friend today. If a guy like you ever came along, I might change my mind about the religious life."

I melted.

Soon, we headed in different directions at the terminal. Disoriented and distracted, I bumped into another passenger and apologized. I glanced back for a last look at her, but she was gone. *Get control of yourself, Clarence. Forget about that girl and focus on getting your rental car.*

Project Manager

The terminal was packed with people. I was drawn by the flow on an escalator and found the baggage pickup area on a lower level. I used the claim ticket to retrieve my bag and searched for the Avis auto rental counter. Since I would be driving in California, the branch secretary had reserved a car. *I never imagined there were so many car rental companies. Ah, there it is.* The rental agent wore a tailored uniform like a stewardess, with a plastic nametag shaped like an auto. She studied her clipboard with a frown.

"We do not have the model you wanted. It needed service and will not be ready until tomorrow. No suitable replacement has been returned yet. Sorry."

Sorry? This could screw up my schedule and the entire test. I had no standby solution for what could be a major delay. I brushed perspiration from my upper lip with the back of my hand. My engineer's problem-solving mind was failing me.

I swallowed. "What now?"

"All we have now are two Volkswagens, a VW Bug, or a Karmann Ghia, neither is as big as what you wanted." She hopefully looked up, "But the Karmann Ghia has added air conditioning."

I pressed my palms to my eyes. "So, there is a car for me?"

"Well yes, but a small one."

I smiled; it was an easy choice. I had long admired the Karmann Ghia's design. It was like a poor man's sports car with its streamlined body lines, and I would definitely need air conditioning in the desert. Soon papers were signed and the car was mine.

Remembering Sunny's advice, I said, "Thanks for helping me get a car with AC. You are very professional."

She blushed and flashed a broad smile. "You are welcome, sir. Be sure to ask for me next time you come to LA. My name is Julie." She stood straighter and aimed her nametag in my direction.

No one had ever called me sir before. Maybe saying "Thank you" did work as an icebreaker.

I drove away from the airport in a brilliant red Karmann Ghia coupe. First, I planned to visit the design engineer, who had built my control sensor. His small company was just outside Los Angeles; we had met once in Huntsville.

When I arrived at the design engineer's office, he treated me like royalty, starting with a VIP plant tour. He introduced me to the company president and later, they took me to a fancy Polynesian restaurant with palm trees, flaming torches, and grass-skirted waitresses. Our table included a formal linen place setting. I was impressed and a bit intimidated. *I think etiquette better be my next self-improvement topic. I should not just learn table manners by watching my hosts.* As a security precaution, my boss warned me about drinking alcohol while traveling, so I turned down their offer for mixed drinks. It wasn't a difficult choice because of childhood experiences with Dad's drinking problem.

The design engineer said, "We quality-checked the control sensor, and sent it to Edwards by courier. It is waiting for you."

"Great. I'll leave for there the first thing in the morning."

* * *

The latest American experimental military planes were tested in the Mojave Desert at Edwards AFB, where there was enough wide-open space. Moreover, security was assured because it was an isolated location. I didn't know what to expect driving in the desert, so I had packed extra drinking water. I had the image of the scorching Sahara I knew from movies. From what I could see when I got there, the Mojave Desert wasn't as harsh, but on this day, it was hot, dry, and windy. The Karmann Ghia's AC couldn't keep up with the desert heat, so I was compelled to open the windows. During the ninety-mile drive to Edwards, I stared at gray hills on the horizon and an otherwise flat landscape like Kansas, but without much greenery. There were numerous low shrubs and Yucca trees in the vicinity and wind-blown tumbleweed nudged the car.

A few miles from Edwards I heard a pop and felt the steering wheel shake violently. I knew what it meant — a flat front tire. I maneuvered to the gravel shoulder. I knew how to change a tire from owning my old Chevy, but I needed to hurry to stick to the schedule. I located the neatly packed tools and went to work. One truck whizzed by, but for the most part, I was alone. Blowing sand got into everything, including my nose and mouth. I was glad that I had brought extra water to wash away the grit. A half hour later, red-faced and sweating, I pulled back on the road congratulating myself for winning the race with the schedule.

I approached the entrance gate wondering if any of the famous test pilots who had been breaking supersonic speed records were on the base. An Air Force guard in a booth greeted me with a questioning expression. He looked like a teenager.

He said, "You have grease on your forehead."

"Oh?" I did my best to wipe the dirt off, as I sat there.

"Name?" he asked.

"Clarence Arnold."

After a long pause, he said, "You're not on the list. Pull off to the right and turn around."

"What do you mean, I'm not on the list? I have an important meeting in ten minutes. I'll be late; I can't turn around."

He raised his voice. "You're causing a holdup!" I glanced in my rearview mirror and saw one car. "Now turn around or I'll call the MPs. And then you will be delayed further if they take you into custody." A high-pitched voice made it difficult to take him seriously, but the gun on his belt helped persuade me.

I frantically tried to think. *I can't let this guy keep me out.* I recalled Mom's direction, "Never give up." Desperate, I shoved my ABMA travel papers at him.

I raised my voice. "Look at this. See my name is here? I'm supposed to be here."

His nostrils flared. "I don't need that. They'll check credentials at the building entrance. You're either on my list or not." But he couldn't avoid glancing at the papers that were now pushed in his face. "Is this you? Clarence — A R N O L D?" He spelled out the last letters.

"Yes, yes." I strained to hold my ABMA photo badge next to my face and posed with an awkward smile.

"Oh. I was looking for an Arnholt." He checked again. "Now I see you're on the list." The motorized gate slowly swung open and he smartly saluted. "Move forward."

With a relieved sigh, I drove further, looking for the right building and the Flight Officer, who was responsible for the F-105 test.

The brief exchange with the guard reminded me that Mom thought my name was special and I realized that even Edwards AFB knew me as Clarence. *Forget that nonsense and concentrate on your job.*

When I sat down with the Flight Officer, I learned that my test would be one of several during the next scheduled F-105 flight. While it was a top priority for me, it was routine at Edwards. I was disappointed when the test pilot didn't attend the meeting with the Flight Officer and me. *I guess there was no need for him to be there because he would be given the required test maneuvers just before takeoff.*

The Flight Officer said, "Looks like we have a problem. We didn't get your package from Huntsville, so there will be a delay till it gets here." He slid my test file to the side.

I thought *Oh no, another screw-up.* I felt a little less desperate this time, just uneasy. *Screw-ups seemed to be a routine here. Hopefully, we can get this straightened out.*

I said, "How can that be? I just talked with the contractor yesterday. They sent it more than a week ago and they called here last week to confirm its arrival."

The Flight Officer turned his head to the side and looked over his reading glasses at his aide, sitting at a desk by the wall. "Check if his secure package for the next F-105 flight has arrived."

"Yes, sir." The aide left the room.

The officer returned to desk work, ignoring me. With nothing better to do, I casually glanced at my trouser leg and saw a large grease stain from the tire-changing chore.

I quickly crossed my leg to hide the dirt. *I'm not making a favorable impression.* After several minutes of awkward waiting, the aide returned.

"We have it, Sir. It came from Pasadena, not Huntsville."

I took a deep breath. The test was back on schedule for the next morning.

The aide escorted me to a large test hanger in the back, where I encountered the F-105; it was a large, sleek war machine. It looked way too heavy to fly. I stepped back for a better look and saw that most of the plane consisted of a huge jet engine.

The Air Force Sergeant in charge of the F-105 was all business. This afternoon I would help him prepare for the test. My responsibility was to ensure that the sensor worked on the plane's nose boom by checking the output signals. I immediately encountered another problem when I tried to enter the room. He would not let me near 'his' plane.

He held his hand up like a traffic cop. "Wait right there, Sir."

I stopped abruptly. "What do you mean? We only have a few hours to be sure that the sensor is working properly on the boom."

He pointed down. "You can't come past that yellow line."

"Why not?"

"Security reasons."

"But how…?

"You stay there and tell me what needs to be done. My men will take care of it."

"But that will take longer" I insisted.

"Regulations, please don't object."

I took another deep breath and started calling out directions to him and his crew. The task took twice as long as necessary, but the process preserved the Sergeant's ego and the plane's security. Before I left the hanger for the night, I looked up at the F-105's long, pointed nose boom that supported my sensor. Light glinted from the polished cone shape and I smiled with pride. *It looks like the future.*

The next morning I shook the test pilot's hand before he got into the F-105. He looked bored. The Sergeant told me that the pilot needed to log more flight-testing hours, even if it meant doing a lot of routine flights like mine. While he was not one of the celebrity pilots, it was exciting to be working at Edwards with a professional test pilot.

Once the fighter plane was airborne, I had no information until it returned. Outside the air was dry and the sky was clear and blue; there was not a cloud in sight. I sat in the shade on an old storage crate next to the hanger, wondering if my sensor would work and return in one piece. The plane returned safely an hour later. I stood and waited with anticipation as the test pilot climbed down the F-105 ladder and approached the hanger. He proceeded through the door, without a glance at me and my open mouth. I was desperate to learn what had happened, but when I entered the sergeant was conversing with the test pilot in a glassed-in office, behind the closed door. They finished talking, came out, and walked past ignoring me again. *Superior*, I thought. *I suppose they have a reason to act like that.* By the time I caught up with them, I was disappointed to find that the test pilot had gone for the day. I had rehearsed a short thank you speech as an excuse to talk with the pilot once more before I returned home. A few days ago, I was proud to be a NASA project manager, but now I felt unimportant and ignored. The sergeant said that the sensor worked fine and my test was finished. My boss was pleased when I called to report that we were one step closer in the race with the Soviet Union.

Because all went well, I now had two free days to see the sights, courtesy of my boss, who had provided glitch time in his inexperienced project manager's schedule. During the drive back to Los Angeles, I daydreamed about Sunny, the attractive young lady on the Constellation. *Perhaps I could have met her if she had been available.*

I conveniently forgot that she was planning to be a nun. *Too bad, now it's back to my quiet, date-free life in Huntsville.*

Before returning the rented Karmann Ghia, I decided to pretend that it was a real sports car and drove it to see the sites in Hollywood. I drove around Beverly Hills and toured the Paramount Studios. I experienced the excitement of fast tailgating, which was typical travel of the LA freeway. Unlike the slower, two-lane highways that I had used while crossing the country, multi-lane modern freeways allowed higher speeds. Once, as a new driver, I had been on the Pennsylvania Turnpike for a joy ride, but LA driving was far more exciting for a young man, who enjoyed going fast; it seemed like controlled chaos. I drove on it for more miles than necessary because it was so much fun. In fact, it was like being at an amusement park.

On the flight back, I selected a window seat to experience the 20,000-foot view that I had missed on the previous flight. An older guy was sitting next to me and reading a book, so it was a quiet ride, which I welcomed. I needed an opportunity to digest everything.

Overall, it was an exciting trip with many first-time experiences; it was exhausting but exhilarating. I learned a lot while avoiding any major mistakes. My boss was happy and because of my time with Sunny, I returned with new confidence. *With a little more improvement, I might finally be successful with women.*

Back in Alabama, my friend Steve, who was aware of my commitment to self-improvement and my desire to find a girlfriend said one day, "Playboy Magazine features an article each month with useful advice and tips on being a hit with girls; you should read it. I renewed my subscription if you want to see my copy."

"Sure. Thank you."

I had always been skeptical of advice from a non-expert. Steve had read *Playboy* for a year and still didn't have a girlfriend, but I did borrow his latest issue. The articles seemed reasonable, and I liked the photos. Too bad, I didn't have much opportunity to practice *Playboy* techniques in Huntsville.

One evening, about ten days after returning from Huntsville, I received an unexpected phone call.

"Hello," I answered.

"Is Clarence there?" The female voice sounded familiar.

"Speaking."

"Hi, Clarence. This is Sunny. Do you remember me? We met on the flight to LA."

Sunny, how could I forget? "Ah, yes, of course, I remember you."

"I thought that I may have given you the wrong impression as we parted. So, I am calling to rectify that." She paused. "I want you to know that I would enjoy seeing you again someday. How about if I call you next time, I get back in the States?"

"Oh sure, that would be great," I replied.

"Good." She paused again. "Umm…I can't talk, so I'll say goodbye for now."

"I see. Okay, goodbye." My head was spinning. I didn't know what to think. *What could this mean? She seems to be encouraging me. I'm sure she had said she planned to be a nun. Something sure doesn't add up. She is charming and sexy, but it may not matter because my chances of seeing her again are probably slim.*

* * *

I decided to focus on potential friends here in town. While there were no likely girlfriends, there were remarkable people working here, like the famous German rocket scientists, who immigrated to the US after the war. By the time I got to ABMA, most of them were mid-level managers. Werner Von Braun had a corner office on the top floor in a nearby building. He was a celebrity in the US, and I could never meet him, but I did get to know one German engineer, who was outgoing and liked to talk with Americans.

Kurt was middle-aged, stocky, and sociable. He was still an engineer, not a manager. His most prominent feature was a three-inch scar from the corner of his mouth to near his left ear lobe. The scar looked thin and white on his ruddy skin. I invited him to eat with my regular lunch group.

Most of the Germans preferred socializing with each other, but Kurt liked to eat with the young and impressionable Americans. His English was good because he had gotten a lot of practice. We were always glad to see him because he was both intelligent and entertaining. Eating with our lunch group one day, he asked me, "Arnold! Were you always interested in building rockets?"

"No, in fact, I wanted to design light planes."

"In our engineering training near Berlin, we made a high-wing, two-seater plane out of wood and canvas." He smiled with pride. "When we finished, it flew. *Ja.*" As Kurt intended, I was a bit jealous; however, he wanted to impress the entire table. He looked around and spoke loudly, addressing everyone, as he touched his cheek. "That's where I got this scar — at the university's fencing club. We used to fight with a special sword called Schlager. It was razor sharp and we had little protection." He made a dismissive gesture with his hand. "Not like English fencing with safety equipment; this required guts. It was easy to get your neck cut. Then this happened — *Schusssh*," He made a hand gesture across his face with the corresponding sound effect. "At the University, a fencing scar is a sign of bravery. This got me plenty of girls, *Ja.* It is from a real fight, not a fake scar." He hesitated, checking if we were all still listening. He confirmed that he had our rapt attention and dramatically whispered, "Do you know, some guys wanted a scar a lot, but they were afraid to fight a real duel. So, they make a thin cut with a razor and put a boar hair in. It gets infected and leaves a scar. *Ja.*" He smiled.

Most of us had heard Kurt's story before, so I tried to redirect the conversation. "Kurt, were you always interested in building rockets?"

"No, the German system decided for me. When I was a boy, I dreamt about flying gliders. We have many high-performing sailplanes in Germany. I fantasized to break sailplane records — for distance and altitude. Now that is a big challenge, to fly without power." He stared into the distance. I guessed he imagined himself flying in a sailplane between towering cumulus clouds. Kurt continued, "Rocket design was not my first choice. I was a good engineer student, so I got picked to help with the top project. Now, I love to design space rockets. It is both exciting and difficult."

I described my experience of flying gliders with the Wichita glider club. Kurt was intrigued by the way we launched them with a pickup truck. He became silent again, thinking as we ate. Then he said after a while, "Isn't it interesting; when I was a boy, I wanted to fly gliders, but I built a powered plane in the university. When you were a boy, Arnold, you dreamt about building a plane, but then instead, you flew a glider. Now, we both build rockets for space, and this is the dream of today's little boys. Maybe someday both our old dreams will come true, I will fly a glider and you will make a plane. We are still young, after all. Maybe I'll even start a glider club here in Huntsville, similar to the glider club you were in."

My eyes opened wide, "I'll join your glider club, Kurt. I miss flying."

"Good!" he said, "I'll see to it someday."

I liked Kurt but assumed nothing would come of his glider club idea because he seemed like a talker and not a doer.

Talking of flying reminded me of Cousin Jason, whom I had not heard of since moving to Huntsville. Jason was undoubtedly a doer and I had no way of knowing that he was about to come back into my life in a big way.

* * *

Everything was going smoothly in the Instrumentation Branch. I had completed my first big project and received the promised pay raise. Then one day my boss called me into his office and I saw two men in dark suits. My boss sat at his desk with a frown. The men flashed their FBI badges.

Maybe they are here for my security clearance.

I started to perspire after one investigator handed me a grainy eight by ten black and white photo. *It looks like the nun I met on the plane.*

The agent said, "Have you ever seen this person before?"

I wiped my left palm on my shirtfront and held the photo closer. "Yes. I think she sat next to me on a plane ride to Los Angeles."

"We are gathering background information and are setting up a tape recorder in the conference room. We will ask you to tell us all you remember about what transpired with her."

"Nothing transpired..." My boss gave me a critical glance. I said, "Oh sure, I can do that."

"Has she contacted you since?" they asked.

"Well, yes...she did call a week or two later to say she would be in touch."

"Did you have any other contacts with her?"

"No" I replied.

"Do you know where she is now or how we might locate her?"

"She went back to her orphanage in Kenya. At least, that's what she said. Her parents live someplace in Los Angeles. What's this all about?"

The agent glanced knowingly at his partner and handed me his card. "If she contacts you again, call me immediately at this number. Also, call if any stranger contacts you about your work. You may wait at your desk now. We will bring you back when the recording tape is set up."

As I left the room, my boss said, "Remember, you know secrets that others would like to know."

My palms were damp. "Yes, I know." I turned back at the doorway because I had another thought. "You know what, she called me, but I had never given her my phone number and it's un-listed...strange." One FBI agent made a note, as I left. I waited to be called back in and was unable to do any work. *I don't remember telling her anything classified. Did I? No. Could she be a spy? That would mean that she isn't studying to be a nun.*

* * *

Life had settled into a routine, a dull routine for my love life. I knew that change was required and it was up to me to make that happen but, I didn't really have any good ideas.

I had been working in the space race for two years. Now ABMA was officially a part of NASA and proudly carried the new name on an impressive entrance sign. Three other major space agencies around the country, and several research laboratories and test facilities had the same honor. NASA was a large and growing organization.

The proven control sensor was waiting to fly on a Redstone rocket. I was satisfied with my performance as a new project manager and was ready for the next challenge. The Branch Chief told me to finish the final report because he had another project ready for me.

"To improve is to change; to be perfect is to change often."

— WINSTON CHURCHILL —

CHAPTER FIVE

Chasing Dreams

Airplane Dream

Huntsville, Alabama — 1960, Age 25

That evening after spending the day writing the final report, I was in my room reading Steve's *Playboy,* when Cousin Jason called. In the past, whenever he contacted me, an exciting adventure was sure to follow. So, as I listened to him talk about his family, I couldn't help but wonder what it might be this time.

"Clarence, remember when we talked about the aircraft company I'd start some day? Well, I'm ready to do it now."

"Really?" I paused to let the news sink in. All I could reply was, "I can't believe it!"

"Yes, my dad was vacationing in Florida, when he met a wealthy land developer, and they decided to back me to build the J-2. I went down last week to iron out all details. We're forming a start-up company at an airport near Boca Raton. The land developer wants this company to be in Florida."

Jason's father had been a successful inventor. His latest invention was a superior industrial paint sprayer. He sold his company for a lot of cash and now lived on dividends and royalties. Jason had a talent for innovation, just like his father, who apparently passed on the creative genes to his son. Now, Jason's dad was also passing on his business advice and financial help.

I was so surprised that I couldn't even think of questions that I assume I should have been asking. I just mumbled, "I can't believe it!" But, I did want to believe it. "You are really going to start the company?"

"Yeah" I heard the smile in his voice. "I'll build the twin-engine, short-takeoff-and-landing version. We will call the prototype XJ-2. I've been refining it on paper during the past few years. The design is much better than when you saw it in my last sketch. Now I'm ready to build a prototype. Are you interested in joining us? I'd sure like to have you on board."

"Yes, I'm interested. That would be great!" *It's better than anything I had dreamed of — a chance to follow my wish of designing airplanes and to do it with someone I respect.*

Jason talked fast. "Good. I talked to two other friends, who are with us. You may not know them. One's an experienced designer, a pilot, and he can do many other things well. He bought a surplus T-6 trainer, fixed it up, and is flying it. When we're finished talking, I'll call another friend, who is a super aircraft mechanic. He rebuilt his '40 Chevy, and it won an award for the best-restored car. If he joins us, our team will include a superior airplane mechanic as well."

Jason stopped to catch his breath, before continuing, "We will start as a small group, so we will each do a bit of everything."

By then I had recovered enough from his surprise call to ask a question, "Tell me more about financing. Your project could cost a lot."

"My dad's putting up half of the start-up money. His Florida partner will put up the other half. After we fly the prototype, we will get private placement investors. Dad's lining them up now and we will use the initial investment to set up a production line. Also, we'll get government certification so that it can be sold to the public. The production model will be a twin-engine business plane. The third-phase is a public stock offering. Dad's Florida partner has already done it before."

I didn't understand much about financing, but Jason sounded like he did, and I trusted his judgment. I also trusted his father's business sense. Jason said, "We would like you to be the Vice President of Engineering. In the beginning, you won't get much salary, but you'll get company stock and will be on the Board of Directors." We both understood without saying it — I'd get the important-sounding title instead of a good salary. It was all right with me since I was in for the adventure. There was no need for me to think it over because I had dreamed and hoped for this day since we discussed the possibility years ago. It was a big risk that I embraced for the possibility of a bigger gain.

"Tell me about the airport and the place we will be working in."

"Boca Raton was used to ferry military airplanes during World War II. Now the airport is owned by the State of Florida and is being offered for commercial use. The runway is long enough to handle B-29 bombers and we've leased a former Air Force utility building for our workshop. It's small, but right off a taxiway leading to the runway, which makes it very convenient. Jane and I rented a house in Delray Beach, and I'll be moving down next week with her and the children. I hope to have the entire team start by next month. When can you come?"

I had been thinking the same thing. *It's going to be great fun building an experimental airplane. And, I bet we will all be rich someday.* I said, "I'll check with my boss. I just finished a project. So, I guess, I could give him a two weeks' notice. I'll call you back in a day or two and I'll be there as soon as I can."

"Great. We're going to have an exciting time."

I put the phone down and started pacing. I had to talk to someone who would understand and share the excitement. I went to see if Steve was in his room. However, I was disappointed to hear Steve's reaction.

He said, "It is a dumb move. We're in on the ground floor here. You will be exchanging a secure space career for an impossible dream."

"It isn't impossible, just challenging."

"It's unlikely to succeed."

My decision to quit the space program for a childhood dream was not considered rational by any of my Huntsville coworkers. While my boss pointed out reasons for me to stay, I was grateful that he was less vocal about his criticism than my friend Steve. There was another important but at that time unknown reason to stay. In a few months, President Kennedy made his "We choose to go to the moon..." speech. In a few years, NASA made history by putting a man on the moon, the centuries' greatest space achievement. I had made a tiny contribution with the Redstone control sensor and could have done more if I stayed.

I had not seen the race with the Soviets becoming more than a satellite launch. Even if I had foreseen NASA's future, I was compelled to pursue my airplane dream. Striving for the brass ring was far more adventurous than a prestigious career. My youth charmed me into embracing the challenge and discounting risk. Also, I saw this decision as only a job change, and not a major life turning event that it actually was.

New Adventure

Boca Raton, Florida — 1960, Age 25

On a pleasant day in June 1960, I drove from Alabama to Florida to begin working with my cousin Jason. I was elated, looking forward to the new challenge, and enjoying the drive through the sunny South. *Life is wonderful.* The car windows were open and my left arm rested on the sill. The sweet smell of honeysuckle was in the air. My used Ford station wagon, which I had just purchased with this cross-country migration in mind, was packed with possessions. They included my favorites, a Grundig high fidelity record player in a polished mahogany cabinet, and a collection of long-playing records. My preferred music was jazz followed by big bands. I also owned three classical records to impress any sophisticated girls that I might meet some day.

My head spun with relocation plans. One thing I wasn't thinking about was sunburn ripening my left arm.

I had been invited to bunk with Jason and his young family in their Delray Beach home until I could find an apartment. He described it as a typical middle-class Florida house — no basement, all rooms on one level, low maintenance terrazzo floors and, since this was Florida, a small swimming pool. Optimistic Jason planned to buy a bigger house after the company was a financial success.

When I knocked, Jason' front door was answered by Jane's friend Suzanne from Cleveland, the object of my high school cafeteria infatuation. She displayed a wide smile and held Jane's new baby on her hip. I took a step back. "What —?"

"Hi Clarence," Suzanne said. "Jane told me you were coming. I just arrived from Cleveland for a week. I can't say I remember you well from school but have heard a lot about you from Jane. I can't wait to hear about the airplane project. Isn't Florida great? This is my first visit."

I took a breath and all I could reply was "Hi."

Suzanne looked beautiful in a gorgeous, white sundress. Her hair was pulled back, which gave the impression of a more mature and stylish woman than the teen I remembered. I tried to say something interesting but found no words. I was still as attracted to her, as I had been when I first saw her in the school cafeteria. Ready or not, seven years after we graduated from high school, Suzanne and I were about to get acquainted.

She had taken the Greyhound bus because she could not afford to fly. Years later I learned that she was also afraid to fly. After a tiring two-day bus ride, she unpacked her bag in the only extra bedroom. This meant I had no place to sleep.

Ever cheerful Jane joined us at the door with a toddler trailing behind. She said, "Don't worry Clarence, there's plenty of room for both of you; we'll set up a cot in the hallway." After one look at my red arm, Jane went to look for the sunburn lotion.

She returned holding the lotion, took the baby from Suzanne and said, "Would you please apply this on Clarence's sunburn?"

"Sure."

During the next few minutes, lotion was gently applied to my arm by an angel. My eyes glossed over.

Suzanne said, "There, your sunburn isn't too bad."

I cleared my throat, "Thanks…Well, I guess I better get my things from the car." I walked out.

As I left I noticed Jane give Suzanne a disappointed glance. *What could that mean?*

I did know what it meant if I could be honest with myself. *Jane is disappointed in me.* I was delighted to see Suzanne, but she presented a new challenge to my shy nature that left me speechless and worried that I was making a complete fool of myself. My brief exposure to *Playboy Magazine* had apparently not helped a bit. I was so flustered I didn't even remember to try the "thank you" advice.

During the next few days, I learned Suzanne was a legal secretary at a small law firm in downtown Cleveland. She and her widowed mother lived in a second-floor apartment on West 95th Street. Suzanne's meager salary was their primary income. I was relieved to know that she was not yet married. Soon after moving to Florida,

Jane remembered her friend back in Cleveland and invited Suzanne for a sunny beach vacation, which was gladly accepted. Suzanne also wanted to help the couple celebrate their good fortune.

That evening I became the target of Suzanne's playfulness. She had retired to her bedroom and me to a folding cot in the hallway near the bathroom door. The layout was such that Suzanne would pass my cot to get to the bathroom, so out of modesty, I waited until she was in her room before occupying the cot.

The house was quiet and dark, except for a tiny nightlight in the hallway. After I was settled for the night, but not yet asleep, Suzanne breezed past me in a filmy, flowing nightgown, which brushed against my head. I lay there and held my breath waiting for her return trip. A few minutes later, she stopped on her way back, kissed me on the forehead and whispered "Sweet dreams." Then she disappeared like a phantom in the dim light.

I couldn't speak. Wide-eyed, both literally and figuratively, I was unable to sleep for several hours. *What did it mean? Was she teasing me? Was she flirting? Did she like me?* Just before finally drifting off, I pictured her dazzling dark eyes just inches from my face.

The next morning at breakfast, Suzanne acted like nothing unusual had occurred. By all accounts nothing had. At that stage of my masculine immaturity, I was naïve about how young women thought and acted, and was still too reserved to make the move expected of a young man in such a situation.

During the remainder of the week, we were occupied with different activities. I looked for an apartment to rent and spent time with Jason at the airport. Suzanne and Jane went shopping and to the beach with the children. After a week together in the same house, I found her even more captivating than in our high school days. Then her vacation days ended, and she departed for Cleveland. I was left frustrated and without answers to my questions about what it all meant. Years later I learned that she and Jane assumed that I was not interested. I avoided confronting my missed opportunity by keeping myself fully involved with the new aircraft company. I wondered if we would ever meet again. Then I admitted to myself that I gave up without trying. That's when I made a promise to myself. *If I ever get another chance I will do better.*

* * *

Similarly, with the new company, I was sure if we didn't try, the result would be the same as failing, but without the possibility of success or opportunity to learn. The goal of our fledgling company was clear — to design, build, and fly a revolutionary airplane; and do it before running out of money. The undertaking was just short of impossible, or it could be called highly improbable, but Jason's optimism kept everyone confident. I joined the venture expecting an exciting ride leading to a successful finish. To my friends back in Huntsville, it was like a person trying to fly by jumping off a tall building. That too would be exciting, — for a short time. We may have been inexperienced, but isn't it usually the clueless pioneers, who make great discoveries? By definition a pioneer ventures into the unknown, while accepting all the risks.

After Jason introduced me to the Boca Raton airport location and described what he planned, it was hard for me to imagine where to start because there was so much that needed to be done. Our leased building was a basic wooden box constructed hurriedly during the war. It looked like a military barrack with about as much space as a small house. We found the building empty, waiting for its new purpose. Jason and I stood inside the entrance, discussing what to do first.

He said, "My dad wants me to talk to an out-of-state investor, so I'll be away for several days. You can get started here."

"Okay, I'll line up the workbenches and power tools, so everything is ready to start fabricating the prototype when you get back." Other team members were also on the way.

The airport's agent had prepared our rental space, except that the small bathroom had been used and needed cleaning. It was my first job as the Vice President. *I wonder if this is what Jason meant when he said we would each do a little of everything.*

Pretend Playboy

After my latest failure with Suzanne, I resolved to learn to be a playboy as a way to improve. The bungled opportunity made me more determined to overcome shyness. I was not even sure that changing my personality was possible, but I decided to try harder. My recent exposure to Suzanne and the girl on the airline gave me hope; in both the cases, the women seemed to like me, although I suspected Sunny was only flirting with me to extract some information. As someone who believed in self-improvement, I figured I would start with research. Recalling Steve's advice, I ordered a personal subscription to *Playboy*. The magazine featured the articles about being successful with girls — sexy centerfolds were a bonus.

Each month I learned more about being attractive to the opposite sex by looking sharp, as well as saying and doing the right things. After study came practice. I was now in the best place for being a pretend playboy, the sunshine state's Atlantic coast paradise. It was exotic and chic with an abundance of attractive women. I had moved from bachelor purgatory to bachelor heaven.

As one article recommended, I tried to bolster self-confidence by dwelling on my other achievements. For example, I had earned an engineering degree and flew an airplane. Talking to a good-looking female couldn't be any harder than those accomplishments.

During my limited leisure hours I immersed myself in Florida's resort lifestyle. I traded the boxy station wagon for a sporty used MG-A Roadster. It was my first real sports car. It had brilliant black paint with sumptuous red leather upholstery — the perfect little playboy car. Just don't ask it to take a heavy load up a steep hill; it was too underpowered, but fortunately there are no hills in Florida.

After working long hours for six days, the team was inclined to loaf on Sunday, but I decided if a girlfriend was in my future, I had to get out and experience the tropical resort environment. So, I treated the beach like a playboy practice field. Typically, I spent

172 · LAWRENCE SCHNEIDER

Sunday afternoons at Fort Lauderdale Beach. I strolled along the shore enjoying what the sea offered — cool surf, scents of sea life, and treasures on the sand — including bathing beauties. When I caught the eye of a cute sunbather, I would stop to try some *Playboy* advice.

Once I saw three attractive gals lying in a row on beach towels. They appeared to be sisters between about 19 and 25. They watched me approach and encouraged me with smiles. I paused, took a deep breath, and spread my arms dramatically.

"Thank you for enhancing the beach by being here."

The oldest looked amused. They rejected me by turning over like dominoes to sun their backsides, oldest to youngest. I blinked, then turned, and continued walking. I was embarrassed by my failure, wondering what they thought about me. *What did I do wrong?* Then I remembered advice from one of the articles. *Learn from each failure.* I continued walking thinking my line was corny and insincere.

I was determined to try again and knew how to improve. First, I dropped any attempt to be dramatic or clever. That was not the real me. I found it more effective to introduce myself and inquire if they lived nearby. If there was interest, I asked if they would mind if I stop to get acquainted. Some gals were curious about me and my career — if the conversation got that far. A few gave me a phone number that led to a date. I discovered the value of risking rejection or embarrassment. I learned by trial-and-error to be cautious with my comments. I made adjustments in my approach. Month after month, I improved, as measured by the number of gals who would talk to me. In time, I decided women were nothing to fear.

There were many elegant, yet low-cost options for dates, such as going to one of the many nightclubs featuring live music and headline acts or taking a sunny drive along Ocean Boulevard with the top down in my sports car. In the beginning, it was hard to shed my shy disposition, but eventually I realized that most of the young ladies wanted to find the right husband. However, my head was in another place — on airplane design. I wasn't even considering marriage. Also, I took home a subsistence salary and had no savings. These facts were evident to the ladies soon enough, so none of my new friendships matured or endured. Nevertheless, I had a great time meeting bathing beauties and cruising in my sports car. More importantly, I became highly comfortable talking with women.

Creating an Airplane

When Jason's two aviation friends arrived from Ohio, we made four workbenches and a large layout table. Jason had ordered two aircraft engines, aluminum, and fiberglass; which arrived. We started building the JX-2 as soon as Jason returned from his meeting with the investor.

The team had his overall design, but few detailed drawings; however, we had something even better, Jason himself. Our approach was to improvise as we built the prototype. He worked with us most of the time. He seemed to be able to solve any new problem, no matter how difficult it was. We were like comrades doing whatever was needed and helping each other. It was exciting, challenging and, because of the fast pace, intense. Both stakes and stress were high. We continued until exhaustion stopped us late each evening. Several employees were added over the next few months — a draftsman, two airplane mechanics, and a part-time secretary.

As the prototype took shape, tension increased because new shareholders were slow to invest and our working money dwindled. It became a race to finish the JX-2 prototype while the money lasted. Over time, we argued more but progressed less. By the fourth month, it became clear that stress was too high because both harmony and productivity suffered. A natural leader, Jason was quick to recognize the problem. One afternoon he left for about half an hour and returned with several toy airplane kits, enough for each person, including the secretary. These were simple, easily assembled balsa wood gliders, which were available from the neighborhood hobby shop.

Jason said, "We're going to see who can glide their plane farthest and highest. You have ten minutes to assemble your glider. Modifications are allowed."

We each marched our finished gliders to the concrete taxiway adjoining the workshop. For the next hour, we flew toy airplanes, laughed, and forgot all about money and deadlines. To the guys' dismay, the secretary's glider performed the best. She had not made any changes.

We came back reenergized and ready to get back to the real airplane. Because the stress reliever had fostered teamwork and morale, productivity seemed to double. Whenever we passed the acceptable stress threshold, Jason came up with a new diversion. One time we flew kites in a friendly competition, another time we made go-carts from old lawnmower engines and surplus airplane parts. Progress was important, but so was having fun.

The twin-engine plane included the same ideas that Jason had described to me back in college. It was intended that it would fly from any local airstrip or patch of flat ground. In his sales pitch to potential investors, Jason predicted that the production version would land and take off from a large parking lot.

* * *

Early on a Sunday, I donned bathing trunks and sunglasses and headed to Fort Lauderdale Beach, as usual. This was now my favorite way to relax. Before walking to the surf, I sat on a bench to remove my sandals. A cool sea breeze balanced the sun's warmth. Someone had discarded the back section of the *Miami Herald* on the bench and I noticed a familiar face. It looked like the same photo that the FBI agent had shown me of the girl I met while flying to Los Angeles. The caption read, "Suspect Spy Deported to Cuba." No details. I leaned back and closed my eyes, imagining some of the bad things that could have happened if I had been less reserved. *I might have been involved with a spy. Was I her target because of my work or was it a coincidence?* I sat there captured by anxiety and unable to move for several minutes. After the FBI investigators had interviewed me at work, I was suspicious of Sunny's real intentions, but she was an attractive woman and I couldn't get her out of my mind. Now I needed to face the truth. The mounting sun forced me to stop worrying about what I'd never know and get on with my day. I tossed the newspaper in the trash and ambled towards the water. *I like to think that dedication to do a good job prevented me from pursuing Sunny with more vigor. But in truth it was shyness or I guess I was just lucky.*

* * *

A little over a year after we started at Boca Raton Airport, Jason prepared to take the JX-2 on its first nail-biting flight. We all knew something big was about to happen, we just didn't know if it would be good or bad. Months of our work, a lot of money, and our futures — all were at risk. We also understood that while Jason was a talented pilot, he was not a professional test pilot. But the fact was that there would be no company without him.

The long runway next to our shop was not used much, making it ideal for testing. Test day dawned calm and clear. We pushed the prototype to the tarmac next to the runway and poured over it like ants, checking and double-checking everything. The JX-2 was pronounced ready and we gathered around Jason.

He cleared his throat. "I'll taxi up and down a few times at increasing speeds with flaps at various positions, just to get the feel of it." He imagined the steps and gestured twisting his right hand in front of his face to represent the airborne prototype. "Then I'll lift off a few feet and do several runs in ground effects." His palm lifted. "Then I'll climb to about thirty feet and fly back and forth at least twice more." His hand came back to earth. "At that point, we will bring it in for a complete inspection."

It sounded like a conservative plan, but I watched and worried as he taxied away. No one said a word. With furrowed forehead, I thought about all the things that may go wrong.

He did the slow taxi runs as planned, but then everything changed. Instead of skimming the ground, the plane jumped up 20 and then 30 feet high. I gasped. *What's he doing?* "Looks like he misjudged and got too high," I said to no one in particular, "He should land before reaching the end of the runway. There's still space."

Jason kept climbing. Soon, he passed the point where he could safely land. So, he flew the traffic pattern and then came around to land. Like a plump pelican settling on water, the slow-flying plane wallowed slightly and then touched down. It was not graceful, but it was our beautiful creation and a successful first flight. We waited for him to taxi back.

I had mixed feelings about what I just saw — thrilled at the successful flight, relieved there was no accident and annoyed at Jason for risking everything by deviating from the plan. He climbed out of the cabin with a triumphant smile. I was envious of his skill and success, which caused me to sound unduly critical.

"What happened?"

"It worked great. I can't wait to go again."

"Why'd you go around so soon?"

"It wanted to fly." He replied like the answer should be obvious. "Before I knew it, we were too far to touch back down."

I considered saying more about the risk he took, but his success forgave it all. Subsequent fights demonstrated that the JX-2 could take off and land in the width of the runway, a notable accomplishment. The plane did what it was designed to do. After a lot of joyful and wide-eyed banter, we put the prototype to bed for the day to celebrate.

However, the team did not celebrate with abandon because we faced a big problem: our resources were almost exhausted. We desperately needed investors. Jason stepped up the promotion efforts, scheduling flight demonstrations for potential investors and other important people. This natural salesman now had an impressive, slow-flying plane for show-and-tell. It had many unique technical features that he enjoyed demonstrating. The employees put other work aside to spend time giving demos and promoting the company. We entertained writers and editors of popular aviation magazines like *Flying Magazine* and *Aviation Week*. They published complementary articles celebrating Jason as an aviation innovator and the JX-2 as a light airplane breakthrough.

With working funds dwindling, the company was desperate to proceed with the next phase of financing. Unfortunately, the economy did not cooperate. While we had been busy building the prototype, a recession slowed businesses and finances in the United States. There was little interest in high-risk investments. The Florida land developer backed out and the team morale plummeted. This slowed the pace of our enthusiastic work. However, I was sure that the situation was temporary. *Recessions do not last forever.* Perhaps my dismissal of our looming financial problem was wishful thinking, but we were not about to give up the dream without a fight. Unfortunately, this economic downturn lasted long enough to make survival questionable.

We adopted a defensive approach to prolong survival, including cutting expenses and raising money by selling stock to a few small investors, who seemed to arrive as saviors to invest a little when it was most needed. We were like a tired swimmer clutching at a series of toy life preservers. Each investment kept us afloat a short time. Employees took a survival pay cut. We avoided calling it a layoff by telling them that we could not pay the complete salary, but they could get IOUs. No one wanted to leave, but about half of them did. I learned how little is needed for a personal survival budget if one is willing to make lifestyle adjustments. It also helped that I was single and had some savings left. I conserved money by moving into a rented room and eating often with Jason and Jane. Fortunately, my car loan was paid off.

As a Board member, I was involved in decisions about financing, but inexperience and lack of contacts prevented me from helping much with this crisis. Several experienced Board members urged desperate action — an entirely new approach. Jason responded with a bold proposal. After much discussion, the Board agreed to use the remaining cash to create a simpler airplane design; one that could be certified faster with less investment, and which would make it easier to attract investors when the economy emerges from its holiday.

He unveiled a drawing of his JX-1, one of several paper designs he reserved for the future. He promised that the team would fly a prototype in nine months. I had not seen Jason working on a schedule, so I asked him when no one else was around.

"Do you really think we can fly a JX-1 prototype in nine months?"

"Sure, because we will run out of money in nine months. The estimate is based on our need; it must be done in order to survive." He grinned. "Also, that was how long it took Jane to make our son, which was much more difficult."

I laughed, "So you picked the estimate out of thin air?"

There was a twinkle in his eye and I noticed a slight smile. "Not at all; the alternative is to give up, kill everyone's motivation, and quit now. I know the team can rise to this challenge. Now we will see if I'm right."

It would not be easy with our smaller team. The JX-1 would be a two-seat, low-wing sports plane. It looked similar to other airplanes of that class, but the fuselage was made of bonded panels with a honeycomb foil core sandwiched between thin aluminum sheets. Panels were made in volume by a large manufacturer for military and airline use, and were available to us at a discount. By using modern materials, Jason promised a much lower selling price than the older two-seat planes made with riveted aluminum sheets. Everyone knew of his overoptimistic estimates, but the Board agreed to this high-risk approach as our best hope. The team was happy to throw itself into something they loved — creating a new airplane.

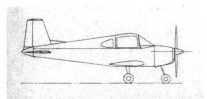

Securing government certification of the JX-1 would require additional investment, which we hoped would come from one of the several possible investor groups that expressed interest. The most promising group was in Ohio. The lagging economy caused mayors and city managers in many towns to form industrial development offices to attract companies and jobs. One such town was Springfield, Ohio. At a presentation to our Board, a Springfield representative promised to find private placement financing and to provide a suitable factory building at their airport; provided the company would relocate. Jason and I were invited to visit Springfield to meet the city leaders and view the proposed site. We traveled from Boca Raton in Jason's Cessna 195, which was a four-seat, high wing plane that cruised at a comfortable 170 mph. Jason bought it a few years back when the company had big plans and a fat bank account. Now, he would be compelled to sell the Cessna right after we returned.

The visit convinced us our company could succeed in Springfield, so Jason agreed to make the move to Ohio with a handshake commitment. The next day we headed back to Boca Raton in the Cessna. We soon faced a new problem.

* * *

Flying since early morning, it was now mid-afternoon. We were alert because the weatherman had predicted a line of thunderstorms to our south.

Jason said, "I see the front ahead." The front was moving east so it would soon cross our path on its trip to the Atlantic. "We'll look for an opening in the clouds and cross to the other side."

As the only other person around, I served as a copilot. I didn't see any openings in the black wall. "According to the map, our refueling stop is on the other side. We could be pushed over the Atlantic if we are forced to stay on this side. In fact, we might have to make another plan to refuel."

"I want us to stick with our flight plan, but look for an alternate airport on this side, just in case we can't cross."

As we approached the mountain of dark clouds, small raindrops splattered against the windshield and then instantly streaked back as they were stripped away by the wind stream. Jason turned southeast to travel parallel to the storm. We continued to look for a gap. It was a solid wall of clouds. The reliable engine droned as we flew on.

Jason remarked, "I'm tired. Take over the controls, so I can take a twenty-minute nap." He had been flying without rest for several hours and it looked like his flying skills were about to be tested. The weather would determine how much longer we might be in the air.

"I've got it." I sounded more confident than I felt. While Jason had several thousand flying hours, I was a new pilot with less than 200, who hadn't even been checked out in the Cessna. *But I should be able to keep it on course.* I could see flashbulb-like blooms of lightning deep inside the cumulus, with vivid flashes passing from one cloud cluster to another. *It looks like a strong storm, one that could easily tear our small plane apart, if we venture too close.* The clouds churned and constantly changed. I was well aware that if we went through the wrong gap we could be trapped if the weather closed in.

Jason slept soundly. I looked at him and bit my lip. *I could never sleep in this situation.* I planned to wake him up if I noticed any sign of the elusive gap in the clouds to safety. The rain suddenly became heavier, so I backed to a more comfortable distance away from the ominous black wall. Now lightning flashes were more frequent and intense. Perspiration dampened my grip on the wheel. A loud thunderclap made me jump and also woke Jason. I was relieved to return the control to him.

After another half an hour, Jason said, "It'll be dark soon, and gas is low. We will land on this side." More time passed and now instead of a gap in the clouds, we looked with urgency for any safe place to land. It was getting too dark to see the ground. I looked down at a few isolated structure lights and creeping headlights on some unknown road below. Jason had been searching for an airport radio beacon but without luck. There was nothing but static and distant stations on the radio. My pulse raced.

I said, "We're someplace over North Carolina, but I haven't been able to point to our exact location on the map." *We're lost at night in a thunderstorm and low on fuel — this isn't good.*

We flew on, both of us straining to see through the dark drizzle and searching for some sign of a landing place.

Jason pointed east, "Look over there! Isn't that an airport beacon light?"

I saw a faint point of light in the distant darkness. It blinked white and then green, at about every two-second interval — dim glimmers of hope. He headed for it, as we huddled in the Cessna cabin. If it was an airport beacon, it might include a radio station, provided it was still open. Jason tried to contact the anonymous airport's radio, but there was no response. Our eyes locked on the beacon's position, expectantly waiting for each pulse. It could be our refuge. Seconds passed with little conversation. I tuned into the sound of the radial engine's unique rhythm. Eventually, I noticed a glow on the ground between the beacon pulses. I asked, "Do you see it?"

"Yeah."

It turned into a dim line of lights that gradually became a solitary runway with landing lights on each side. The sight pleased us more than anything else, but there was little time to talk about it.

To save gas, Jason made a direct approach to land just in time. It rained harder as we touched down, which further decreased the visibility, but the plane with its relieved occupants was finally on the ground. We had landed safely!

There were no taxiway lights, so Jason did his best to steer towards what appeared to be a small building. He turned off the engine when he could no longer see. We became aware of raindrops drumming on the Cessna's aluminum skin. After a few seconds, Jason exhaled a sigh of relief. "Well, let's get out and see what's here."

We found the building locked. It was a wooden structure about the size of a double garage. By peeking through the windows, we guessed this was the small airport's office. There was a mail slot in

184 · LAWRENCE SCHNEIDER

the door, where we could leave gas money, but the pump was locked.

Jason raised his voice above the rising sound of rain and wind, "We'll have to sit it out till morning. I think it's going to get much worse as the front passes over."

I said, "I don't see any shelter. We shouldn't stay in a metal plane during this storm. It's going to be a rough night."

Jason tramped around studying the soaked grass with his shoe. "We will have to secure the airplane. There must be tie-downs someplace, but I can't find any in the dark."

I pointed to a mound next to the building. "Looks like a pile of lumber covered with an old Army tarp. Maybe we can tie the Cessna to the planks and spend the night under this cover."

We pushed and heaved, slipping on soaked grass, in our attempt to move the bulky plane. With a lot of effort, we got close enough to tie it securely with nylon cord from the cabin.

It was a bit drier under the tarp. The downpour became steady as rain thudded on the canvas and sounded like a quick ting, ting, on the Cessna's aluminum skin above our heads. Soon, the sound became a continuous clatter on all sides, like a machine gun. The heavy canvas flapped and pulsated noisily in the gusts. Thunder claps and lightning occurred more often. Despite being exhausted, I couldn't sleep as the thunderstorm raged. It was a long night in our makeshift sanctuary. I lay there with eyes closed, wondering how primitive peoples must have felt huddled in their shelters during such a downpour. I thought of the bed I hoped to sleep in to-morrow night.

At first light, we pulled the tarp back and crawled out. The tarp's pungent mildew smell had given me a headache, and the odor was now a part of my clothes, like a persistent skunk spray. It would be mine to keep until I got home to shower. I limped around in an old man's crouch learning to walk again.

Now, storm clouds were far to the east, as was evidence of morning sun. I saw patches of blue sky and the air was warm and humid. We were weary, damp, and dirty, but relieved that we got through the night without any serious harm. I wondered if the tempest was a bad omen for the Springfield deal.

When the airport operator arrived he was surprised to find two scruffy guys in need of gas. We ate a vending machine breakfast of Hershey bars and Ritz cheese crackers. There were black coffee and coke to drink. Then we filled the gas tanks and continued on our way home. It was the start of a new day.

As we traveled South and crossed the Florida State line, Jason celebrated by dropping low over the eastern shore surf. Every ten minutes or so, he alternated his track between flying on the ocean side of the shoreline and then on the land side, so we got a look at the surf from each angle. I waved to sunbathers and people who were just arriving for a day at the beach, even though I knew they couldn't see us inside the Cessna's cabin. We were almost home. I put my head against the side window and tried to dose off.

Suddenly Jason yelled in surprise, "Damn!" At the same moment, he threw the Cessna into an aggressive right bank. My head, which had been resting against the passenger-side window, was forced upright. I opened my eyes wide to see the right wing pointing straight down at the ground.

He shouted, "Restricted Area," and then leveled the plane when it headed back North. After a few minutes he turned inland to fly a course around the prohibited government space. I looked down at an unoccupied Cape Canaveral missile launch tower and saw another tower in the distance. We were alarmingly close. He left the area fast. Jason speculated on the possibility of scrambled fighter jets. We sat staring expectantly until we were sure that none would come. The flight was calm after that, but I couldn't sleep.

I arrived home fragrant and fatigued, happy to be a stinking survivor. Removing the mildew smell required two showers and a liberal application of deodorant. My smelly clothes went into the trash.

The company was desperate for working funds, so the Board accepted Springfield's offer on little more than promises. We were running out of money, so it was the best of the bad options; obviously, it was, better than bankruptcy.

During a rainy week in the fall of 1961, the company moved from Boca Raton to Springfield, where a few Ohio businessmen became investors. It was not enough money to complete the prototype, but the infusion kept us going.

I hated to leave warm and exciting Florida for cold and dreary Ohio. We arrived to greet winter and I wasn't optimistic about my future social life. I traded my impractical MG sports car for a winter-friendly vehicle. I selected a 1959 Olds-98, four-door sedan. It was a large, comfortable car that we hoped might impress the potential investors. I rented a furnished apartment, which Jane helped decorate. I had improved much during the past two years as a pretend playboy, and now I was learning about a proper bachelor pad.

* * *

The JX-1 sports plane made its first flight one week short of the nine-month deadline. It was another design success for the experienced team. Jason spent all his time promoting this latest innovation. It attracted a lot of media attention in publications like *Popular Mechanics* and *Air Progress*. I also spent most of my time talking about the plane with visitors, reporters, and investors. Favorable publicity increased the demand for the attractive, low-cost JX-1. Many buyers made deposits for future deliveries, even though the plane wasn't yet government certified.

The team shifted from prototype development to order processing, like chameleons adapting to a changed requirement. Deposits went into an escrow account and were not used for current expenses. The growing deposit balance indicated to potential investors that a strong demand for JX-1 existed.

Then, Springfield's initial promises started to fall apart. We were told a factory at the airport had to wait, until we got sufficient financing to complete the certification, but town fathers were not able to find the financing. Before moving to Springfield, they had offered, and we had accepted to use, a vacant auto dealership near the town. It was to be a short-term arrangement. The old building was spacious and suitable for fabrication, but its location was far away from the airport, which was highly inconvenient. The frustrating situation in Springfield meant that our search for financing had to continue.

Downy Head

Springfield, Ohio — 1962, Age 27

During a visit to my cousin's house, Jane asked me to hold their newborn while she prepared dinner. Even before the company moved to Ohio, I had become a regular fixture in their household. Jane felt sorry for me as a bachelor, living apart from relatives. As a consequence, she frequently invited me to be part of her family. Now, I found myself in the unfamiliar position of standing with a tiny downy head cradled against my cheek. The baby had just been bathed and nursed, and I couldn't believe how small and fragile it was! Wrapped in its white cotton blanket, she was a contented little bundle, smelling of baby shampoo and powder. The infant and I watched Jane work at the sink. I glanced down at the child and was unexpectedly overwhelmed with emotion. A shiver went up to my spine. Not wanting to be embarrassed by an unmanly display, I leaned against the door frame for support and closed my eyes, so that Jane wouldn't notice the tear. I was struck with awe by being in the presence of something much more significant than my current aspiration for success. I clearly saw that this baby was what life must be all about. *The child has an opportunity to experience a wonderful life because her parents have hope in the future. My life lacks a life-giving purpose, the kind that comes with love and children.*

Having my own family was always a distant possibility, nothing more. This downy head caused me to reconsider. I knew that I too could be party to creating new life. All I had to do was marry and start a family — a life altering consideration, which I had refused to seriously entertain until that moment. The thought of so much responsibility was scary. Also, there was the annoying fact that I still did not have a girlfriend. It was too much to deal with, so I wiped my eye with a sleeve and pushed the idea to the back of my mind. But from that day onwards, the memory of the downy head on my cheek remained just under the surface.

* * *

One day that winter, I was again in Jane's kitchen holding the baby while Jane made the salad for dinner. Taro, our new test pilot, was also invited.

Jane said, "Did Jason tell you that Taro won't be coming because his father died?"

"No..."

"Taro won't be back from Kansas for a week."

"That's unfortunate." I paused. "Where is Jason?"

"He went to the Greyhound station to pick up Suzanne. She is coming for a visit this weekend. You remember Suzanne? You met her in Florida a couple of years ago."

"Yes." I tightened my hold on the baby.

"I told Suzanne she would meet the new test pilot. Now that won't happen. Though, she will be glad that you are joining us."

"I'd like to see her again. But won't she be disappointed when the dull Clarence shows up instead of Taro?"

"Not at all," Jane smiled. "You are not the same guy she saw in Florida. Don't worry about Suzanne, just be yourself." Just then the doorbell rang. "That must be Jason with his hands full bringing Suzanne and her luggage. Would you help with the door?"

"Sure."

When I opened the door, I encountered Suzanne face-to-face. I never saw a more surprised expression, as she witnessed me holding the baby. She was as bright and beautiful as I remembered. She greeted us with a dazzling smile and offered sweet baby talk to the infant in my arms.

This time I was more prepared to socialize and welcomed her with enthusiastic conversation. "How have you been Suzanne? What have you been up to lately? You look great." I passed the baby back to Jane and continued the chatty talk that I had learned from Playboy articles.

Suzanne and I double dated that weekend with our hosts. She seemed to be trying to figure me out because her mood was serious, instead of flirty. One evening we went dancing; holding her close and smelling her fragrance overwhelmed me. *I can't let her get away this time.*

The day before Suzanne was to return to Cleveland, Jane said, "Clarence, would you like to show Suzanne your apartment? I've been telling her how I helped you decorate your living room."

Before I could answer, Suzanne said, "Yes, I would like to see it."

* * *

It was early evening when we arrived at my bachelor pad. The winter sun had set, so I flicked on the lights as we went in. The wall switch also activated the FM radio in my Grundig, and high fidelity music filled the room. Like a bowerbird's display, it was meant to make a favorable impression on the young ladies. Suzanne was the first to enter my bower. Her expression indicated disbelief and then curiosity. I proudly showed off the fashionable black modular furniture and white shag rug. I neglected to say these furnishings were either borrowed from Jane or rented with the furnished apartment, but I suspected she knew. To top off the attempt to impress, I furnished some chilled wine.

That day Suzanne looked sexier than the first time I glimpsed her at the high school. She surveyed the room. "You have no art on the wall; I'll just have to paint you a picture for your birthday."

She must be teasing, "Well you'll have to hurry up because my birthday is in three weeks." She bit her lip and I detected concern. *Maybe she is serious.* Then her face relaxed. I learned much later that she figured she could get help from her brother, who had gone to the Cleveland Institute of Art and was Art Director at an advertising agency. He had painted an impressionistic landscape that hung over his fireplace and she figured he would coach her through the reproduction of a similar painting.

She sashayed around, inspecting the room and making more decorating suggestions before settling on the black couch. She clearly enjoyed my bowerbird nest. A smile invited me to join her.

In an enthusiastic attempt to slide in place, I misjudged the slickness of gabardine trousers and bumped her hip a little too hard. She giggled and kissed my cheek — just a peck. That was all I needed to initiate our first real kiss. Suzanne's reaction was unexpected — she broke into tears.

I asked, "What happened? Why are you crying?"

After several seconds, she sputtered, "This is not going to work."

"Why?"

"Jane thinks you are all wrapped up in airplane designing, and that doesn't leave much of you for anything else."

She must really like me. Don't screw this up. "No, I will make time for you; for us."

"And, we live far from each other and I have my mother to take care of in Cleveland."

I gently took her hand and held it to my cheek. "Look, you are my girl now. There may be problems." I tried to think of the right thing to say. *Be yourself.* "But first tell me, do you want us to be together?"

She nodded. "Yes."

"Then we will solve all the problems together. Are you ready to give it a try?"

She looked up. "Yes. I think I have loved you since Florida."

She grabbed me around the neck again, which started another series of kisses, making a loving partnership with our own downy heads foreseeable. *Together, it would be wonderful if we could always be together.*

Jane had guessed a long time ago that I was attracted to Suzanne, so she had always hoped we would fall in love. It never occurred to me that the two of them would conspire to bring about what they figured was in everyone's best interest. Suzanne loved children, and we were not getting any younger. Jane did what she could to bring us together in social settings, but she was always discouraged when I seemed to only focus on aviation, but Jane had hope for us, so she never gave up. Now I'm in love and need no other encouragement.

When Suzanne returned in March to bring my birthday gift – the painting, I was ready to ask her to be my wife (even if the painting turned out to be terrible). I had been infatuated with her for years, and now Suzanne had decided that we would be a couple. Nothing else mattered to me.

But there was a problem. I had not saved enough money to buy a ring, much less support a wife and family. *Would she consider me a poor marriage prospect?* I rehearsed a proposal speech.

When the time arrived, my head seemed to belong to someone else. It could not be me about to propose marriage to my high school dream girl. I could only think about one thing — not screwing up the proposal. I could not foresee all that might transpire in our future — the possibility of growing old together, holding a newborn grandchild, celebrating family reunions, being the father of the bride, watching our children and grandchildren play sports, having downy head babies or even going on a honeymoon.

Finally, we were together, and it was time for me to act. My lips did not want to do my bidding, but I managed to blurt out a few words. "Suzanne, please sit here with me. I have something to tell you." My hands were fidgety, and I rubbed my upper arm.

"Yes?" Her eyes were wide, and her lips held a slight smile.

Once I launched into my speech, words spilled out faster than normal. "I love you, and I would like us to be married. I don't have a ring to give you. But I think we make a good couple and could be a great family someday. What do you say?"

She jumped up even before I finished the last words. "Yes." She gave me a tight bear hug and repeated "Yes." When I mentioned my savings shortfall, I discovered that an engagement ring was not important to her at all.

"I think we should get married soon. How do you feel about that?" I asked.

"Yes." She did not try to restrain a joyful squeal.

Suzanne accepted without a doubt or hint of surprise. Now, we would paint our life's canvas together.

She said, "Oh, I can't wait to tell Jane. She will be so happy for us."

I said, "Let's go tell her, and Jason too." I was grinning. "Wait, I have a better idea. I'll ask Jason to be my best man."

"Great!"

I paused and added, "We are forgetting one important person." I paused when I saw Suzanne's questioning look. "Your mother!"

Suzanne said, "Oh…yes. I've been thinking a lot about her. She will be so happy for us. But, I worry…"

"I'm driving up next weekend and we can talk to her then."

* * *

I received a big hug from MY GIRL when I knocked on Suzanne's door the next Friday. I had met her mother a few weeks before, when I had picked up Suzanne for a date but had never actually been inside their apartment. The upper level of a single family house had been converted to a small, three-room apartment. Everything was clean and organized. Three of us sat at the kitchen table to have a piece of apple pie, which Anna Novak had made to celebrate her daughter's engagement. I waited as long as possible to bring up the topic that worried me — what was to become of Anna after the wedding.

I said, "Anna. It seems like your life is about to change too. Are you worried about that?"

"No, my son needs me."

Suzanne added, "My brother's wife just had another baby and my mother is the only grandmother in their family. She will go live with them for a while."

I looked at Anna. "Does that mean I have your permission to marry Suzanne?"

"Yes. You are a good boy, and smart." Anna's expression brightened, "Someday I will come to help Suzanne with her baby too."

Suzanne blushed and looked down. "We hope so."

"Then I might ride on an airplane when I visit. I never did that." We all laughed.

* * *

Over the next few months, we enthusiastically planned our future. Six children seemed like a perfect family; therefore, there was no time to waste and we scheduled the wedding for August at Suzanne's neighborhood church, St. Ignatius Catholic Church on Lorain Avenue in Cleveland. Cousin Jason was my best man, and Jane was the maid of honor.

Suzanne's family and my family celebrated with us, including my Mom, Dad, sister, and Grandpa Joseph. I was pleased when my friend, Steve from NASA traveled from Huntsville to be with us.

He said, "Congratulations Clarence. You finally got yourself a girl."

"Yes, she's my dream girl. How about you? Have you found someone special?"

"No, I'm still looking. You know how it is in Huntsville."

"Yes, I remember." *I bet I would also be alone if I had stayed.* "Do you still play poker?"

"Yes, but I limit myself to one small glass of moonshine per game." We laughed.

"How is your career going Steve?"

"Outstanding. I got a big promotion to Section Chief. Can you believe it, the United States is going to the moon? I love it."

"Well, then congratulations to you as well." *I wonder what my career would have been like if I stayed. I suspect I would not be as happy as I am today.*

* * *

Since we had almost no money saved, the wedding was simple and the honeymoon short. I have since concluded love, not an ego wedding, is the only requirement for happiness and marital success. With the help of her children, Suzanne's mother was happy to move to a one-bedroom apartment, close to one of her sons.

When we arrived back in Springfield after the honeymoon, Suzanne, a gifted decorator, converted my bachelor pad into our newlywed's nest. She wanted to store the birthday painting in a closet since it had served its purpose, but I insisted that her artwork must retain its prominent place on our living room wall. It was more than a decoration, it was a symbol of our love.

One evening, a few months later, as we sat in our comfortable living room, Suzanne said, "Clarence, I have good news."

"What?"

She lowered her eyelids. "I'm pregnant."

"Wow! That's great. It's what we hoped for."

Her smile was wide. "Yes."

I took a deep breath. "That news is the best gift I have ever got. Thank you!" We were in each other's arms with tears in our eyes. I said, "Let's go out to celebrate."

"No, let's stay home tonight. This is nice." She kissed my cheek.

* * *

Each day we learned more about the challenges of married life. Suzanne had an immediate problem adapting. She hated driving the large, boat-like Olds 98 sedan. She didn't own a car and hadn't driven since the driver training course she took. Confidence and the skill she once had were long gone. After a few practice runs, she reluctantly accepted a personal set of keys, and it became 'our' Olds.

One morning Suzanne dropped me off at work before going shopping. When she returned to get me after work later in the evening, the car scraped a stone retaining wall, which was next to the building's narrow driveway. It wasn't a big dent, just a scratch on paint, about twelve inches long and one small piece of dislodged chrome trim. Co-workers rushed out to offer help and advice, which added to her embarrassment. Her face registered distress, and her cheeks were stained with tear streaks.

I was troubled because I assumed it was my new responsibility to protect my bride from all unhappiness, yet this was not engineering, and I had no experience in solving such a problem. My voice took on a pleading tone, "The parking space is too narrow for large cars. You made a minor mistake with only slight damage. It's fine. Relax!"

The word 'damage' started a new round of weeping. I sat down and held my head with both hands. I later learned her reaction was not only about the car. During the next few years, I discovered that pregnancy tended to lower the weeping threshold of Suzanne. With today's accident, we experienced perfect crying conditions.

In spite of my assurance that this was only a scratch, which I followed that evening with a red rose intended to cheer her up, she refused to use the Olds again. Later, she stood in front of me with hands on hips, "I'm not going to drive your monster car, so don't expect me to!"

"But this is nothing. Anyone can have a minor accident."

"No! I will never drive it again." There were more sobs before she said loudly, "End of discussion" and slammed the bedroom door.

I had heard about the rigors of pregnancy but never thought much about it as a bachelor. I had no inclination on what it would be like as a new husband. I soon decided that it was more stressful than my first attempt to land the Piper Cub.

When I mentioned the incident to Jane, I didn't get much sympathy or support. "You know, it's even harder on Suzanne." The fender scratch was not the only time Suzanne was distressed by the Olds. A few weeks later I came home from work to a nonfunctional homemaker, which was immediately apparent in her dull complexion. After a low groan, she managed to say, "I can't deal with preparing raw food tonight." It seems that pregnancy made her more sensitive to certain food odors.

Like most engineers, solving problems was my specialty, so we went to McDonald's. Suzanne only ate a few bites of a cheeseburger before we headed home. It was dark as we approached the apartment parking lot. Suzanne's nausea was now sending an urgent message.

"Clarence, I think I'm going to throw up."

"Oh no, not in the car. Please." I quickly pulled into a parking spot. "We have an important visitor coming early tomorrow. I'll be picking him up. Quick, roll down the window."

I was relieved to see that she got her head out before releasing her burden. She was ashen when I helped her to bed a few minutes later. All Suzanne had needed from me was understanding and sympathy, not a solution, and especially not fast food. It took years of me looking for perfect solutions for her problems before I learned that lesson.

* * *

The next morning Jason and I conferred about the expected visitor, who was from a wealthy American family. We hoped that he would become an investor. He planned to fly his twin-engine business plane into Springfield airport. I would drive him to our facility in town for a meeting and tour. Jason didn't want to use his car because it looked and smelled like a well-used playpen. My freshly polished Olds was perfect for this occasion.

I sat in the Olds and watched the would-be investor's plane land and taxi to a stop. I drove up to it as the propellers stopped turning. I ran around to the passenger side door ready to open it like a well-trained chauffeur. I was stunned by what I saw. The door looked like an abstract painting. It was covered with the remains of Suzanne's cheeseburger, now dry and almost odor free. It was obvious what it was. The visitor, a perfect gentleman, ignored what he too had noticed by now.

In the evening, when I told Suzanne about the incident, she expressed hope that his decision of not investing had nothing to do with her. I assured her it didn't.

The pregnancy challenges made the importance of family clearer. At a logical level, I knew my family would be central to my future, but before the impending birth, I was too career-focused to feel it emotionally. I'd soon learn that career and family were often at odds, requiring time-honored choices that our parents must have also encountered.

Our first daughter came into our world the next summer. It was a wonderful thrill to hold her downy head against my cheek. My education in family life was beginning. I discovered that babies often come with surprises. That night as I walked the floor with a screaming infant, I learned about colic. It was just the first of several such nights. Our first baby was treasured so much that we did it again, and again, and again.

* * *

When it became clear that Springfield would not deliver on its financing promise, Jason began looking for options. He had learned a lesson about cementing deals in writing, but that did not help us now. The team was aware of his efforts, but after so many disappointments, they held little hope of success. I was more involved in what Jason was doing and was also more hopeful. Then one day, Jason called the employees together. He looked relaxed. Jason's father, the person who had made it all possible, was visiting.

"I have good news!" Jason exclaimed.

The few remaining team members brightened and gathered around.

"Before I share with you the details about our newest financing prospect, you need to know the background." Jason pulled a chair closer for his aging father.

Jason stood straighter and paused to look at everyone. "Several years ago Cleveland's mayor asked key business leaders to form an

Industrial Development Group. His goal was to attract small businesses to the city. If they helped finance new companies, the businessmen could have ground-floor investing opportunities, so they might make money, while also helping their city. The group has been operating for the last few years, and I've met with them three times so far. They are impressed by the JX-1 and the advance orders and have just made a generous proposal. There is also talk of a future public stock offering after we start production."

Someone said, "Great!"

However, another commented, "Doesn't it sound like Springfield's empty promises."

"We're not about to accept promises without careful vetting this time," Jason said. "We checked everything with our lawyer. These guys are pillars of the community. Also, they are all wealthy. One owns a major part of the Cleveland Browns football team. Another industrialist is on *Fortune Magazine's* list of the richest men in America. Their offer is backed by a solid legal contract."

There were no more critical comments and the team waited to hear more. "Here is the deal — there will be sufficient up-front private-placement money to pay all employee IOUs and even hire a few more people. We will have enough to complete JX-1 certification and build a production line. One of the investors will finance a new factory east of Cleveland at the county airport in Richmond Heights. Also, he'll lease the factory to us at a reasonable cost. The new investors get forty-nine percent ownership and seats on our Board. That's good because they are the best business minds in the city. However, we still retain fifty-one percent, which gives us a voting majority."

We closed our operation for the rest of the day and went out to celebrate. Since Jason had ensured that the founding employees had modest stock ownership, we imagined riches in our futures. Some pessimists still had doubts but, to optimistic Jason, this success was expected and overdue.

We were ready to charge ahead. Investment funds were soon deposited into the account, proving that it wasn't an empty promise.

We got busy — one group designed the production line and another worked on FAA certification. The Federal Aviation Administration was the all-powerful government entity authorized to give us a load of trouble if they suspected that we might try to sell an unsafe design.

While the team worked on the airplane, Jason recruited future dealers in cities around the country and orders kept coming in. I worked with the architects, providing them with our factory requirements, including a simple conveyor system for JX-1 production. The building quickly progressed with the help of an experienced construction company. In the spring of 1965, we moved into a brand-new factory, still smelling of fresh paint. Another dream had come true.

A few new employees came on board, although we still remained a small cohesive team. Morale was again high and the work pace rapid. We made much progress during the following two years.

Because the JX-1 was to be a sports airplane, it would be certified for aerobatic flight. Therefore, the FAA required extensive static and flight testing beyond what was normally required for commercial light planes. I designed the static test fixtures and supervised the testing. We hired an experienced test pilot at the insistence of the Board, who did not want Jason at risk of a possible accident.

Certification proceeded according to the plan until everything the FAA required was completed and sent to them for final approval. Again, our working funds were almost depleted, as we waited for FAA to grant final approval so that we could proceed with the public stock offering. Weeks passed and there was still no decision. FAA employees did not share our sense of urgency. They said that they were working on it and the JX-1 was not their only project.

Because of the delay, the company was coming close to announcing another layoff in order to avoid running out of money. We knew that if something like that happened, some furloughed employees would find other jobs and would be unavailable when we were ready to resume work. We needed to do something, and soon.

"Fear is the path to the Dark Side. Fear leads to anger, anger leads to hate, and hate leads to suffering."

— YODA —

CHAPTER SIX

Facing Ordeals

Predator

Cleveland, Ohio — 1965, Age 30

When the company most needed it, one of the Board investors contributed a substantial loan, which was enough to sustain operations, while we waited for FAA certification. The investor was the wealthy owner of several Ohio businesses. He was a clever money-maker, respected by peers, and hated by those on the wrong end of shrewd business deals. For years, he and his family had supported major city projects and were known for their philanthropy. His idea of success was to maintain his family name, build his wealth, and keep ahead of his competitors.

The investor disagreed with Jason's aggressive promotion style. Their differing views resulted in heated debates about efforts to recruit additional dealers. At one of the board meetings, the investor said, "I insist that we stop spending the development money to form new dealerships. FAA might not approve this version of the plane and then you will run out of money again."

Jason responded, "FAA assured us that approval will come soon. If there is a delay, which is unlikely, we will get another loan. Signing up more dealers now will mean higher sales immediately after certification."

"High sales are good only if we earn a profit on each plane. We don't know if the JX-1 is profitable at the stated price. If not, you will be in the red with each deposit."

"I stand by my production cost estimate. I'm sure we will earn a profit."

"How can you be sure? You have never produced anything in your life." The investor's gestures were slashing, and his face was red.

Jason wouldn't back down. "You've never invented a new product before."

The investor stood and placed both hands on the conference table in front of him. His tone became measured and softer. "You don't know what you are talking about —." He was about to say more but decided to keep it to himself.

There were more such disputes at future meetings, which started as a difference in attitudes about risk tolerance and led to arguments between the two adversaries, who clearly disliked one another. When the Board voted on Jason's risky ideas, Jason always won because he and his father held a majority ownership.

As predicted, after a few months, funds again became depleted, so Jason proposed seeking another loan as insurance against a further FAA delay, which now seemed quite possible. The opposing investor pledged money for a second loan because it protected his initial investment. With the additional loan money, the pace of work resumed.

Several months later, the FAA presented us with a shock. The FAA director responsible for final approval was concerned about the safety of inexperienced pilots, who had ordered the low-cost JX-1, thinking some of them would try risky acrobatic maneuvers. So, to be safe, FAA required extra flight tests, including additional spin tests. The team was compelled to use what remained of the second loan to conduct the tests, but it wasn't enough to complete everything. So, Jason went back to the Board for a third loan. The investor, who signed the first notes refused and demanded immediate repayment of the first two notes, which were now due under these circumstances. A sequence of financial and legal events quickly led to the bankruptcy of the struggling company.

We soon learned that while the team had been busy completing flight-testing, the investor in question had quietly prepared takeover documents. Before we knew what happened, he had legal control and Jason was asked to resign as the president.

Jason and the original team who had started romping together in that first Florida workshop now had a predator in our midst. We were confused and angry. Jason called a team meeting and everyone was anxious to learn more. He looked as if he had not slept for days.

"We all got this same letter from the lawyer explaining the terms of the takeover," Jason said. "I also got a letter from the Board asking for my resignation." Jason waved his letter overhead. "They have asked me to continue guiding engineering operations. That won't happen because I plan to resign and leave. As far as I know, they don't plan to make any other staff changes."

I blurted out, "I'll leave too." Then other voices shouted, "Me too!" "Me too!" Most of the rest of the team agreed with me and said they would quit. We assumed the company couldn't continue without Jason's creativity and the team's technical expertise. We may have been right, but it didn't matter. The predator had struck, and his plan would run its course.

He consumed his prey, but in doing so, eliminated the company's creative force. Jason was the source of ideas for follow-on airplane designs. Without him, the company only had the JX-1 and a limited future. The company's future was of no concern to the predator, who planned to sell and cash out as soon as possible. This was a planned takeover by an experienced and clever businessman and we never saw it coming. Our dream enterprise seemed to disappear in a puff of takeover smoke.

That evening, after the children were asleep, Suzanne and I talked about the situation. She had become an important personal advisor. I was emotionally invested in the outcome, so I needed her clear thinking. We sat together and held hands. Suzanne said, "You look terrible like someone stole your dog. Are you sure it's that bad?"

"It is worse…I feel like someone stole my future. I can't believe Jason would let something like this happen to the company."

"You can't blame it all on him; it sounds like several people let it happen." She looked thoughtful. "This might not be so bad. You still have your engineering degree and a creative mind."

I reached for her hand. "Yes, and I have you."

She shed a tear and kissed me. "So what are you going to do?"

"First I'll ask Jason about his plans."

"What's most important to you now?"

"Caring for you and the family," I replied

"We should still able to feed the children and buy shoes for a while. It's all right with me if you stay with Jason for as long as our money lasts. But I would feel better if we were less dependent on what he plans to do."

"Yes. The alternative is another job, which would probably not be as creative."

* * *

Jason resolved to continue building airplanes — in other words, to start over. He rented a space on the other side of the airport. I was determined to hold on to my 'never give up' motto. Most of the other team members could not afford to stick with him.

Soon there were only three of us, including Jason, a newly hired designer, and me. To survive, we would need working funds and a new product. Since we had limited development money, our product had to be simple. We decided to sell plans for a do-it-your-self homebuilt plane, which would not require FAA certification. We built and flew a primitive open cockpit prototype that could provide a mechanically inclined pilot with low-cost flying fun. Sales of the plans were satisfactory for a few months and several planes were built and flown by do-it-yourself pilots. However, we soon discovered that selling plans was not enough to support one person, let alone three.

There were not enough potential customers capable of building and flying even a simple airplane. I told Jason that I didn't think I'd have enough to support my family.

He frowned and said, "I understand, well, thanks for sticking with me so long and thanks to Suzanne too. I know this is no way to raise a family. It has been six years now that we've worked together. I'd understand if you decide to find another way to support them." A slight grin formed, "But in the meantime, I want to celebrate this mile-

stone by giving you the pay raise you would get if we had money. For now, it can only be an increase in your stock ownership, because we can't offer any more."

I laughed and replied, "You're right, it may be time to start looking. Suzanne and I haven't been able to pay all our bills on time."

"I do hope you can find a way to stay. I'm going to need you for two exciting projects that we can do together."

Here we go again. He is trying to use our friendship to get his way. I can't let it happen.

He said, "One is a record-breaking around-the-world flight. I will fly all the way around the globe without stopping or refueling."

"What? How is that possible?"

"We will put a small gasoline engine on a Schweizer TG-2-32 sailplane and fill the wings with fuel. I didn't tell you before because we were so busy working on the JX-1. I have sponsors lined up and have already discussed the airplane modifications with the Schweizer company."

"So, the financial backing is from the sponsors?" I asked.

"Yes. The other project is a single-seat sports plane that will be the smallest jet in the world. We will sell it as a kit plane. You have seen my drawings of the JX-5, the piston engine pusher plane. A small, light jet engine just came on the market, and we will use it to make a jet version."

I can't let his exciting ideas pull me in again.

I held up my head. "No." I paused when I saw his surprised look. "I wish I could stay, but I can't put that burden on the family."

He shrugged and took a step back. "Too bad. You will miss out on some of the best projects. Let me know if you change your mind."

"Yes, I'll let you know. Jason, I have a feeling you will be famous some day. Good luck." I felt like I had just stabbed my best friend. The situation caused me to think more about the effect of my career on Suzanne and our growing family, which was also a growing responsibility. It reminded me that my risk taking adventures affected not just me, but several others as well. Our family included three toddlers, with a fourth baby expected soon. I didn't have a penny in my pocket. Suzanne said she was doing fine and had faith in my ability to support the family. It helped that she didn't crave luxuries. She was a rare and wonderful wife and mother. *I am lucky to be her choice as a husband.* But if I continue to follow my impractical dream, I won't be able to feed our family. *I guess it's time to face my responsibilities before she becomes concerned.*

I found Suzanne home changing a diaper, "I got a raise today. Guess how much pay I will not bring home this week." She laughed. Then I told her about my conversation with Jason and my plan to look for another job.

"Are you sure it's what you want to do?"

"Yes."

"Must we move at some point?"

"I expect so."

I researched the job market but remained reluctant to take decisive action. Jason was my best friend, and I couldn't imagine having a more satisfying career. His goals were always big, exciting, and fun to pursue. I identified with Don Quixote's sidekick, Sancho Panza, helping Jason chase impossible dreams. We did survive for another few months before completely running out of money.

While it was clear that we failed to reach our goal, it didn't feel like a failure. Lack of success is not the same as failure because it provides a learning opportunity. *I should try to learn from this lack of success, and not rationalize or make excuses.* Since I endorsed his dreams and approach, loss of the company was my doing as well.

Our initial goal was to create a revolutionary short takeoff and landing airplane, which we did, although we never produced the JX-2 because a recession cut off financing. The innovative airplane received national recognition and an honored place in the Experimental Aircraft Association Museum. Our next big goal was to make the JX-1 sports plane, which we did, and were about to find business success before the takeover. Based on our work, JX-1 production and deliveries started later under the new company. While the airplane was a technical success, it was a financial flop for Jason and the team. If success was to grow a business and become rich, we failed. I had learned that wishful thinking is not a serious goal.

So what happened? Jason's business instinct was to move forward aggressively while learning from mistakes and then make essential adjustments. The company takeover allowed no chance to recover from a critical mistake, which was taking too much risk. Was the once-in-a-lifetime opportunity worth doing in spite of the ultimate failure? It  was for me. I look back on the experience with much satisfaction. It was a magical adventure of creativity and teamwork that I'd measure against future career experiences.

While I hunted for another job, I decided to try a completely different creative activity — woodcarving. I was inspired by a magazine photo of a magnificent carved eagle sculpture that was done in a traditional colonial style, with wings spread holding an olive branch of peace and arrows of war. I imagined one like it hanging in our home. I dusted off my drafting tools and drew the eagle at a suitable size. As a subtle war protest, this eagle would not carry arrows in its claws. My weaponless bird would be a sympathetic gesture toward the 1960's peace movement, which was in full swing.

After buying basic carving tools and a thick mahogany block, I began to work at the kitchen table. I told myself I'd clean up after a few hours of carving; however, I didn't get that far. Suzanne irritably pointed out the result of my effort — mahogany dust on the floor, in the cupboard, and in the children's diapers.

She said, "I would love to have an eagle wall hanging, but you can't do this in our kitchen!" She tried to remain calm, but her red face said otherwise. "You need to wait till we have a basement; you turkey." 'Turkey' was her affectionate way of calling me an inconsiderate jerk. So I was compelled to put woodcarving on hold. This added to my frustration because it came easily to me and offered me a lot of creative satisfaction.

While we had little personal savings, I had an optimistic outlook, along with my engineering degree. The economy had slightly recovered, so it was a good time to look for a new job. Although I never expected to ever find one with the same excitement and comradeship that Jason offered, the realization of what I would miss was distressing. Most painful was abandoning Jason as he continued his struggle to achieve his dreams. However my family was the most important, so I looked for another line of work.

Aerospace companies were actively hiring, and I looked forward to receiving higher pay. However, without any aerospace experience, I failed to realize the downside, which was evident soon.

Aerospace

Baltimore, Maryland — 1967, Age 32

Our family of five, along with Suzanne's mother, woke up in a strange city after driving from Ohio to Maryland. We were crowded into two motel rooms. The kids were crying because they were hungry. Unfortunately, Suzanne's nesting instinct had begun and she was intent on organizing our belongings, particularly diapers before we could think about looking for a place to eat.

Our new adventure had started. Until now I had gladly lived on low pay, but now I wanted a better standard of living. No longer motivated by a dream, making money soon became my goal. My initial idea was to stick with a familiar organization like NASA. I applied to work at the Cleveland NASA facility, where I had done the wind tunnel tests years before. They made a job offer. But because aerospace paid higher salaries, I took a job with Westinghouse Space and Electronics Division in Baltimore, Maryland. They made electronic systems for military airplanes — primarily radar for fighter jets. Thousands of technical employees designed, developed, and produced sophisticated equipment. These were large projects, which were executed on a massive scale. The company wanted me because of my credentials, and not for my know-how of aviation design. My early NASA experience would look good on the future contract proposals.

We had moved our family into the Baltimore motel, while we looked for a suitable rental house. Pregnant Suzanne carried our fourth child, so Suzanne's mother came along to assist. Despite her age, Grandma was a vital helper because Suzanne had limited energy and mobility. I worried about everyone's health and safety and the physical challenge this presented to both Suzanne and her aging mother.

Grandma Anna Novak had married in 1923, soon after emigrating alone from Hungary to America at the age of twenty-three. Suzanne was the youngest of her three children. I thought of

Grandma Anna as a perfect mother-in-law because she regarded me as the perfect son-in-law. She cooked delicious Hungarian dishes, like Chicken Paprikash, Apple Strudel, and Palacsinta. She became a savior for Suzanne, who struggled with three toddlers during a difficult move. Also, she treated her engineer son-in-law as the undisputed head of the family, which made my life easier as well.

Several weeks after our relocation ordeal, we moved into a small, two-story rental in a Baltimore suburb; rejoicing to live in a real house for once, rather than an apartment. We had a large fenced-in yard where the children could play and a basement workbench, where I could resume woodcarving whenever job and family responsibilities allowed. It was the start of a wonderful family life. Grandma celebrated this new beginning by making Apple Strudel. The house soon smelled of baked apples and cinnamon as I mowed the lawn on the first warm spring day.

I looked forward to my new aerospace career, and we all anticipated the arrival of our child. Unfortunately, my optimism didn't last for long. Before we finished unpacking, the three children were sick with mumps. I decided that their illness wouldn't keep me from appearing for the first workday, but then the mumps got me too. My boss and I had agreed on a start date, but now I wasn't able to show up on time. I lay in bed with a high fever and wondering if I might lose the job. Clear-headed Suzanne called my boss to get everything straightened out. Maryland tested us as a family, and we passed the first test due to the strength of two mothers.

* * *

I lay in bed thinking about my new job responsibility to provide project managers with the latest techniques and tools like project scheduling, resource budgeting, component reliability, and change control. I expected these all to be boring subjects, far removed from the creative designing that I was involved in. Computers were used more in business, and my new boss planned to computerize some of these techniques. Computerizing meant writing simple code from scratch to run on large mainframe computers. I faced learning several new and different subjects. I might have been more concerned if I understood what was required of me. But I figured I could learn anything if I applied myself and persisted.

Finally, I recovered from my illness and was ready to start. The new workplace near Baltimore's main airport looked like a giant hanger encompassing several square blocks. A secretary escorted me to my department.

"The boss will stop by to see you later today. Make yourself at home."

Looking around the large room, I was stunned. There were hundreds of undersized gray steel desks jammed together in clusters of four — no windows, no partitions. Several men occupied the desks — no women. I recalled from my engineering classes that universities didn't seem to encourage women students, so few graduated and moved into aerospace jobs. Each cluster of four engineers shared one phone on a fixture, allowing it to rotate among the occupants. *I guess management doesn't expect us to make many calls. This setup seems primitive and degrading.*

After introducing myself to the neighbors, I checked my desk. The company didn't spend much on housekeeping. I found office debris in the drawers. It appeared that the prior occupant snacked on Twinkies; I tried not to let my annoyance show. I smiled at the guy next to me, who wore a suit and bow tie. We exchanged first names.

I asked, "Where'd you go to school?"

"Purdue, Mechanical engineering. And you?"

"Wichita, Aeronautical engineering. Been here long?"

"Almost two years. Do you want to eat lunch with our group?"

"Sure, thanks for inviting me. I don't know anyone. You like the job?"

He forced a smile. "Can't beat the pay."

"There are a lot of guys crowded in here. I wonder why?"

He glanced to the side, slid his office chair a bit closer, and lowered his voice. "So, you noticed our primitive working decor?"

"Well, yeah. I guess there must be a reason?"

His expression turned serious. "Our time is charged to projects, and billed to the government. The company adds overhead and profit, so more workers result in more profit. Small desks are crowded together to accommodate more engineers. That is the primary reason why there are so many of us in this room." He didn't hide his discontent. "Long ago, a division vice president decided that our workspace shouldn't be better than the Navy guys, who are here to test and buy our stuff. They are our customers and we must work side-by-side." He motioned down the aisle at a group of four uniformed Navy lieutenants sitting at a quad of desks. "That's the reason for these cheap desks."

I didn't know what to think. In contrast to the undignified space, engineers were dressed for business. They seldom removed their self-validating suit coats and ties. *It must be attire dignity.* They reminded me of zebras, each with unique stripes but indistinguishable in the herd as individuals. *This job is not looking encouraging.* Recalling the generous salary, I decided to withhold judgment.

I heard indistinct conversation at the entrance. The noisy room hushed. A silver-haired man in a silk business suit entered the room with an Admiral in tow. My bow tie neighbor nodded his head at them and whispered, "He's our VP, conducting a high-level customer tour."

Engineers stopped gossiping, picked up their ballpoint pens and slide rules, and pretended to solve some difficult technical problems. The vice president talked nonstop to the Admiral as they proceeded down the center aisle and out of the rear door. They never looked at anyone. My neighbors relaxed when they exited.

Before the day ended, I noticed the slow work pace. There was no urgency in the room. Engineers seemed to move in first gear, which contrasted with the swift, high gear urgency when I worked at NASA and then built planes with Jason. Despite the apparent lack of mission importance, this job felt like pure labor. The other jobs were definitely more fun.

At the end of the day, I arrived home exhausted. After putting the children to bed, we curled up on the couch. I closed my eyes and held my forehead. "I'm afraid I got myself into a fix with this new job. I doubt I'll ever like the work." I described some of the day's events.

"I could tell that your day was crap, as soon as you walked in. What are you going to do?"

"I'm tempted to quit now before I get in deeper."

Her expression shouted, "Are you kidding?" Then she asked, "Would you be able to find a better job?"

"I don't know. Most high-paying engineering jobs these days are in aerospace. I wonder if all aerospace companies with government contracts operate this way."

"Well, I wouldn't want to move again so soon. Moving with the kids was hard, and I like this house."

I closed my eyes. "Yeah, I agree."

She smiled and tried to sound hopeful, "I suspect there are good and bad points with every work situation. Remember how my last boss would put his feet up on his desk, right on top of the legal brief with three carbon copies that I just typed?" I laughed.

She said, "It wasn't funny!"

"Yes it was, when you first told me that story, you said you bit his ankle. That was very funny."

"Not for him." She grinned. "Your company offers high pay and other advantages, like insurance and vacations. These are more benefits than we ever had. You wanted such a job, right?"

I glanced down. "Yeah." After thinking a bit more, I added, "It's just that I always enjoyed the work too."

"There is no rule that says you must love your job. In fact, the Bible says that we earn our bread by the sweat of our brow."

"You might be right, but I never accepted that as a given."

"Well, I hope we will not move too soon."

"Don't worry. I won't quit. Maybe things will get better after I figure out what it takes to be successful here."

After few months I was able to tell Suzanne what success required. I stood and started pacing. "Above all, engineers in my group value promotion and vertical movement. That means being a manager, which provides more money, greater status, and a bigger office. It is also competitive, even cutthroat. Since college, I only experienced teamwork and cooperation on the job, not competition among team members."

"What will you do?"

I set my jaw. "I'm stuck. It makes me mad, but it's my fault, and we have family responsibilities. I'll just have to start competing." So, I bought another suit and became the new zebra in the herd. In time, I got used to a big salary and even embraced the promotion game. After six months I convinced myself that I too might be a manager someday, not because I had a vocational calling, but because this company valued managers and paid them well. While I had never liked games growing up, if there was little opportunity to be creative, I thought I might find fulfillment playing this game. I also needed a new goal to revive my work life, so I was ready to head down a new path towards management. I knew if I achieved such a position, my focus would shift from doing engineering to managing others. Perhaps, it was not a bad decision, but only time would tell if it was a good one.

I soon learned that becoming a manager was not easy. According to my boss, I needed improvement in two areas, learning how to manage and becoming more outgoing. I also required credentials to prove proficiency. I figured a master's degree in management should do it. I had been thinking about a Master of Business Administration degree, so I enrolled at George Washington University. Rather than an MBA, I picked the Master of Systems Administration. The MSA program substituted some business courses for those in the computer department. GWU offered off-campus classes in the Baltimore area and the company paid the tuition. I worked on my own time. This job did not tax my energy, so studying evenings and weekends were not a burden. But it was a three-year night school commitment.

I didn't understand that a trivial decision like picking the MSA over the MBA program might affect my future, but I soon learned that seemingly small decisions can have big consequences.

When making career decisions, I often overlooked the effect on Suzanne. I assumed my commitment to work harder would only affect me, but soon I discovered I was wrong. Suzanne, who did a lot of work caring for family and household, had agreed to edit and type my papers. As a former secretary, she was most qualified, and lingering dyslexia caused me to be a poor speller. While I did schoolwork on our kitchen table, she found distractions for the children. She never complained when I didn't seem to have time to help with her work; or when I kept adding new self-improvement challenges to my schedule, like the latest — public speaking.

I was less shy now than in the past but was still terrified of speaking in large meetings. So, I joined Toastmasters International as a way to gain poise and confidence. It required me to do what I feared — speaking to a group. I was soon participating in a variety of practice settings with the local Toastmasters club. During the next few years, I developed better speaking skills and self-assurance.

Public speaking wasn't the last of my self-improvement projects. In the 1960s, there was much media attention on meditating for health. Celebrities like the Beatles music group were promoting Transcendental Meditation. In addition to personal health benefits, use of meditation was touted as a way to end war and suffering in the world. I did not believe that conjecture, but I did experience much stress and tension.

I told Suzanne, "I plan to learn meditation to reduce my stress."

She smiled and said, "I bet you could reduce your stress and mine if you stopped adding self-improvement activities to your day."

"I'm sure you're right, but I like learning new things. I will not take the lessons if you object."

"No, it's okay. I'll let you know if it gets to be too much."

So I learned meditation and after several months, I did feel more relaxed. Meditation became a life-long habit. It helped reduce tension and, in time improved my creativity, which was an unexpected bonus. My current job didn't require original thinking, but creativity would become more important to me in the future.

Suzanne tried to keep four playful toddlers quiet and off my lap, while I meditated, which was an impossible aim. She was supportive and understanding throughout. Like a typical husband, fixated on my mission, most of the time I was oblivious to her feelings and needs. I didn't guess this could lead to trouble.

* * *

We felt our relationship change as family and marriage matured. I was busy with work and night school, while she cared for four children and me. Our feelings for each other were as strong as ever, but we spent less time exclusively focusing on each other. Suzanne became aware of the problem first. One evening she looked at me with moist eyes and tightly pressed lips. "Your public speaking skill might be improving, but we don't communicate with each other anymore."

Her comment surprised me, and I started to object but thought better than saying something that might increase the tears or start an argument. She seemed to have more on her mind. She said, "I heard about this program for improving communications called Marriage Encounter. It's a weekend program. The next one is this weekend at the Holiday Inn, and I want us to go. We could use an overnight vacation from the children, so I registered and lined up a babysitter."

I took a step back. "No way! I need to write a paper this weekend."

She narrowed her eyes. "Last week you said you wished our marriage was more romantic like it once was. According to the person I talked with on the phone, this could help." She tilted her head and smiled, which always worked as personal persuasion.

I kissed her cheek. "It sounds like bribery."

Suzanne pursed her lips and pretended to punch me in the chest. She said, "No, this should last longer than one weekend."

I recalled how my Dad always said "No" to Mom's requests. I did not like hearing him say "No" because it made her sad, which was the last thing I wanted for us. "Well... How do I learn more?"

Suzanne was ready with answers and after a few minutes, I agreed to attend. I learned a new skill of how to express my feelings. It might seem odd that I had difficulty expressing feelings to my wife, but I discovered that it was a common problem for all busy couples and husbands in particular. Going to Marriage Encounter was one of the best things we did as a couple, since our honeymoon. Our communication and love life certainly benefitted from it.

While a communication problem could start with either of us, I was usually the cause. After the Marriage Encounter weekend, rather than crying, arguing, or pouting, Suzanne would call for a discussion.

"Clarence, we need to talk."

At one time, I'd dread those words because tears and an argument usually followed. After Marriage Encounter, we sat together, held hands, and took turns telling each other how we felt about an issue. It took practice for me to limit my comments to feelings, and not dump logical or defensive thoughts on her. We were in love, so this method usually led to understanding and resolution, since we tried our best to put the other's well-being first.

I avoided discussing my work problems with Suzanne, using the classified nature of my job as a reason to keep things to myself. At times, this contributed to communication problems because I was still unhappy with my job, and this affected my disposition and our home life. This unresolved work situation festered and remained a problem. In the meantime, it helped to talk about how we felt as I pursued my unsatisfactory aerospace career.

During the next few years, I worked on several technically advanced and secret airborne military projects. I was not involved in the design or anything creative, and I disliked contributing, even in an indirect way, to make lethal weapons. The realization nagged me.

222 · LAWRENCE SCHNEIDER

I knew I had to accept it as part of the company's mission, at least
until I'd be in a position to change jobs. I felt negligent for not actively pursuing a move. Rather than looking for another job, I became ever more comfortable with the life that a large salary
provided.

After about five years of saving a big chunk of my pay, we had a
substantial down payment for our first house. Owning a home had
been my desire since getting married. Suzanne didn't mind renting,
but I was chasing the American dream as portrayed by the media
and real estate companies. As with many such dreams, it was motivated by culture more than need.

We liked the neighborhood of our current rental, so we bought
our first house on a nearby cul-de-sac, the perfect suburban home
for a family of six. There were three bedrooms in the two-story
house. The lot was small and well shaded with mature oak and
beech trees. We were surprised a few months later by how many
leaves those trees produced. Leaves were the least of my surprises. I
soon learned that if I procrastinated too long, fate would kick me in
the butt.

* * *

Westinghouse lost a major government contract and a ten percent cut in engineers followed, which was an unexpected shock. I
discovered job stability, even at the large aerospace company, was
much less than expected. The herd of zebras panicked. Most of the
work stopped for water cooler meetings.

I talked with a more experienced co-worker who had survived the
last two layoffs. "I just bought a house. What's going to happen?"

He said, "Well, for layoffs they use a somewhat objective process
called 'relative worth.' It means higher paid engineers, who haven't
kept up in their field go first. Of course, the guys who get canned
don't think it is objective or fair."

"Should I be worried?"

"Probably not, but there is no way to know for sure."

I was new and had not seen many pay increases, but was worried because I felt the responsibility for my family.

Electronics, not aeronautics, was needed at the company. So after the first layoff, I uneasily waited and believed that the ax may fall at any moment. Fortunately, this time I retained my job, but a possible future layoff became a real concern. I had learned that engineers were an expendable commodity in aerospace. I became alert for an opportunity to jump ship. I did not like to passively place my fate in other hands, so I decided to act.

I tried to think of a way to make my situation more secure. After completing a basic computer programming course, I wrote a simple application to automate a project management process. My boss appreciated my initiative, but it wasn't enough to win praise at a higher level or promotion to management. However, what it did was increase my appreciation for the future of computers, and I seriously considered shifting my career in that direction. I was no longer doing aviation related work. My main goal was still to be a manager.

After three years in night school, I received the MSA degree and was now equipped to apply for management jobs within the company. Several unsuccessful attempts caused me to look closer at qualifications of the managers. In addition to having advanced degrees, they were electrical engineers. Most had master's degrees, but they were Masters of Electrical Engineering, which made sense because our division developed complex electronic products and these managers led the innovative design. An aeronautical engineer, even one with an MSA degree like mine, was unlikely to be promoted to management ranks. It was unfortunate and I became angry at myself for learning this important fact now rather than three years earlier.

That evening I told Suzanne, "I don't belong here. I need a different job and a better plan if I'm ever to become a manager. I'll concentrate on finding another company."

Manager

Baltimore, Maryland — 1973, Age 38

There were two areas, where past experience could help me find a better job opportunity as a manager — airplane design, or computers. I favored computers because they were the future, but I lacked a way to break into the field.

One of my responsibilities at Westinghouse was to recruit experts to speak at project manager training meetings. I became friends with one speaker, an Air Force colonel stationed in Washington, DC. Because he knew I would be impressed, the Colonel arranged for me to attend a project management briefing at the Pentagon. It would be my first time inside the distinctive and historic building.

I was excited and eager that morning. I allowed extra commute time for the significant event. However, I misjudged the DC traffic and after a hectic two-hour drive in the rain during rush hour, I arrived in urgent need of a restroom. By the time I got through security and into the building, the meeting participants had moved into a large briefing room. The hallway was empty, so I hurried to find the nearest restroom. It was empty too, but something seemed wrong. I looked around with eyes darting everywhere — no urinals. My frantic mind quickly guessed a reason. *This must be a ladies room!* I rushed out looking from side to side, relieved that no one noticed. I soon located the right restroom, before finding a seat in the back of the crowded briefing room.

I saw a long table on the stage populated by military officers, decorated with ribbons and gold bars. I was one of the few civilians in the room. The restroom debacle blocked my concentration during the first half of the presentation. I imagined how I would have felt if one of these decorated officers had seen me come out of the ladies room, or worse if I had surprised a lady officer.

I did absorb enough of the briefing to conclude that I was not interested in configuration control of airborne radar, which was what my current position entailed. This insight confirmed that I needed a different job.

The drive home provided two hours to think about my situation. I knew it was time to leave; not just career satisfaction but self-respect demanded it. I devised a plan to get a more suitable job. It involved asking my new friend, the colonel, for career advice. It would be the first step in persuading him to hire me. He recently retired from the Air Force and was now a manager at the Social Security Administration (SSA) headquartered in Baltimore. I called him the next day.

"Hi Clarence, I'm glad to hear from you. How was the Pentagon briefing?"

"Thank you for arranging it. It was an impressive place and an interesting experience. I almost got kicked out for walking into the ladies room."

"Wow! I expect you are exaggerating, but it sounds like an entertaining story."

"I'll tell you all about it next time we meet, which I hope will be soon because I need your advice. I'm ready to find another career position with more opportunity to move into management."

"Well sir, as I have hinted before I would like for us to work together. So keep that in mind. SSA is a professional outfit. I'm sitting here in my third-floor office looking out of the window at what could be a park. These are spacious quarters and a great place for meaningful work."

"What might I be responsible for?"

"You would report to me, sir. I'm the Planning Branch Chief in Data Processing. Our mission is to create SSA's first long-range plan for the next generation of mainframe computers. For the first time, Headquarters computers will be linked directly to all SSA locations around the country. It is an important mission." He lowered his voice. "I inherited a gaggle of employees who have no idea how to manage such a project. You do, and we need you here."

"What about future growth?"

"You say you aim to be in management? Well, sir, you would have a good chance to get my position when I retire in five years."

I said, "So this could benefit us both."

"Yes. Come in next week for an interview." He hesitated. "Be warned, getting a government job can take a long time."

It sounded perfect. Then I recalled my bungled aerospace job selection, and decided to give this career move more thought. I spent several days documenting pros and cons before talking with Suzanne. On one hand, SSA had a good reputation as an employer and an appealing social mission. I liked and respected the Colonel. He would be a good person to work for because he was a leader and not just a boss. Federal employment included valuable benefits and job stability. The planning project could provide the creative challenge of starting a new discipline at SSA — long-range computer planning. Moreover, the opportunity to step into management seemed much better. Also, since SSA was within commuting range, the family household would not need to move.

Those were the positive reasons to switch. On the other hand, the job offered a lower salary. More significantly, it represented a career change; I'd abandon any connection to aviation to embrace computers. Because of continuous advances in technology, in a short time, it would be difficult to return to aeronautical engineering. There would be much to master with this job — new computer career, new social mission, and a new employer.

In the evening, when the house was quiet, Suzanne and I talked about it in our favorite place to consider important decisions, side-by-side on the couch holding hands. After I described my job research, she said, "I don't see a clear choice; there are too many factors."

"Well, let's try it another way, sometimes using intuition works. I believe in the mind's ability to access subconscious knowledge that might not be apparent."

Suzanne said, "Well, it does seem like a good job. And we wouldn't move. I prefer not to move again soon."

* * *

Two days later I headed to SSA's national headquarters, which occupied several square blocks in a Baltimore suburb. I walked toward the entrance and past manicured azaleas and mature oaks, The American flag fluttered on a tall pole surrounded by an expansive lawn of green grass. *It looks like strength and stability.* I smiled. *And the grass is greener.*

Three receptionists stood behind a long, polished granite counter in a large lobby. The two-story high wall behind them was matching black granite. There were few seats in the lobby for visitors, and I discovered why — I did not wait long. I was soon on my way up to the third-floor, escorted by the Colonel's secretary. *These workers are not like the stereotype of inefficient government employees, it is more like NASA.* We exited the elevator, and I couldn't repress a self-satisfied smile because I had already decided this is the place for me.

The Colonel greeted me warmly, but he looked concerned. My smile disappeared.

He said, "The position isn't a sure or a near thing. I did a lot of selling with the Bureau Director to approve a planning slot for you and it could be yours if you want."

"I'm ready to start as soon as you can arrange it," I replied.

"Let's not celebrate too soon, sir. You must compete with every person here who wants a promotion, qualified or not. Sometimes I wonder if current employees even bother to read the job description. I think they Xerox their application and submit it for every possible opening. Civil Service rules require each job to be filled competitively. There is no way around it."

I cleared my throat. "It sounds like it could take a few more weeks."

"More like months, not weeks. Here are the forms. Mail them back to me. I will track them through the hiring process to avoid a delay. At some point, there will be an interview, maybe more than one."

I went home and waited, and then waited longer. I assumed it was government bureaucracy. Months went by, but nothing happened. I called the Colonel often, only to learn of difficulties with regulations and budgets. After three months he said, "The planning position is approved. Next, I must get Agency approval to spend money on the salary, which is a separate step. I'm working on it with the budget group."

Two more months passed before I returned for an interview with a committee of three computer managers, who asked a few easy questions. They seemed to be more impressed with me than I was with them. They treated me like a technical wonder because of my background, which they assumed was grander than actuality. However, no offer followed. Then two weeks later, I was again summoned, this time to see the Bureau Director, the executive in charge of all computer systems at SSA. The Colonel said that such an interview was unusual when filling a lower-level job.

The Director had been the mayor of a medium-size Maryland city before he lost an election, followed by his current political appointment. The Colonel said the affable Director had little technical knowledge and favored social gatherings to structured interviews. He didn't know what I might expect.

An attractive assistant led me into the Director's spacious corner office. Outside of movie versions of executive suites, I had never imagined such an impressive workplace. I looked around with mouth open.

The assistant announced, "Clarence Arnold is here, Sir."

He stood and came towards me smiling, and with hand extended. "Come in Mr. Arnold. I hear you are a rocket scientist."

I nodded once. "Well, not exactly. A few years ago at NASA, I played a small part."

He glanced at my resume "And you are a graduate engineer with an advanced degree in systems management?"

"Yes."

"Wonderful. I'm planning a project that might be of interest. We will soon build a new Computer Center here at SSA. I understand you once worked with architects on an aircraft factory building."

"Yes, a small factory. I prepared the requirements."

"Good. I think you can be a big help. Let's get some lunch. We have a small executive dining room down the hall. I will tell you about some ideas that I have for our Computer Center."

Two hours later, I left his office more confident that the job would be mine.

The hiring process took almost a year. By the summer of 1973, I was a planning analyst, reporting to the Colonel. While I never ate again in the executive dining room, working conditions were first-rate. Suzanne and I easily adapted to my lower salary. I worked in a spacious cubical with a phone and a window. Other long-term employees in the Colonel's branch learned of my background and bestowed on me an unwanted celebrity status. They regarded me as someone different and special — a rocket engineer and an airplane designer with an advanced computer management degree. I didn't feel special in this new situation because, unlike my colleagues, I knew little about SSA's business processes or mainframe computers, while they were experienced experts. Nevertheless, I savored the undeserved stature for as long as it might last. It was a good beginning, this working relationship of mutual respect.

I had expected to develop SSA's long-range computer systems plan. However, after the Director learned of my experience with architectural requirements for the aircraft factory, I was selected to work on a different project. SSA had received Congressional approval to build the Computer Center, and I would work with the architects. Because I was new, an experienced SSA employee would assist.

* * *

Over the next ten years, the job progressed as the Colonel predicted. SSA completed the Computer Center, and after the Colonel retired, I moved into his Branch Chief position, which meant that my goal to be a manager was achieved.

My enthusiasm to do a good job as a manager persuaded me to apply every planning, organizing, and directing technique that I had learned while earning the MSA degree. My boss was pleased with the result, but my subordinates were not impressed with my leadership style. They did not like being pushed to work harder and meet deadlines. In the 1960s, most university management programs did not emphasize leadership. I now discovered that managing was not the same as leading. I had become a typical demanding boss and didn't feel successful because of my subordinates' discontent. I observed that most SSA managers were mediocre, and I joined them. I considered putting on my self-improvement hat to learn leadership but decided my problem wasn't lack of knowledge, but the lack of talent. I was an introvert with a little natural ability for leading others, which requires communicating a vision, and motivating others to support it. While I might learn better leadership skills, management was unlikely to ever be my strength.

Promotions continued in spite of my shortcomings. It seemed high-level executives thought telling people what to do and cracking the whip was the best way to manage. So, in time, I reached the executive level — a manager of managers. Promotion came with a larger office, underground parking, and a higher salary. It also came with more office politics and several top-down reorganizations.

Years later, one of those reorganizations provided an opportunity to move into a senior staff job. Because I didn't like being a mediocre manager, I had stopped applying for promotions and was glad to become a high-level SSA computer consultant. It offered less status but a chance to do what I had come to SSA for — long-range planning of computer systems.

The Colonel's friendship led to another stimulating opportunity. He taught a course called *Project Management* as an adjunct instructor at the University of Maryland's Baltimore campus. Because project management was one of my specialties, he often consulted me when developing his course topics and asked me to substitute when he couldn't teach. I enjoyed the experience and felt exhilarated after conducting a class. When the college's Computer Science Program expanded, I was invited to join the part-time teaching staff, a position I enjoyed for eight years.

After achieving my goal to become a manager, and then discovering I was mediocre, I still did not feel special. As I grew older, I wondered if there was still time to accomplish whatever special destiny Grandpa Joseph foresaw for me. Doubts led to a crisis of self-confidence. I grasped for something that might make me feel better. I discovered a possible solution one day when I joined one of my sons, whose hobby was drag racing.

Mid-life Crisis

Baltimore, Maryland — 1999, Age 64

It was a warm summer evening when I arrived at the Carroll Dragway. An attendant at the gate asked, "Watching or racing?"

I smiled proudly. "My son is racing."

As our children became adults, there were fewer opportunities to do things together. We were all busy with school and careers. I regretted not setting aside more time to enjoy the family when they were younger.

Our youngest son, Phil, and I shared a love for cars; however, he took his interest and experience far beyond mine. From the time he was in high school, he loved powerful muscle cars, and as an adult restored and collected fast cars. His passion led him to race at the drag strip. One day he invited me to watch as he tried to surpass his best time on the quarter mile track.

I parked and walked towards the staging area. In the distance, I heard the sendoff screech of racing tires blending with the roar of a high-powered engine. There was a glint of sunlight from moving cars and smoke visible over spectators' heads. My adrenaline increased. *I may be too old to race, but I can still get a kick by watching Phil.*

I found him next to his Fathom-Green 1969 Camaro SS. Two friends were assisting. The car hood was open, so I assumed they were making last-minute adjustments. I said, "Is there a problem?"

He said, "I just made a run and the engine is cooling. It's running fine."

He had worked many hours to tune the car for maximum horsepower. I glanced under the hood at a gleaming engine. He looked at a small slip of paper containing the time of his last run. "I'm not happy with the result. I can do better. It takes practice to anticipate the green light after seeing the yellow because the car's inertia causes a delay. So to compensate, I need to hit the accelerator a moment before seeing green. A fraction of a second makes the difference between a good and a bad run. I'm a little rusty today."

It required several runs down the track before he was satisfied. I was jealous that he was having so much fun, while I could only watch. He promised me a ride, even though my extra weight would slow his car. "Okay Dad," he said. "Are you ready to go with me?"

I knew from similar experiences in amusement parks that fear can be fun if danger doesn't get out of control. It's like a natural high. So, I settled into the Camaro's passenger seat and secured the buckle. Only then did I realize that my mouth was dry, but it was too late to get a sip of water. He performed a burnout to improve traction, causing a deafening screech and we were enveloped in smoke. Burning rubber irritated my nose, and I wiped tears away. Even that was part of the excitement. For my benefit, he demonstrated how to time the lights. We shot forward, the screech became a roar as acceleration pressed me back. Before I could blink, he had reached the end of the track and pushed the brake preparing to turn back. My hands were trembling and I laughed with the thrill; Phil smiled to see my reaction. On the return driveway, he stopped to pick up an electronic record of his time. I was hooked. Feeling scared and excited was addictive.

The sounds, smells, and sensations of racing were thrilling. I hadn't felt so alive for a long time. After that ride, I wanted to experience even more of life's highlights, while I still had time. *This isn't just about a fast ride. It's about living the rest of life to the fullest.* I decided to buy myself a replacement commuter car suitable for drag racing. Called a street-legal car, it was a compromise that wasn't best for either task but ran satisfactorily on both the track and in traffic. I didn't want to be too scared. I was reaching for another thrill before retiring to a rocking chair, not trying to hurry the process.

Suzanne didn't object when I mentioned my desire. She looked at me with a questioning expression and muttered something about a mid-life crisis. The new car I wanted would be expensive, but as in the past, when it came to financial decisions, she had confidence in my ability to provide what we needed. This time she was more concerned about my safety.

I said, "A former pilot should be capable of driving a short distance in a straight line." But she took our son aside and asked him to watch out for me.

I bought a new 1999 Pontiac Firebird-Formula. Phil helped select optional equipment to enhance its racing ability, and I ordered it from the factory to get what he recommended — a fast street-legal car. I was willing to wait several weeks for delivery.

* * *

The first time I took the dark blue Firebird to the track, the gate attendant said, "Watching or racing?"

I smiled wide, "Racing."

He gave me a quizzical second look, just before directing me to a staging area where I was required to pass a safety inspection before meeting Phil at the racing lanes. I didn't mind that the safety inspector saw me as an unlikely race driver with gray hair and hunched behind the wheel. His bifocal glasses  were peering out from under an oversized, borrowed helmet. I was there to capture the thrill, not to impress anyone.

After receiving Phil's final instructions, I entered a short queue leading to the starting line and then inched the Firebird forward until a red light indicated the car was on the mark. Timing was electronic. There was another driver in the adjoining lane. He wasn't a competitor because we raced the clock rather than each other. The other car was a distraction, so I tried to ignore it. However, its presence added to the excitement and tension.

I held the Firebird in position with my left foot on the brake, and right hovering over the accelerator. Moisture trickled down my side. I stared unblinkingly at the starting lights, not wanting to miss the green. Lights on the starting tree flashed YELLOW and then GREEN. I stomped the accelerator to floorboard with a complete lack of skill or finesse, getting away from the line a fraction of a second late. Tires squealed as the Firebird's powerful engine worked to overcome inertia. The launch pushed me back against the seat. Clutching the steering wheel tightly with both hands, I plunged forward surrounded by the engine's roar. Time stood still. I blinked my eyes only to discover I was across the finish line at about 95 mph. By the time I remembered to brake, the speed had passed 120 mph. I feared I might overrun the end of the track, so I pushed the brake hard — too hard. The Firebird sailed over a slight rise marking the end of the track and came to a skidding, shuddering stop in a cloud of gravel and dust.

I sat there breathing heavily. *What just happened?* When my mind caught up with reality, I recalled that I should keep moving to make way for the next car. I quickly pulled ahead. On the way back to the starting line, I forgot to get my time slip. I moved ahead, and heard a voice on the loudspeaker, "Will the Firebird driver pick up his latest time slip at the announcer's booth?" *This is embarrassing. He just told everyone I'm a beginner. Well, I guess that's what I am.*

I improved with each run. My best performance for the day was 99.9 mph and 14 seconds to cover one-quarter mile from a standing start — not bad for an old guy in a standard, factory-built car.

This brief drag racing experience was a thrill to be remembered and just what I needed to perk up my disposition. The exciting father-son event reminded me of the Lake Erie fishing adventure with my father long-ago.

The Firebird became my commuter car until I retired. Rumbling echoes of the engine in the underground SSA parking garage caused heads to turn whenever I drove in.

Surprise

Baltimore, Maryland — 2001, Age 66

My primary care physician, a gentlewoman from India with dark eyes, moved her skilled fingers over my neck. I noticed a slight hesitation and her eyebrow rose slightly. She repeated the sequence of finger moves with eyes fixed on my neck. *Something is wrong.* Then she pushed into my neck again.

I bit my lip. "What is it?"

"Umm...There is a swelling here in your neck."

I cleared my throat as if that could make it go away. "What is it?"

"I don't know yet, but it needs to be looked into. I'm going to send you to a colleague with an office in this building. He is moving his practice here and he may be able to see you today."

"Good, I am anxious to take care of this."

This was my annual physical exam, the inconvenient ordeal I forced myself not to skip because it might save my life. I decided not to call Suzanne yet because it might be nothing, but I had a bad feeling.

Fortunately, my internist's assistant was able to get me an immediate appointment.

A few minutes later, I rubbed my face briskly, found my courage, and pushed the door of his office open. There was no receptionist and no one else was in his small waiting area. The open inner-office door allowed me to see him talking on the phone, leaning back in a swivel chair with his feet on the desk. His loud voice meant I couldn't avoid his part of the conversation.

The surgical doctor said, "You should expect pain after such a procedure. Try to deal with it."

He listened, and then said, "Do not be such a weakling. There is nothing more to be done. You should start feeling better tomorrow. If not, call back."

After a few minutes, he called me in, listened to my complaint, and felt the lump.

He said, "It is abnormal, and you will need treatment. More tests are required to determine the cause. I will make arrangements and contact you."

I left his office thinking; *He seems unsympathetic and less than competent.* Later that day he called our home. Suzanne answered. He identified himself and said, "Is Clarence Arnold there?"

"No, he is at work. Do you want his phone number?"

"No, tell him I think his abnormality could either be thyroid cancer or a goiter. I would like him to come back in next Monday at 9:00 AM for initial tests."

She choked back a gasp. "I will give him the message."

She called me immediately, frightened and ready to cry. "What is this about? Cancer! You never said anything about cancer."

I stumbled through an explanation of what I still did not understand. *I need time to get a handle on the situation.*

I immediately called the surgical doctor to vent fear-motivated anger. I shouted at the phone, "It's bad enough that you tell me it might be cancer before even doing any tests. Now, you tell my wife, before I had a chance to talk to her." My voice was shrill. "You are incompetent. I will have nothing more to do with you." I slammed down the receiver, closed my eyes and took a deep breath.

As soon as I regained my composure, I called my primary care physician, who apologized for her colleague and the unsuccessful referral. I was more interested in resolving what seemed to be an urgent crisis.

I asked, "Who is the top doctor in the area to treat my problem?"

"In this area, it is likely to be someone at Johns Hopkins or the Chief Surgeon of the Head and Neck Center of the Greater Baltimore Medical Center. I never met him, but he was named Baltimore's best doctor of the year."

"Would you refer me to him?"

"I do not think he will treat you. He is much too busy now that he is famous."

"Please just try. Give his office a call?"

"All right, I'll ask."

I was obliged to wait about six weeks for an appointment with the Chief Surgeon. The Head and Neck Center had a well-appointed and staffed suite on the fourth floor of the medical center's West Pavilion. Suzanne accompanied me for the appointment.

After taking a needle biopsy from my neck, he said, "You have a treatable thyroid cancer, and luckily, it is not an aggressive type."

The news was like a hammer blow. I had absorbed one word, cancer. I didn't know much about it, but I assumed cancer could result in rapid and painful death. I sat with elbows clamped to my sides and stared straight ahead.

The Chief Surgeon said, "The tumor is larger than we like to see and I suspect the cancer cells have invaded the lymph nodes outside the neck. We will know more about its spread after we perform a scan. This type is slow growing and can take up iodine. We can apply radioactive iodine to the cancer cells to kill them. Standard treatment is surgery followed by iodine radiation. Neck surgery can be delicate, but we have performed this procedure many times."

I listened with eyes wide. I looked at Suzanne and saw fear. My gut response was to get the invader out of my body immediately, a reflex reaction like brushing a poisonous spider out of my hair. I didn't want to leave without deciding what to do. My practice was to discuss major decisions with Suzanne, but my survival instinct said act now.

I focused on him. "Will you do the surgery?"

"Yes."

"Let's schedule it as soon as possible."

I glanced at Suzanne. Her eyes were squeezed closed with right hand on her throat. She radiated the fear I felt. She opened her eyes and noticed my questioning expression, her eyes widened and she nodded. *She is with me, as always.* Tears came to my eyes for the first time since I heard the bad news, not for me, but because of what this was doing to her.

When we got home, Suzanne and I sat on the couch staring straight ahead. We said nothing for several minutes but held hands for comfort, each of us full of worry. Mine was about the curse of mortality and a future I may not have. *One thing that will die with me is whatever chance I had to be special. It's my time, but I'm not finished living.*

Suzanne said, "Look, we have to be strong for the family. We have to get through this as a family. We aren't even sure what will happen."

"You are right. Everything might work out fine." *I want to believe that.* "We are strong enough to face this together."

She whispered, "Yes. Together, we are always together."

Our ordeal had begun.

* * *

That summer I gave myself over to the Head and Neck Center for treatment. There was no assurance, but there was hope. After several weeks of tests and exams, we returned for the results. The doctor entered his office, I leaned forward and looked up. He said, "As I suspected multiple cancer cells have spread into the chest cavity. It may require two or three radiation treatments, but I'm confident that we can destroy them. We will admit you since radiation treatment will require twenty-four hours in isolation."

I got right to the point. "What are my chances of surviving a few more years?"

"We have had considerable experience with this type of cancer, and it is treatable. We will know more about survival probability after you recover from the surgery."

Suzanne said, "How long do such operations last?"

"About four hours."

"What about recovery? How long will he be in the hospital?"

"A few days in the hospital, before you can take him home. He will recover faster and be more comfortable there. You will need to provide basic nursing care and our staff will train you."

Suzanne looked concerned. "What's required?"

I knew what she was thinking. Suzanne did not like blood. Whenever one of our children had a play accident that caused bleeding, she came running to me for help.

He said, "You will keep the surgery site clean, change dressings, and empty drains."

Suzanne bit her lip. "I should be able to do that."

"Also, he would have to be isolated from small children for several days, after we give him each radiation treatment."

"I see." I guessed Suzanne was thinking about the well-being of our first grandchild, a toddler.

I said, "I understand that thyroid cancer can be triggered by past radiation exposure, and I had x-ray treatments for acne as a teen. Could it have been the cause of this cancer?"

"It is possible, even likely."

I was angry about what was happening to me and wanted to blame it on something, or someone. I decided, if anything, it was my fault as a teen for insisting on unnecessary x-ray treatments. I also decided that blame wasn't a useful feeling. I needed to think of Suzanne and the family first.

Surgery was scheduled in five weeks, for early September 2001. Waiting became extremely difficult. It was like being on death row. I had plenty of time to think and spent many hours worrying. When I learned cancer had metastasized to multiple lymph nodes in my chest, I reasoned that I would die soon, maybe not this month, but I would not live to be much older. *So why should I bother doing anything?* I thought about what it would be like to die. I did not feel afraid to die, which surprised me. I felt sorry for those I loved and who would grieve after me. I thought about unfulfilled opportunities.

A week before surgery I was stunned, along with the rest of the world, when I heard the news of the 9/11 terrorist attack. Word spread through my workplace like a wildfire, stopping everything but concern and speculation. That evening, I watched the TV News replay the moment the planes hit the Twin Towers.

The next day the Head and Neck Center called about my surgery. They were preparing to receive many injured people from New York City, so all elective surgeries would be canceled, including mine. Catching up and rescheduling the backlog resulted in a six-week delay. My anxiety remained high and my life was on autopilot. I had more time to worry.

When the rescheduled surgery day arrived, life seemed to speed up. Suzanne and our children gathered for support kissed me with worried smiles, and I was rendered unconscious for most of the day. Weeks of recovery were a combination of discomfort and boredom. But in time, after surgery, radiation treatments, and follow-up exams, I was pronounced ready to return to a normal life. Suzanne did what was needed to be done — overcame her fears, and endured all in the name of love. The doctor praised her for "keeping the surgery site cleaner than my best nurse could." During the one-year follow-up exam, I asked again about the survival chances.

He said, "I am pleased with your outcome. You have ninety-five percent probability of surviving five years. You could live much longer." *Five years doesn't seem like much time to me.*

Next to the relief of overcoming cancer, had been the thrill of approaching death and beating it. I would have a hard time surpassing such an intense experience, not that I wanted to. I did have a life extension and resolved to use my remaining time to the fullest.

* * *

"I'm not really satisfied with my job," I told Suzanne. "I guess I'm getting a little bored." We were back on the couch for another serious discussion.

She said, "Think about what you do have — a good salary and benefits, interesting work, a nice office, even undercover parking."

"Somehow those things no longer seem important. I never thought much about it till now. My time here on earth is limited and if there is something that needs doing, I better get on with it.

We do have enough money to retire, and I'm the oldest person in the office. They call me the old man."

"What do you think still needs to be done?"

"It's just a feeling I have," I replied

"Like being special?"

"I guess so. But that is so vague I don't like to admit it."

"It sounds like you are ready to leave."

"Right."

"Will retiring make you happy?"

"Well, I've been in this job for a long time. It isn't the same as it was. In retirement, there would be more time to do creative things like woodcarving."

"Your retirement will change things for both of us! It sounds like the end of the story."

"It might be an end of one story, but it might also be the start of a new one. I feel like I am running against time. The Head and Neck Center gave me a little more time. I would like to use it to do something..."

"To do what?"

"Oh, I'm not sure... something beneficial."

Suzanne shrugged, "You should slow down and think about what is important before making your decision."

"Yes, perhaps you are right." *Life moves on whether or not we are ready.* After a few more months of deliberation and discussion, I decided to accept the reality of life and retire. We started planning for the extended vacation called retirement and began our search for a retirement community.

"One day your life will flash before your eyes. Make sure it's worth watching."

— ANONYMOUS —

CHAPTER SEVEN

Finding Answers

Self Actualization

Hunt Valley, Maryland — 2005, Age 70

I got bored just three months after moving in.

We realized that retirement communities were like resorts, where most of the needs of the residents are tended to, and there are few concerns about house maintenance, house-keeping, or health care. Suzanne was interested in living space, gardens, and health; I looked at their woodshop, where I might do a little wood carving. I imagined myself relaxing with the current bestseller book. We chose a community called Brookfield.

I soon discovered something new about myself — I needed action to be happy, not rest. And it needed to be creative action, not games or busy work.

Three months after moving in, I told Suzanne, "I'm ready for something new. I miss not having meaningful accomplishments in my life."

She faked a surprised look, "Are you saying taking me to the movie yesterday wasn't a meaningful accomplishment?"

"That was foreplay."

Suzanne couldn't suppress a squeal, followed by an explosive laugh. After recovering, she said, "What were we talking about?"

"Foreplay."

She grinned, "No. Foreplay is when you take out the trash without being asked."

"Well, that too."

She smiled broadly. "You are a turkey. Now I remember what we were talking about. What sort of meaningful accomplishments are you thinking of?"

"Like doing things that are creative, or inventive, or that might inspire people."

"That's a really big agenda for someone who is retired."

"I guess I don't want to be sidelined anymore" I replied.

She shook her head and continued ironing.

* * *

Suzanne liked to invite her friends for what she called "tea parties." Because they engaged in girl-talk and our apartment was small, I was encouraged to find something else to do. So I began to spend more time in the woodshop. The woodshop was spacious and well furnished with equipment that many prior residents brought with them and donated to the community. There were two large rooms, one for making things, which accumulated dust and dirt; and another for wood finishing, which was kept dust free. There was even a small, well-organized tool room for workers to use.

Members of the retirement community, who worked in the woodshop organized themselves into a formal group with a budget and elected leader. They raised money by repairing things for other residents. Woodshop members came from a variety of backgrounds and possessed varying skill levels. A typical member was a retired male professional with little shop experience. Some members went to the woodshop daily for fellowship. I was a daily member, but I preferred to work alone making woodcarvings. To work more efficiently, I bought the latest power tools to supplement my hand tools. I learned to appreciate the inherent beauty of wood and preferred using furniture-grade hardwoods selected for grain color and figuring beauty. I also started to create abstract shapes.

About that time several Brookfield residents who knew of my woodcarving hobby suggested that I put a few completed pieces in a lobby display cabinet so that other residents could see them. The exhibit generated more attention than I expected, especially from folks involved in the Maryland art community. During the next two months, one person after another complimented my work and compared it to what they saw in art galleries.

My items had never attracted much interest in the past, so I figured the residents were offering inflated compliments as a way to welcome their new neighbor. However, some of those who said they liked my carvings seemed to know about such things, as compared to me, who knew almost nothing about art. Their compliments flattered me and enticed me to listen to what they had to say. One large man, who was on the board of a museum was the most convincing. He favored a dark suit and a serious expression.

In his deep voice, he declared, "You have an obvious talent for direct carving."

I dismissed the idea with a wave of my hand. "How can anyone know that?"

He gestured toward the display cabinet. "You said it was easy to carve that eagle. You claimed that you had no formal training, and the eagle was your first attempt. Most people would find that really difficult, if not impossible. You use direct carving, which is the hardest way to make a three-dimensional figure."

"I don't think it is so hard. Why do you think it is?" I asked.

"Because with direct carving, you can only remove material, and, if too much is lost, it is irreplaceable. If you think it is easy, that means you have a talent for it, which is rare. It is something that you have an obligation to nurture."

"Well…I don't know about that." I had no better response.

He said, "Think about becoming an artist. Start making sculptures rather than woodcarvings."

His surprising comment was compelling, but I wasn't ready to be burdened with an obligation, even if it came with well-meaning flattery. Then pride caused me to reconsider my initial objection. *Could it be true? Do I really have talent?*

I finally asked, "What would being a sculptor involve?"

"It would require more effort and time than hobby wood-carving, but that is not important. First, you need to decide if you are a true artist. Being a real artist is a calling, not a choice. The effort becomes a pleasure for a true artist because he loves doing it." He motioned towards the display. "Did you feel a need to make these items? Was it a passion?"

"I would not say that. I enjoy carving and plan to continue, but I'm not sure about being a full-time artist. To be honest, I always thought of art as right-brain fluff — all about intuition and feelings. I spent my working life in left-brain careers involving logic and machines. I figure I'm a left-brain thinker and not an artistic type."

He touched my shoulder and smiled. "Could you at least be open to the possibility? You do have the talent."

I was pleased by his remarks, "Sure. I will think about it."

I had conflicting thoughts about what the museum guy said. *Would this be my next adventure? People do seem to admire famous artists. A successful artist might even be considered special — perhaps this is my last chance. I would probably like expressing ideas with art, but I don't think I'm good enough. I did enjoy making the woodcarvings, and it's relatively easy for me. I have several ideas for future woodcarvings as well. I'd like to try those designs, but I'm too old. Most beginning artists are young and well educated in art. I'd like to do something challenging and satisfying during whatever time I have left. What does he know? He might know museums, but he's not an artist.*

I knew an artistic path would involve not only making art but also rejection and stress. Someone told me that being a full-time artist was like starting a small company. As usual, Suzanne and I discussed it.

I said, "On the plus side, others will see my work and have an opportunity to think about the themes. I'd also enjoy the craft challenge of fabrication, just as I do with woodcarving."

She said, "But doing it full time to meet deadlines could be a lot of work."

Here is what clinched the decision; Suzanne looked at me unsmiling. "If you become a professional artist would you be away from the apartment more?"

"Yes, I suppose so. I'd find a place like the woodshop, where I can work, and I'll spend time there."

Her face lit up with a sweet smile, "Then go for it!" We laughed and then Suzanne added, "I'll be glad to get you out of my hair, so I can invite some of my new friends for girl-only chats."

Then my expression turned serious, "All right. I have just decided to become a sculptor." She gave me a high-five.

"I guess you are serious because it didn't take much of a push from me."

"Do you know what this means?" I asked.

"What?"

"I just decided to reinvent myself — from an engineer to an artist."

Irene said. "That seems like a big change from left brain to right brain thinking. Is that even possible?"

"We will see."

* * *

My first objective was to practice making art while learning the business side of being an artist. I received advice from several new artist friends. One of our neighbors was a retired businessman and a serious art collector. He understood both sides of art. Mal was enthusiastic about my work and was anxious to help. He agreed to be my mentor.

Members of the retirement community, who worked in the woodshop welcomed my conversion from woodcarver to sculptor, even though it meant more commotion, noise, and dirt. They agreed I should have one corner of the shop for my exclusive use as a studio. They used some of their tool budget to upgrade the dust collector to dispose of the extra wood chips and dust I would create. Also, they were readily available whenever I needed advice or help.

I decided to pursue abstract shapes as my sculpture style. I liked the challenge of representing ideas about being human with conceptual forms. Abstract art also offered viewers an opportunity to add their own interpretation to the original meaning of my artwork.

For my first sculpture, I tried to represent an interesting attitude of workers that I had often observed. Most people dislike work but love to play. In fact, a majority of us just tolerate work to survive. Yet, I feel that work and play are identical in many ways. I remember coworkers who hated to come to work each morning and looked forward to weekends when they could have fun. Sometimes one person's play is the same as another's work. For instance, a professional golfer works on a golf course, while an amateur is there for enjoyment.

This was fascinating to think about but was not a three-dimensional shape that I might make. *How does such an idea become a unique sculpture?* I waited for inspiration, but nothing happened for several weeks.

I had continued to practice transcendental meditation every day since learning it years before. One day, while meditating, the image of *Work & Play* popped into my mind. I assumed it emerged from my subconscious, which might explain why it occurred when I was meditating. The shape looked like gears (work) intertwined with a ribbon (play). I hoped viewers would also find the idea intriguing and the form pleasing in appearance.

I categorized using imagination in this way as *artistic* creativity. Apparently, it didn't require art training or years of practice because I had neither. With an image in mind, I planned to rely on my engineering training for the fabrication step, which I labeled *design* creativity. The engineer in me had experience with fabrication and an abundance of confidence. I figured I should be able to build almost anything I imagined. Without this overconfidence, probably I would not have attempted direct carving.

I sketched the imagined shape and planned how to construct it — selecting materials, tools, and steps. Each project was a unique challenge, which is what I liked about fabrication, and I enjoyed taking risks. For example, I intentionally made the wood ribbon of this *Work & Play* sculpture thin to the point of breaking. I feel that taking a risk is exciting; ask anyone on a rollercoaster. Taking risks while carving added to the challenge because it required more skill to execute a shape that was pushed so close to failure. I hoped that observant viewers could recognize the unique craftsmanship in my artworks.

I reached an artistic milestone with the completion of *Work & Play* and felt privileged being able to visualize and then make my first real artwork. I would never claim that I created it, similar to the mother, who would never claim that she created her baby. Creation is magical and beyond human control. I had simply completed a series of art-making steps.

In the process, I discovered something wonderfully personal about art. However, it is hard to describe it in words — it might have been the pleasure of being lost in a creative zone during fabrication, or the wonder of producing what people value, or simply making something that did not previously exist. The entire process was highly satisfying for me. If limited to use just a single word, I would call it joyful.

However, completing the first sculpture caused a dilemma, since I was unsure of where to head next. I called my new mentor to warn him about my doubts. Mal invited me to talk and we soon met at his home — a showplace for fine art.

His eyes gleamed playfully, "You still look more like an old guy than an artist. Your hair isn't long enough." We laughed. "So tell me, how is it going?"

I frowned. "Well, I don't feel like an artist. I wish it were as easy as letting my hair grow."

"So what's the problem?"

I replied, "Those who have seen *Work & Play* seem to like it, which is encouraging. In fact, it's heartwarming, but I'm not sure where my so-called art career is going."

"I think you need to plan, and before that, you will need a specific goal."

"You think that is my problem? I do not have a plan?"

"Yes, you could benefit from some direction." He touched his fingers together like a steeple and leaned way back in his swivel chair. "Some experts say experience is the enemy of creativity. You have plenty of creativity, but not enough experience as an artist. It takes time to acquire experience, but there is a quick way to get enough of it to decide where you want to go next and how to get there." He stopped to let the words sink in. I waited with raised eyebrows.

"You can learn from an expert, and I know just the expert you need. He has been a successful Maryland sculptor for the past nineteen years. Make a list of questions and we will visit him. After we get answers, you should be in a better position to select goals and decide the steps to achieve them." Mal smiled at me. "Bert supports a wife and two daughters by selling his work. That is difficult for an artist without any other income. The art economy is booming and he has benefited from it. He just renovated his barn into a spacious studio. He also hired an assistant to help with sculpture preparation and can afford a part-time marketing expert to advise him about promotion."

* * *

A month later Suzanne, Mal, and I were on our way to see Bert. After a bumpy ride on a country road, we came to a contemporary house built on land carved from a large farm. There was a new-looking sign on the renovated barn, *Sculpture Studio*. After introductions, Bert gave us a tour of the property, which included showing us several works-in-progress. We talked as we followed him through the recently completed studio space.

I asked Bert, "What is required to be a successful artist."

He tilted his head back. "You should learn to do many things and also do them well. I'll mention a few that have been the most important to me. Firstly, your work must be original and unique. It can't be too similar to what another sculptor has done. I don't find this too difficult myself, but some artists find this challenging. Secondly, sculptures need to be large, and more so if they are made of wood like you use. A small work might be regarded by viewers as a less-serious woodcarving and larger works are more likely to be considered art. In my opinion, they should be at least two to three feet high to sell well. Here is an example. Come with me."

He led the way into his primary workspace. At the center was a twice life-sized clay sculpture of a stylized lion. I learned this represented Bert's signature style. It took my breath away. Impressive would be an understatement. It was the perfect example that size did matter.

Suzanne voiced what I felt too. "Wow!"

Bert said, "This clay model will be a bronze sculpture for a public library."

Just then Bert's marketing expert, Helga, came into the room. In addition to helping Bert with marketing, Helga was an instructor at the Maryland Institute College of Art. She was a middle-aged woman, attractively dressed in a feminine business suit.

I asked her, "I don't know much about selling. Can I still be a successful artist?"

Helga said, "Success follows promotion and marketing of your art. You can create art without it, but that is not enough to be successful. Preferably, you should direct your promotion effort yourself as you understand your work best. Or, you get someone like me to help. It makes it easier if an artist likes to interact with people. Are you comfortable with people? Do you think you would like to do promotion?"

I touched my cheek. "I doubt I'd like it. Marketing would be a distraction from creating art. Also, I'm a reserved person, some would even say that I am shy."

Suzanne added, "He's an introvert."

Bert smiled, "Me too. I can only manage with Helga's help."

"There is a direct relationship between the appeal of artwork and the reputation of the artist. A well-known artist's work is valued more highly by buyers than work of a lesser-known artist." Helga explained.

Mal agreed "That sounds right from my experience. As a collector, I always prefer art made by famous artists, but can seldom afford it."

Helga said, "You must promote yourself. You can do it by getting publicity, entering juried exhibits, giving artist talks, and networking at art events. I would suggest that you hire someone. Of course, there would be an expense. But you can also consider getting a part-time art student. That could work out well for you and provide the student basic experience."

I thought about the extra cost and doing things I didn't like. Promotion sounded like work.

Helga noticed my disappointment. "Becoming a successful artist is difficult and requires time. It takes from ten to twenty years to become known as an artist, which assumes that you know your craft and have developed the skills in the chosen media." After a pause, she added, "You look concerned. What are you thinking?"

I cleared my throat. "What I love about being an artist is the opportunity to be creative. I have missed that for many years before finding art. I think I can make high-quality sculptures, but I'm surprised by your ten to twenty-year estimate. I don't know if I have enough time left. It's not just my remaining lifespan, I'd also need to be fit enough to handle the creative and physical work for another ten to twenty years. At that rate, I will be eighty or ninety years old before I'm known, and maybe I will still never be successful."

Helga replied, "It is going to be a difficult challenge. Or you could always enjoy art as a hobby."

I pursed my lips, "Doing it professionally provides an incentive for me to go to the studio regularly and be creative. Now that I've discovered that I love making sculptures, I want to share my artwork with others. I'm not ready to give up on the idea of being a professional artist. Do I have a chance?"

"Tell me more about what you want to accomplish as a sculptor, not aesthetically, but as a career. Then I will offer you my opinion. What is your goal for success? Do you want to sell enough to support yourself or just cover the art expenses?"

"We have sufficient retirement income to live, so I would be happy if I cover the cost of making art." I glanced at Suzanne, pleased to see that she was smiling. "So, this means that I only spend what I can earn."

Helga said, "That is probably doable. In the beginning, the expenses could be much more than what you will earn, so you will need a starting investment. You'll be competing with other artists for attention and sales. There are a lot of talented artists trying to sell their work — so, basically there is more art available than the collectors to buy it."

Helga paused to gage what we thought of her comments. Then she added, "In the beginning, plan to spend at least half the time promoting your work."

"I never expected that self-promotion would be so important." *Or time-consuming.* "I wouldn't feel comfortable doing it. I think an artist should create art, not show off. I'd like to think the artwork would stand on its own if it's good enough."

Helga shook her head and smiled knowingly. "How will you know, as an artist, that you have achieved success? Do you have a certain sales target in mind? Is your goal to exhibit in an upscale New York gallery, or is your dream to be a famous artist someday?"

"I never like to underrate myself. I guess I'd want to be good enough to be famous some day."

Helga smiled, "Famous! That is admirable but unrealistic, and if your goal isn't realistic, you will get frustrated and give up. We could both name famous artists throughout history. There are very few, and most did not make it until after they were dead, sometimes even long after."

"Well, that describes me. I'm old, but not yet famous. You could say I'm almost dead and almost famous." Everyone laughed.

Helga looked thoughtful. "Almost dead and famous; that could be a marketing slogan."

I said, "When I think more about it, I would not want to be famous, even if it is possible. It sounds appealing at first, but not for me; I'm reserved. I'd hate all the things that come with a lot of attention, like crowded events and meeting new people." I continued thinking out loud. "When I recall celebrities in the news, most do not seem to do that well in life, do they? No, I definitely would not want to be famous."

"Well, that settles it." Helga chuckled. "Your goal is *not* to be famous. History tells us it is highly unlikely that you will be in any case."

With a bemused smile, I added, "After I'm dead, I wouldn't mind being a little famous, though." We laughed again.

I added, "Seriously, what is a reasonable goal for a beginner like me, who is seventy years old?"

"You are never too old to learn something new and to achieve success pursuing a new career. Also, you have valuable and useful life experience. That is a big advantage. But, as I said, it takes ten to twenty years for most emerging artists to become known. This is a more reasonable goal for you, which is hard enough, considering your age."

Bert and Helga had run out of time, so our visit had to end, but I still had questions. *How many people must know an artist before he is considered a known artist?* It was a typical left-brain question that would remain unanswered.

So, we thanked them and left. I had much to consider.

While driving back, Mal said, "The visit was interesting but discouraging. It seems you may not have enough time to become a professional artist."

"But I can try; the ten or twenty years is just an estimate. I'm not going to sit around and think about what I can't do. I've decided to continue creating art, even if I'm never a known artist."

"What about self-promotion? What do you want to do about that?"

"Well, I will not brag about myself, but I do not care what other artists do. I'll exhibit my best work, whenever I have an opportunity and let it do all the talking."

Mal looked thoughtful. "I wonder if that will be enough. To be appreciated, abstract sculptures need to be studied, and viewers need a reason to stop and look. What would their reason be if not to see a known artist's latest work?"

"Becoming known could be my measure of success. I just hope my work can speak for me."

This was the first of several such visits with art professionals. I had decided that time spent learning from experienced artists could be as valuable as time spent earning an art school degree.

Looking Glass

My journey from an engineer to an artist was like Alice stepping through the looking glass. It included surprising discoveries, interesting encounters, and new challenges. Above all, there was much to learn about this strange new world called art.

I was on firmer ground since I decided my goal was to become known, although I was still unsure how success could be measured. I executed the next steps with a career plan based on the advice from Mal and others. It included making sculptures half of the time and conducting business tasks, like promotion, forming a business entity, and finding the right gallery, during the other half. After my initial overwhelmed feeling, I got to work.

I started on the familiar path of using hard work to succeed. Since initial sales did not offset expenses, I started spending savings, hoping it was an investment in my new career. For example, taking promotional photos seemed like a simple task, so I took my first three sculptures to a local photo studio. The photographer did his professional best, but I was not satisfied with the result. I knew what I wanted, but found it impossible to communicate. It was difficult to explain my subjective concepts to someone with little experience photographing art. Rather than paying someone else to take more photos, I figured I could do it better myself. Then I would not need to describe my elusive impressions of why a photo was not acceptable. This "I can do it better" attitude was a personality failing. Years before this had made it harder for me to be an effective manager. I was an impatient perfectionist, in this case, determined to get high-quality photos.

I knew little about photography and would need to learn quickly since my age didn't allow for spending months in class. I decided that my learning method would be trial-and-error, which required equipment — a high-quality camera, backgrounds, and lighting — in other words, a poor man's photo studio.

Suzanne was perplexed, "Are you planning to pay all that money for a few photos?"

"Yes. It's the best way to get the quality images I need."

Her frown turned into a slight smile. She said nothing, but I knew I was being compared to the Thanksgiving bird.

I said, "Thank you for not laughing out loud."

I wasn't a starving artist, so I bought the equipment with the hope that I could recoup some expenses by not paying a photographer.

There was no room for a dedicated photo studio in our small retirement apartment, so Suzanne helped me improvise. Each time I finished a sculpture, we removed the living room furniture and installed photo gear before capturing the images and then reversed the process to turn it back to a usable space. I discarded many images before producing a few acceptable photos.

The next product on the schedule was a promotional brochure. After my discouraging experience of hiring a photographer, I went right to the computer to design it myself.

Mal diplomatically said, "It is a good starting point." Then he used more words to pronounce it inferior.

Suzanne was more direct. "It's crap-o-la."

So, I decided to pay a professional graphic designer and the resulting brochure was outstanding.

At that time, websites were new in business, and few emerging artists used them, but Mal thought a high-quality website would be useful as a digital gallery, so I added it to the plan. Available website development tools were limited and required specialized training. Since I didn't know how to program a website, I visited several website companies and learned that it would be too expensive.

That weekend we went to a party, where I mentioned my website need. Someone said, "I know a programmer in Los Angeles who can develop it for less."

I looked up. "Los Angeles! That's too far away."

He smiled. "No, you can communicate by email and phone. He'll do it for about half the cost."

So, that's what I did, all in the name of becoming known. The primary purpose of the website was to introduce myself as an artist and showcase my work. With these promotion tools in place, I imagined I might be a known artist someday, but I was still not confident enough to call myself a sculptor when someone asked what I did for a living.

I was always on the lookout for inspiration. My next idea came from Suzanne. She had recently started attending a writing class. One evening she showed me something that she'd been working on. It reminded me of our dancing experience long ago and provided the inspiration I needed for my next sculpture. This was her version of our dancing story.

HOW I GOT MY MAN TO WALTZ

"Dance like no one is watching! This exhortation is often advanced by the followers of the 'live in the moment' philosophy. I have heard this expression a lot and it made me think of how resistant my husband usually is when it comes to approaching the dance floor.

It really takes a lot of prodding and encouragement. In general, I guess that encouragement factor becomes essential in order to bring males to the dance floor. And even then, dynamite might be more productive in getting the guy to move his feet. The guy is willing to latch onto the gal and hold her in his arms in a socially acceptable connection, but moving his feet to music is another thing altogether. I married a guy whose basic idea of dancing was to shift his body weight from one side to the other, period. His two sons inherited the same proclivity in spite of Mom's efforts to teach them a few variations. This shifting from one foot to the other usually involves a small pivot, which guarantees that the couple will never travel far from the spot where they have drilled themselves into the floorboards. It also assures the couple that they can cling to each other with their eyes closed because there is no necessity to see where they are going — they are going nowhere! And then the gal falls in love with the guy and it doesn't matter whether he dances or not, as long as they are in each other's arms.

Year after year I beseeched my guy to learn the waltz, particularly since that is my favorite dance music. And his answer was always negative: "No way" he said. "Don't bug me about it anymore", "Forget-about-it already", No kidding — CASE CLOSED!" But I persisted with my request for twenty years or more, and finally — sadly — I surrendered to the fact that I would not be able to waltz with the man I love.

Imagine my enormous surprise then when at our twenty-seventh wedding anniversary dinner, the guy makes this announcement to me at a classy restaurant, "I made arrangements for us to take private waltz lessons."

My hysterically happy reaction was to keep squealing: "I don't believe it! I don't believe it!"

And the guy said: "I can't believe it either. I can't tell you how many times this week I was tempted to cancel the lesson." I told him over and over again that he was giving me the best anniversary gift; and besides, I reminded him, that in addition to making me happy, he would be well prepared to dance with his daughter at her wedding.

He did not cancel. We went to the private dance class and at the end of the hour, we were waltzing! The recording that the instructor played for our first complete dance together was an instrumental version of "Amazing Grace." I laughed and cried at the same time. The guy had a happy prideful look stamped all over his face. We, as a couple, were one with the music and completely in the zone of moving together with "amazing grace."

And I wanted the Whole World to be WATCHING THIS DANCE!"

As the Guy in her story, I really was excited to see how happy she was as we waltzed together for the first time and I treasured the memory in my heart. *I wish I had said "yes" when she first asked me to learn.* Now about eighteen years after that waltz lesson, I poured the memory into a *Dancers* sculpture. Suzanne cried again when she first saw it, and then she looked for a recording of *Amazing Grace*, so we could do a little more waltzing then and there.

Dancers became my very first sculpture sale, validating the investment I had made to have a high-quality brochure and website. A friend had mailed my brochure to an art collector in Massachusetts.

A few days later, the same friend called me. "Clarence, I have good news, the art collector wants to buy one of your sculptures, the one called *Dancers*."

"That's great. Does he want to see it in person first?"

"No need, the photo is good enough. He said it will be placed in his entrance hall, so that visitors see it as soon as they come in. Just ship it to him with the invoice."

"Will do. This is my first big sculpture sale. Thanks for your help. There is only one possible problem, I fell in love with *Dancers*, while I was making it and now I won't have it anymore. It is like giving a daughter's hand in marriage."

"Maybe you will get over it when you put his check in the bank."

When I told Suzanne about the sale, we did a "happy dance" together.

* * *

After the *Dancers* sale, I expected more strong sales, so I decided to make a bronze sculpture because it seemed like a romantic idea. Bronze is a traditional material for sculptures and casting bronze could be a way to reproduce multiple copies of my designs. Since I knew nothing about making a bronze sculpture, I took the cherry wood version of the finished *Work & Play* sculpture to an art foundry and asked the owner, "What would it cost to make this in bronze?"

"No, can't do it."

"Why?"

"This polished wood finish will be damaged when we make the mold and we can't guarantee that your wood sculpture will not be broken. Can't take the risk."

"How can it be done?"

"Make an expendable model for us to use."

Since I was obliged to start a different model from scratch, I made a new design rather than making another version of *Work & Play. But what would be a suitable image?*

Many sculptors start with the shape, I typically began with an interesting theme. For my first bronze sculpture, I selected the theme 'success in life.' It had only been a few years since I left the workday world of organizations, where success is important, and I believed that I had figured what success required.

The success image came to me as I watched a championship soccer game on TV. A sports team is a perfect metaphor for success. During the game, one player scored and another team member ran towards him. They jumped and met with right hands together in the air — a high-five. I saw what looked like two athletic ballet dancers when the TV network replayed the goal in slow motion. I took pencil and paper to quickly sketch the abstract image in my mind, trying to capture the graceful twisting motion using thin ribbons.

The next step was to fabricate a full-size foundry model. Like most sculptors, Bert made his models with clay supported by an armature framework. As a woodcarver, I'd make mine of wood and plastic resin.

I called my son who lived nearby, "Phil, I need help with my next sculpture. Would you give me a hand?"

"Sure."

Rather than carve the hands, my idea was to start with plastic castings of our right hands. On Phil's next day off work, I took body-casting materials to his house.

We mixed alginate powder with water in a pail, and I put my hand into the thick, gray, mud-like mix. Instructions cautioned to remain motionless for 15 minutes. I was relieved when the timer sounded, and the mix was a rubbery consistency. I carefully removed my hand so as not to crack the freshly jelled mold. Then we poured urethane resin with hardener into the cavity where my hand had been. After ten minutes we removed a plastic hand from the mold. Then we repeated the process with Phil's hand.

During the next few weeks, I carved two ribbons of poplar wood and mounted the two plastic hands to the wood. I delivered the finished model to the foundry for casting. Several months later I picked up a bronze sculpture that I called *Success*.

My new art career looked promising. I learned more about the art market by searching online and reading art publications. They all said the same thing; art collecting was popular, prices were increasing, and this trend was accelerating. I figured my path to becoming known was clear. I bragged to Suzanne that my first sale would be followed by many more. *I wonder if I'll be able to keep up with future demand.* It was not to be as no sales followed.

I didn't realize it then, but the recession of 2008 caused the bottom to fall out for the art market, and big dollar art sales ended for emerging artists. It was another economic storm that seemed to come along as soon as I forgot they existed. I didn't know what to do other than hope that sales would improve and commiserate with Suzanne.

"The economic depression put a damper on art sales and has me more disheartened."

"It sounds like your expectations are too high."

"I guess so, but it has been more than a year now with no new sale. I wonder if this is all I can ever expect."

"I think economies go up and down in cycles, and the art market will turn around some day."

"But it's hard to stay motivated and make more sculptures that remain unsold. And I'm not so sure things will ever get better."

"You know that economies move in cycles. You must remain hopeful. It will get better and you should keep working with that in mind. Remember how good things were when we were in high school? That was several years after everyone was in despair during the Great Depression, then everything gradually improved."

"Yes, that was a good time to grow up." I had benefited from being caught in the updraft after the depression. I was able to finance an education, find a job, and secure my future. I remembered how painless it was to pay my way through college with part-time Co-op jobs, to graduate without debt, and to have a pick between several good jobs.

"And, things will improve this time."

"I suppose you are right, but there is no way to know how long it will take."

Unsure of what else to do about slack art sales, I redoubled promotional efforts. One day I was asked to give an artist talk to fellow residents at the retirement community. A string of speaking requests to various community groups followed. I discovered that it was fun to brag about my work to the interested and supportive audiences. I gave a dozen talks during the following three years, the most popular was entitled "Almost Dead and Famous."

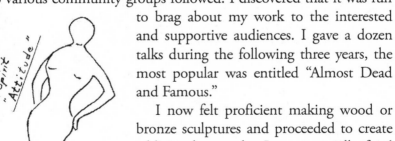

I now felt proficient making wood or bronze sculptures and proceeded to create additional artworks. I was especially fond of my next bronze sculpture named *Attitude.*

One evening while daydreaming with feet up, eyes closed, and head back, I smiled thinking about Suzanne busy in another room. She wasn't by my side at that moment, but I felt particularly close to her. *How fortunate it is that I'm with her. A lifetime together has strengthened our love.* I recalled those days in high school when I anticipated her arrival in the cafeteria. I was attracted to her outgoing personality and shapely figure. As a teen, my dream was to be her boyfriend, but shyness limited her to being my fantasy girl. Then years later she noticed me and decided that I would be hers. I held my breath remembering. *She still has the same outgoing attitude of poise, sensuality, exuberance, self-confidence, and energy.* At that moment, I imagined her spirited personality as an abstract sculpture. It was a powerful image representing a wonderful memory. I knew that the image would not be content in my head, but must become a physical sculpture — the celebration of our love — and the *Attitude* sculpture was born in bronze.

Known Artist

Even with the drag of slow sales, I felt a creative need to produce a steady flow of sculptures during the next years. I concluded that being a known artist was a subjective idea, similar to the idea of being a successful artist. I was still insecure about myself as an artist, so I decided to have fun and not worry about being known or successful. Maybe I'd get a break; if not, I'd remain unknown.

Then Mal brought another opportunity my way. One day he said, "I know the director of the *Green Museum of Baltimore*. I gave him your brochure and told him about you. If you call to ask for his advice, I'm sure he would agree to give you some pointers. It will be beneficial for you to know each other."

A few weeks later I met the director and invited him to tour my studio. He looked at what I was doing; particu-
larly a walnut sculpture called *Hope*. I had been inspired by the idea that new life was hope for a better future, and depicted the stylized image of a mother and baby bird.

He invited me to exhibit six sculptures in the *Green Museum* that summer. I felt encouraged by the invitation because I knew hundreds of people would see my work during the three months. An exhibit in a museum is a milestone that many artists never reach. That solo exhibit was an important confidence builder, as was the director's advice. We met in his office at the museum to plan the coming exhibit, and to select the sculptures for display. He was serious about his respon-

"Hope"
(New Life)

sibility to provide the public with quality exhibits and was explicit in his requirements.

He leaned back in his chair. "Would you like to give a brief talk on the opening day?"

"Yes, I can do that."

"Keep it informal, no slides. I suggest you describe the process you use to make the sculptures."

"Okay."

"We have rules for the exhibit that you must follow. For example, no cameras are allowed and lighting in the exhibit room must be low to protect other museum items."

My eyebrows went up, "But, the sculptures look best under spotlights."

"No extra lighting is allowed. We will try to arrange the works in a way that they get maximum advantage under existing lights. And you may not place business cards or any other print materials in the room."

"Can I do anything to attract possible buyers?"

He shrugged, "You may put your brochure in the rack provided in the back hallway. We can try for pre-event publicity in the *Baltimore Sun*. This is a museum, not a sales gallery."

"I understand."

"I will arrange a separate meeting so that you can brief our docents, who will greet visitors on days when you are not here."

"Okay."

"The museum will provide wine and cheese for the opening."

When I got home, I told Suzanne, "It's going to be a nice exhibit, but I don't expect any sales to result from it."

By the end of the summer, I had much respect for the director's experience. I asked him for career advice at every opportunity and learned many things about being an artist. However, the director's focus was on managing his museum, and not on educating me.

Once he looked at me with his head tilted. "You seem unsure of your ability as a sculptor."

"Yes, at best I think of myself as an emerging artist."

"No. You are an artist because you make exceptional art, which is why I invited you to exhibit." That was the day I became a 'real' sculptor in my heart. *If he believes in me, I should believe in myself.*

* * *

Not all my art-making experiences at that time were so positive. Once I made a stylized female sculpture from beautifully figured tiger maple wood. It was inspired by the fleeting nature of female beauty. I named it *Illusion.* I was highly pleased with the result, which I felt represented the theme and was aesthetically beautiful. It didn't occur to me that the sculpture might offend anyone. It was not a nude, but I learned that a few conservative viewers considered it too sexy. It was my practice at that time to exhibit each freshly completed sculpture in the Brookfield lobby for several days so that interested residents could view it. Less than twenty-four hours later, I got a call from the front office asking me to remove it because it offended someone. I could hardly understand why, until someone confided that the two critics were elderly and ultra conservative. I removed it immediately to avoid upsetting any neighbor, but taking it away provoked complaints from other less conservative residents, who thought that the Brookfield should not censor art.

I had started carving *Illusion's* 'sister' when this occurred. The controversy caused me to make the second figure sexier than the first. Suzanne teased that the devil made me do it and from then on, we called the two sculptures *The Babes.* Until then, I preferred not to depart from the initial inspirational vision, and I wondered if my impulsive revision to make the second sculpture sexier had tainted *The Babes'* aesthetic muse. A few months later, I was pleased when a well-known juried exhibit accepted the second *Babe.*

I was gradually learning and having fantastic experiences as an artist, but unfortunately, I was not selling any work, nor had I found a suitable gallery to represent me. Having such representation is a mark of artistic success, so finding a good gallery remained an unfulfilled objective. I didn't think much about the pros and cons of such a sales approach, but it seemed like a good idea because most artists wanted to be in a gallery. I had visited several galleries but found it difficult to form a relationship as there were many more artists than gallery spaces. Also, my work was expensive for the average art collector, and galleries carrying high-cost work were limited. I talked to Mal about the problem and he thought that I needed a more effective approach to introduce myself.

* * *

While researching suitable galleries, I found one with a prime Charleston, South Carolina art district address. The well-known owner also conducted career consulting for artists. Mal thought a consulting arrangement might provide an opportunity to introduce myself and for her to get to know me. So, I asked her to advise me. I received a long form with many questions. It seemed I would need to qualify to merit her advice. I sent a carefully worded replied and my website link. An email conversation followed. Then she replied, "I can't help you. Your work is first-rate, and the website is professional. I do not think you need a consultant or advisor at this point in your career."

"What do I need?"

"Well, I think you are ready for gallery representation."

"That is good to hear. What about your gallery? Would you represent me?"

"I do not have space for a new artist, however, I like your work, and someday I would like to see it in person."

"You are welcome to visit my studio in Baltimore any time."

"The art market is in a slump. I must tend to the business here in Charleston. Also, I'm busy moving into a larger gallery space, so I'm not making any studio visits now."

Her compliment may be my opportunity. "I can bring my work samples next week for you to view if that is acceptable?"

"Well sure, I can make time to look at it."

The gallery owner and I set a date and time. My son-in-law helped me with the long drive. We drove with four sculptures from Baltimore to Charleston on a Friday, met with her on Saturday, and returned on Sunday. She liked my work and me enough to sign a contract to represent me and she held the four display sculptures for sale in her gallery. Our working relationship lasted several years in a difficult market. However, because she only sold one of the four, the endeavor wasn't financially successful for me.

Then one day, I was contacted by an interior decorator asking if I did special commissions. She said, "We are decorating two identical maternity ward waiting rooms in a large St. Louis hospital. The directors saw your website and liked your sculpture designs, but want the new work to be specific to their family mission. We are reaching out to several artists, would you like to compete for the commission?"

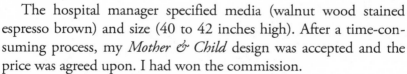

Mother and Child ✱

"Yes. What must I do?"

"Send us a sketch of your proposed design along with the price and delivery date. We need your proposal for a meeting at the hospital next Friday."

The hospital manager specified media (walnut wood stained espresso brown) and size (40 to 42 inches high). After a time-consuming process, my *Mother & Child* design was accepted and the price was agreed upon. I had won the commission.

Many hospital visitors and patients saw these sculptures over the following years. The waiting rooms are open seven days a week and 24 hours a day. At a time when an expectant mother and her family are experiencing their joyful event, my wish was that they might contemplate the sculpture's message of motherly love.

My goal when becoming an artist was to be known before I got too old to make art. I never did learn how many people are required to declare an artist 'known.' I wasn't a financial success, but I felt known based on the many supporters, who appreciated my work. I had reached the ten-year milestone as a sculptor and decided to celebrate the anniversary by publishing a coffee table book featuring my art.

Bus Ride

Baltimore, Maryland — 2015, Age 80

I didn't see it coming; a short ride from Baltimore to Philadelphia provided new insight into Grandpa Joseph's prediction. Suzanne and I signed up with the Baltimore Museum to see a traveling exhibit at the Philadelphia Museum. We held hands and waited for the chartered bus with a group of art lovers.

A well-dressed lady walked our way. She smiled pleasantly, "Hello, Clarence and Suzanne."

We said hello, but I did not recognize her. "I'm sorry I don't remember your name."

"Helga," she said with a twinkle in her eye. "We met long ago at the studio of a Maryland sculptor. I did his marketing. You were starting your career, and we offered advice."

Then I remembered her, but she looked older. Of course, we did too. Helga was interested in my progress. We talked about my solo exhibit at the museum, the period of gallery representation, and my commissions. I told her about my ten-year anniversary book. She now had her Ph.D. in psychology and an office in Baltimore.

"It sounds like our advice helped."

"It was the turning point for my decision to be a full-time sculptor."

"How has it been going?"

"Well, I'm not ready to celebrate artistic success."

She grinned, "Does that mean you are not famous yet?"

I smiled and looked down. "No, I'm not."

"But as I remember, you only wanted to be a 'known' artist, which it seems you are. So, I think you can claim success as a sculptor."

"I don't know about success, but I'm satisfied with my accomplishments."

Helga smiled and replied, "I enjoyed studying the elements of success in grad school. The simple definition of success is to achieve one's objective. I think a better definition is how far one comes in life rather than where one ends up. I think that a person, who is born into a guaranteed successful life and achieves little beyond that, is really less successful than another person, who starts with fewer advantages and achieves success through his or her own diligence."

"For most people, their primary objective or dream is to be rich, but is that really what they want? Or is it to be happy and they believe riches will make them happy?" Suzanne asked.

Helga replied, "It is an interesting question."

I said, "I don't believe having money guarantees happiness, but not having enough can cause problems that make us unhappy."

Helga said, "Yes, money buys necessities and is a measure of self-worth, which we need for happiness. It is used to value our labor and achievements, like the art you make. We tend to equate the value others place on our work with our self-worth, which affects our happiness."

I agreed. "I felt low artistic self-worth, when my sculptures weren't selling, even though I knew poor sales were largely due to the economy. I was satisfied with my skill and creativity, but couldn't avoid thinking that collectors didn't value my work in as many dollars as I did."

"Don't be so modest." Suzanne interrupted and looked at Helga. "Clarence just won the Maryland Governor's Award for 2014 Leadership in Aging, Visual Artist of the Year."

Helga said, "Congratulations!"

We moved towards the bus, which had arrived to pick us up.

She said, "I would like to hear more about your art career. Shall we have lunch together today?"

"Sure, I would like that."

Later, we found a table in the Philadelphia Museum's modern dining room. I felt important surrounded by great art.

Helga looked at me. "Aren't names interesting? We both have uncommon first names. I did my dissertation about how given names can influence our lives." She picked up her napkin. "My thesis proposal was that first names tend to match a person's personality — maybe not at first, but after we have a chance to grow into them. I feel very much like a 'Helga' now. As a child, I hated the name."

"I hated mine too. One day I asked Mom why she named me Clarence."

"Did she say why?"

"Her father told her I needed a special name because I would be special someday. When I was small, I assumed grandpa knew everything, so I believed him. Everyone thought he was extraordinary. He had accomplished a lot during his life." Helga looked at me expectantly, waiting for more. "Once when I was a little older I asked him what special thing I would do. He told me to nurture my talents and, in that process, I would discover why I was special."

Helga said, "Identify your strengths and concentrate on developing them. That seems reasonable."

"But I had a learning problem that blocked my progress. After I gained more self-confidence because I was doing better in college, I decided to embrace my dyslexia and my unique name as inherent elements of my being. I resolved to make the name's uniqueness special by trying to become special."

"Good for you."

I shrugged. "There is a problem. I've searched ever since without success; trying one goal after another during my several careers. It has taken me on a pinball path through life; rocket engineer, airplane designer, aerospace engineer, computer scientist, executive manager, college instructor, and now a sculptor."

Suzanne said, "And now, you are a father and grandfather; don't forget that."

Helga said, "That is some quest."

I ran my hand through my hair. "Yes, but I still don't know why. Why did he think I'd be special?"

"Every mother thinks her child is special, even before he is born. All children are special to their families."

Suzanne agreed, "That's true."

"Well, if a mother knows her child is special before he's born, maybe specialness doesn't have to be earned, or does it?" I stared into the distance and said, "I had just assumed it must be earned." I took a sip of water. "I've been searching to find what would make me special, so I could try and accomplish whatever was required. According to your idea, perhaps I did not have to do anything spectacular to be special. It seems my search has been unnecessary and a waste of effort."

Helga held up her hand. "Not a waste, the search took you on many adventures. And how about the art you created?"

Suzanne added, "And what about the most special of all — our children."

"And all your descendants to follow," Helga said

Suddenly, I was struck with a new insight about what had eluded me for so long.

Achievement is not found in the destination but in the journey. Discovery and accomplishment can only follow if we risk saying yes to the adventure.

I choked up but managed to smile at Suzanne and reached for her hand. "Yes, ours has been an exciting adventure and a wonderful life."

Helga noticed that something had changed in me. "So, now what is your conclusion about being special?"

I felt confident to answer. "I think I know what Grandpa Joseph meant by 'special.' It's not just achieving life's dreams and goals, but also experiencing the journey with integrity while learning along the way."

"And learning to *enjoy* the trip," Suzanne added.

Helga smiled, "I second those comments. The two of you are obviously happy together. What is your secret?"

I didn't hesitate. "Say 'yes' to your partner as often as possible."

Helga smiled at my response. We finished lunch and rejoined our group for the afternoon museum tour.

I took Suzanne's hand as we followed. "I guess my search is complete, and it's time to look for another adventure."

With a bright smile she hugged my arm tighter. "I know just the thing for our next adventure."

"What?"

She squealed like a newlywed, "A second honeymoon!" In the next breath, she added, "It is Saturday you know, and I think you should say yes."

"Ooh... Okay — but we aren't finished with the first one."

"Happiness is not in the mere possession of money; it lies in the joy of achievement, in the thrill of creative effort."

— FRANKLIN D. ROOSEVELT —

Afterword

• The character, Cousin Jason was based on the aviation genius, James R. Bede, 1933–2015, who designed over a dozen unique airplanes during his lifetime. His XBD-2 short-takeoff-and-landing airplane can be seen at the Experimental Aircraft Association Museum in Oshkosh, Wisconsin. Following the company takeover, the new company produced many BD-1 sports airplanes renamed *American AA-1*.

• In 1967, James R. Bede attempted a world record around-the-world flight in a highly modified Schweizer SGS 2-32 powered glider. The flight ended early as a result of equipment failure, but Bede went on to set several distance and endurance records on the plane.

• Bede's homebuilt BD-5J design (the world's smallest jet) flew in several air shows and was featured in the opening sequence of the James Bond movie, *Octopussy*. An early propeller version, the BD-5, can be seen at the Smithsonian Museum in Washington, DC.

• The author and his cousin remained close friends until his cousin died at the age of 83.

About the Author

Lawrence Schneider was an aeronautical engineer and a sculptor. He is most proud of his role as a father and a grandfather.

He and his wife Irene were blessed with two sons and two daughters, followed by four granddaughters and one grandson. First child, Anne Schneider became a world traveler, who experienced her own adventures. The second child, Joseph Schneider with his wife Becca Cavell parented his granddaughter, Sarah Cavell Schneider. The third child, Paul Schneider, is married to Janet Young. They are parents of his granddaughters, Alison and Lindsay Schneider. Fourth child, Karen married Drew Dorbert and they are parents of his granddaughter, Julia Dorbert and grandson, Brady Dorbert.

Like the protagonist, the author became a sculptor late in his life. If you would like to learn more about the sculptures described here, take a look at his book, *Insight in 3D: Ten Years of Sculpture*. The gorgeously photographed coffee-table book celebrates the author's works and reveals the skill and craftsmanship involved in each of his creations. Moreover, Mr. Schneider's commentary provides an insight into the thought, intent, and wisdom that permeated his body of work.

Note from the Author

Thank you for reading *Say Yes on Saturday*. My goal is to tell a story that will inform and motivate my descendants, but also entertain and inspire current readers who might relate to the experiences described. You can help me to reach them by adding your honest review of the book on your favorite book dealer's or book discussion group's website. If you know friends, who might like it, please do recommend this book to them as well.

www.LawrenceSchneider.com

48373697R00174

Made in the USA
Middletown, DE
16 September 2017